ALEX DRIVING SOUTH

By Keith Maillard
Two Strand River

a novel by
KEITH MAILLARD

Alex

Driving South

New York
THE DIAL PRESS

Published by
The Dial Press
1 Dag Hammarskjold Plaza
New York, New York 10017

Lines from "My Dreams" from LIES by John Newlove reprinted
by permission of The Canadian Publishers, McClelland and
Stewart Limited, Toronto.

This is a work of fiction. The characters, names, incidents, places,
and dialogue are products of the author's imagination and are not
to be construed as real.

Manufactured in the United States of America

Second Printing—1980

Design by Francesca Belanger

Library of Congress Cataloging in Publication Data

Maillard, Keith, 1942–
    Alex driving south.

    I. Title.
PZ4.M222Al 1980 [PR9199.3.M345] 813'.5'4 79-21779
ISBN 0-8037-0196-9

For:

Tom Bryson,
Herb Rogers,
Pat and Fritz Temple,
Bob Harlow,
and Willy, who taught me everything I know,
which is why I am so ignorant.

There's a strange dog
puking in my sink
where I wash the dishes.
I wish I were blind.

—John Newlove

One

Chapter One

"Carlyle, you simple shit!"

Evan didn't recognize his friend.

"Come on, fuckhead, you know me."

Evan looked—a huge, muscular man in faded coveralls, short curly black hair, grease on his hands—and then he remembered. There was no way he could have forgotten that pleasantly ugly face and those expressionless brown eyes so pale that they were nearly yellow. "Alex," he said. Then: "Christ, you look different. You've gotten heavier—" Not as though Alex Warner had gone to fat, rather that the boy in Evan's memory had been worn to the bone and the man who stood there now was massive. *Well, here he is,* Evan thought, *the one person in town I didn't want to see.* "You look fit," he said uneasily.

Alex laughed; that is, his single short bark must have been intended as a laugh—"Haw!"—harsh, like a crow. "Fit, my ass!

I'm burning out faster than a racehorse. . . . But shit, man, you look young. You look like a fucking college kid." And again Evan regretted his whimsical suit with its curved lapels and flared pants. Dana had talked him into it; theatrical lady, she loved playing dress-up as a party game, had been at him for months over his flannel shirts and baggy pants—his "leftover sixties conservatism," she said. They'd bought the suit the day he'd heard that his contract had been renewed; he wore it now because it was the only suit he owned. He should have known how it would look on the streets of Raysburg, West Virginia. "Yeah, you really look young," Alex was saying. "I didn't know you till I damn near run you down. Come on, I'll buy you a drink."

It's been over ten years, Evan thought, *thirteen years, to be exact, since I've seen him. Do I want to have a drink with him? What could we possibly have to say to each other now? But Christ, there's no way in hell I can get out of it.*

He had planned to fly in from Toronto, pay a duty visit to his parents, and fly out again, untouched, unmoved, detached as an anthropologist. Worrying about it on the plane, he had decided not to see Alex at all, to keep him fixed in the past, set into those surreal nights that spun in memory like pinwheels: both of them sixteen or seventeen or eighteen, careening from bar to bar in Alex's truck, getting drunk and then drunker, trying half-heartedly to pick up girls, and always ending the night by driving south with a case of beer between them on the seat. Driving south to look at the fiery open-hearth furnaces that burned hellishly (no other word would do) out into the West Virginia night. That's where Alex belonged, Evan had decided, pushed firmly back into the mist of nostalgia that was growing over his high school days—"The Old Friend," a piece of the legend, the central figure in his stock of down-home stories to be trotted out at dinner parties with Dana urging him on: "Hey, tell them about that crazy guy you went to school with. The one who stole all the cars. What was his name?" Alex Warner was his name, and now here he was, a grown man, solid and grinning. At least that cracked, ironic grin hadn't changed in thirteen years.

Evan reached out automatically with his right hand, but Alex turned his palm up to show the grime: "Come on, I'll buy you a drink."

"All right," Evan said. "Sure."

The streets of center Raysburg were wretched and gray enough to match Evan's memory, but small family businesses had once given them a tentative human warmth: a bakery, a used clothing store, a feed-and-hardware store, a small grocery, bars, and diners. His father's place had been here too, T. E. Carlyle & Sons, with its modest sign advertising BLUEPRINTS, PHOTOSTATS, ART SUPPLIES, AND FINE PORTRAIT PHOTOGRAPHY, but the shop had gone long ago, as far back as the late fifties, replaced by a blank, gray bank building. And now everything else he remembered seemed to have gone too, all replaced with concrete and gaudy signs and huge white slabs: a Laundromat, a chain supermarket, a chain drugstore, a chain department store, a McDonald's. Evan hadn't worn a topcoat; standing on the pavement, he shivered. The stifling industrial haze still hung over the valley; even the clouds looked dirty.

Alex turned and walked away so quickly that Evan had a hard time keeping up, going down Main Street toward Twenty-second, and not to a bar as he'd expected, but to a garage. Striding by, Alex slapped a gas pump. "Dry," he said. "The fuckers." The sign painted on the window said: WARNER'S GARAGE—EXPERT AUTO REPAIRS.

"Yours?"

"Yeah. Wonderful, ain't it? Great fucking business to be in these days." Alex led Evan past an automobile hung on a lift. A fat man, an anonymous lumpish figure with a gladiator's visor over his face, was raining down sparks from a welding torch. Alex waved to him, a casual flick of the hand like a salute. The man grunted. Alex pointed to the suspended car: "Needs a whole new exhaust system, but you think they'll let me put it in? Fuck, no. 'Patch it up,' they say. The simple bastards. No matter what you do, they think you're screwing them." From a dispenser at the back wall he squirted cream onto his hands, worked them together, wiped them dry with a paper towel, and then with a measured awkwardness, almost, Evan thought, with diffidence, reached out and took his hand. "Well, you're looking good, you old fucker. You look like you're making money."

"I guess I'm doing all right," Evan said stiffly. "Not great. But all right." He followed Alex into the warmth of the office. Alex unlocked the desk, pulled out a pint of Jack Daniel's and two Styrofoam cups. "I'm getting squeezed out," he said, and then that harsh, humorless bark of a laugh again: "Haw!" He poured each of them two fingers of whiskey. "Had a kid working for me," he said. "He would have been a damn fine mechanic . . . had to let him go." He drank. Evan drank. "Well, what the hell brings you back to the valley?"

"I came back for Christmas . . . came back to visit my folks."

"I haven't seen your old man in years. How are they doing?"

"As well as can be expected, I guess. They're both retired now. . . . Looks like my dad's going to die pretty soon."

"Yeah? Well, my old man kicked off a while back. Men around here burn out faster than light bulbs. Haw! Where you living?"

"Vancouver."

"Vancouver?" Alex put on a puzzled expression. *He's picked up some conventional tricks with his face,* Evan thought. *He probably had to learn how to look sociable to run a garage, but underneath it's still there: that unreadable mask.* "That's in Washington state, isn't it?"

"No. It's in Canada."

"Canada?"

Well, here it is. "Yeah," Evan said carefully, "I was one of those guys who wasn't going to Vietnam."

Alex's face was expressionless. Then, very slowly, he began to smile. "Good for you," he said finally. "I did my time. The army can kiss my ass." He toasted Evan with the Styrofoam cup. "Fuck all of them."

It had begun to snow. Alex was looking away, out the broad plate-glass window. His face was hard and watchful; it gave away nothing. And that was how Evan remembered him: staring off into space. "Yeah," Alex said, his eyes on the falling snow. "Well, do you like it in Canada?"

"Yes . . . yes, I do."

"Fuck, that's good. You ever plan to come back?"

"I don't know . . . not to the valley."

Alex didn't say anything. Still looking away, he lit a cigarette. "Well, shit, yeah, not much to come back to, I guess." He dragged on the cigarette, said finally, "Cold up there, huh?"

"No, not especially. Not where I am, anyway. It's warmer in the winter than it is here. It rains a lot."

And then Alex turned to him. "Look," he said, and his expression was so grave, so weighted, that Evan expected something like "The country's falling apart" or "These are hard times." What he said was: "Come to dinner."

And, "I'm married," with that twisted grin. "Did you know that?"

"I think I heard it."

"Yeah, well I am. Ignorant fucker that I am, I went and got married. Got two kids. How do you like that? Come to dinner," he said again.

"I don't know. . . . Do you think your wife—?"

"No problem. She loves to have company. Gives her a chance to put on the dog."

"Well, if you think it's all right—"

"Fuck, yes, it's all right."

Evan hesitated, still riding the edge of an obscure fear out of all proportion to anything that seemed to be happening. *Does he remember the last time?* he thought. Then he let it go: *Screw, so what if he does.* "Okay," he said. "Sure. I'll call my mother and tell her I won't be in tonight."

"You do that. The phone's right over there." Alex stood, knocked back the remainder of his whiskey. "Snowing like a bitch out there. I may as well close this goddamn place for all the money I'm making."

Chapter Two

Alex was living in a new subdivision improbably terraced down the backside of Raysburg Hill. Evan tried to remember what had been there before, but all he could pull from the past were vague images of trees and scrub, weeds trickling down to vacant lots. But now Alex was turning onto a bland street where small cheap houses were lined up like so many Velveeta cheese boxes. Evan wasn't used to riding in big American cars, that sensation of cruising in a boat; Alex was driving quite slowly and they were rolling by tiny clipped lawns gone dun-colored for winter, strewn with tricycles, bicycles, toys—and children. Alex parked in front of one of the houses, said flatly, "This is it," and before Evan could answer, had climbed out and slammed the door.

Alex stood, scowling, and surveyed the neighborhood. The snow was falling in large, wet lumps. "Shit," Alex said, and lit a cigarette. Evan couldn't imagine what they were doing standing there on the sidewalk in the snow. He could hear, faintly but distinctly, the sound of traffic on the National Road. Looking up Raysburg Hill, where Alex had been gazing, he could see the new Holiday Inn perched on top. And again guided by Alex's eyes, he looked down the descending streets of houses, terraced over the hillside on lots like rice paddies, to the outline, flattened and gray through the snow, of the Consolidated chemical plant. "If it freezes tonight, have a fuck of a time getting out of here," Alex said.

"I don't remember this," Evan said.

"No, you wouldn't. Developers come in and slapped it up in twenty-four hours. Damn fine cardboard they make these houses out of these days, the damn finest they can get their hands on." Having taken no more than two drags on it, he snapped his cigarette away into the gutter and turned and walked toward the house so abruptly that Evan was left again momentarily behind.

"Snowing like a son of a bitch out there," Alex announced to the empty living room.

"Hi, hon. You're home early," from somewhere inside the house.

"Yeah. I closed the garage for the day."

"Oh, Al!" And she was walking into the living room, something on her face that looked to Evan like panic. She seemed too young to be the mother of two children; slender in a sweat shirt and tight jeans, sneakers on her feet, she could have been a high school girl. Quite pretty, he thought, but not a remarkable prettiness; the only startling thing about her was the contrast between her large eyes, so dark they seemed all pupil, and her pale blond hair which had been set into a feathery style, carefully curled. She had a hand out to Alex; the beginnings of words were in her mouth, and then she saw Evan and stopped. He saw her body go tense. She stood motionless, her face confused and unhappy.

"This is Evan Carlyle," Alex said. "He was one of my best friends back in high school." Evan was surprised: *I wouldn't have thought he'd say that.* And, "This is my wife, Sharon." Alex pronounced the words slowly, measuring them out with a droll underlining; he seemed to be enjoying her confusion.

Evan saw the effort it took for her to convert her open face—that miserable O—into the smile that matched the blithe Miss Clairol curls. "Oh, Jesus!" she said involuntarily, wiped her hands on her jeans, leaving a white patch of flower on each hip, and held out a hand to Evan. She wore grape-colored nail polish. It was badly chipped.

He took her hand. Her dark eyes were searching his face. He forced himself to smile. And he was hating himself for standing there in his chocolate-chip suit and high-heeled boots, his hair styled by Mode Uni-Sex, noticing such things as her chipped nail polish and bleached hair. "This isn't me," he wanted to say.

"You've caught me with a mask on . . . the same as I've caught you." But he couldn't say anything. There was nothing in his head, not a single polite formula. Something about Alex's wife disturbed him immensely. He felt his stomach knot angrily.

"Evan lives up in Canada," Alex said, continuing his slow, ironic delivery. "He's one of these draft-dodger fellows." *He's needling her!* Evan thought. But then Alex broke the tense mood as quickly as he'd created it, slid his arm around his wife's shoulders, pulled her into him, and said, "Evan and I used to loaf together. Would you believe it? Shit, between us we damned near put the Iron City brewery out of business." And led her into the kitchen. "What're you making?"

"A cake."

"Oh, a cake. Well, that's just fine. The kids will love that."

"It's just out of a box," she said, the words directed over her shoulder at Evan; her eyes were sad and accusing.

Alex jerked open the refrigerator. "Well, how about a beer, Carlyle? You drink beer up there in Canada, don't you?"

Evan looked at Alex closely, saw for the first time the mischievous glitter on his face that must have been there all along. Evan felt his stomach relax; he thought he knew, suddenly, where he was. "We've got real beer in Canada," he said. "None of this bottled dishwater."

"Oh, you do, do you? Haw! But I suppose you could manage to choke down one of these?"

"Sure, I think I could manage."

Alex popped open two cans. "Never saw a man who could put away the beer like Carlyle here," he said to his wife. "He was just a plain fool for drinking beer."

Evan took a can and grinned at his friend. "To the Queen," he said.

Alex laughed. It wasn't one of his sudden barks, but a belly laugh. He tilted back his head and laughed. "To the Queen, is it? Well, okay, to the Queen." Sharon had been watching the men carefully; now she began to giggle. "Where are the kids?" Alex asked her.

"Alex Junior's at Billy's, and Lori's off being a sugarplum," she said. And Evan was startled to hear in her, now that her voice was relaxed, an echo of Alex's flat, ironic delivery.

"Damn crazy kid," Alex said. "She's amazing."

"Lori's his darling," Sharon told Evan. "She can't do anything wrong."

"How old is she?"

"She just turned six," Alex said. "She takes after me, God help her."

"It's true," Sharon said. "She's got that ugly Warner puss." For the first time her smile was spontaneous and genuine; she smiled at Alex. *I was wrong,* Evan thought, *she's more than merely pretty.*

Alex acknowledged her, sent her back a hint of that old wolfish grin that Evan remembered. Then he swept one arm around Evan's shoulders and propelled him through the door. "Let's leave the kitchen to the women, right?"

"It's a nice place," Evan said uneasily, looking around the living room, which seemed to have been furnished from one of those new discount warehouses he'd seen along the National Road. He settled into one of the chairs in front of the picture window.

"Well, I don't know about that. . . . It's a house." Alex raised his beer can in a salute. "What has it been, you crazy fucker, ten years?"

"Thirteen years. Nineteen sixty . . . that summer was the last time I saw you." *Hold on,* Evan told himself. *Don't say that. Don't remind him.* "But then you went to WVU, didn't you?" he said, speaking quickly to hurry the conversation forward in time, "and then I heard you joined the army."

"Yeah, that's right. Dropped out of school that winter and joined the army. Damn stupidest thing I ever did in my life."

"How was it?"

"What? The army? Well, you ever been in the Boy Scouts?" Evan laughed. "It was stupid, that's all. Just fucking stupid. The only part of it I liked was being in Korea. . . ."

"You liked Korea?"

"Yeah, I liked Korea. I liked the people . . . getting drunk with them in those little funny bars they've got over there. *Makali* houses they call them. Shit, I even learned to speak some Korean, can you believe that? . . . Sometimes I wish I was back there . . . although God knows what I'd be doing in Korea."

"And you missed out on Vietnam?"

"Yeah, just barely. There was a big push on for us to re-up, but shit, I wasn't that crazy."

It was all coming back too fast now, memory so weighted and evocative that it might have been as recently as last week that Evan had last watched his friend look away: Alex continued to stare at the falling snow. *The only times I ever felt comfortable talking to him,* Evan thought, *were when we were riding in a car. He seemed easier then; he had the excuse of watching the road.* "It's fucking cold in Korea," Alex said. "You want another beer?"

"Sure."

Alex returned with not merely another beer but with an armful of cans which he set on the floor between them. "When did you go to Canada?" he asked.

"Sixty-eight," Evan said. "It wasn't easy. . . . It wasn't an easy thing. I was out in California then . . . working for one of the Radio Pacifica stations. It was the first time in my life I'd ever been doing exactly what I wanted to, but then they called me up for the physical—"

"So you put your ass on the road."

"It wasn't that simple, but yeah, that's what I did. We talked about it a lot and—" Evan stopped, hearing the *we* he had just said. "I was married then."

Alex turned to look at him. "Yeah?"

"I'm not any more."

Alex shrugged.

"She wasn't ready to leave the country and . . . well, shit, it had been breaking up anyway." He wondered if Alex understood about these modern marriages that lasted three years.

"The divorce will probably come through this spring," he said. "Looking back on it, I don't think we had a whole hell of a lot in common."

"Yeah," Alex said, "well, who does?" He had turned his eyes back to the window. "So what are you doing now? Still working on the radio?"

"Yeah. Work for the CBC." But then he remembered that those initials wouldn't mean a damn thing in West Virginia. "The Canadian Broadcasting Corporation," he said. "I'm a producer . . . the guy who makes sure the show gets put together and broadcast every day."

"Pay decent?"

"It's all right. Not wonderful, but all right. . . . It's more money than I've ever made in my life actually." *Actually!* he thought. *Christ, that Canadianism sounds strange in Alex's living room.*

"Well, shit, it sounds like you're doing all right."

A knock at the door sent Alex to his feet: "It's that crazy woman bringing Lori back." He was moving so fast that he could have been running away. Evan was left staring after him, confused.

Sharon yelled from the kitchen, "I'll get it."

"Yeah, you do that." Alex's voice receding. "I'm going to take a shower."

Door opening, women's voices. Evan turned in his chair and saw that a small child had come silently to stand next to him. She wore a red ski jacket, too big for her, hanging open; under it a pink tutu and tights, pink ballet slippers soaked through with snow; she'd trailed snow behind her into the living room. There was snow melting on her short curly hair—hair like her father's. And her eyes were like his too, uncannily, the same near-yellow that Evan used to imagine as the color of stale beer. As her mother had done, she was staring into Evan's face. She didn't smile. "Where's my daddy?" she said.

Sharon was right behind her: "Lori, my God, you're getting snow everywhere!" To Evan: "It was so warm this afternoon. I didn't think it was going to snow." As she peeled the jacket off the child, she kept glancing over at Evan, then back at her daughter. "Oh, look at your feet! Go change your clothes right now or you'll be in bed for a week." She pushed the little girl in front of her out of the room. He still couldn't understand why he should find Alex's wife so disturbing.

Women's voices again, the door banging, footsteps, and in the distance the shower running. Evan drained the last of his third can of beer. He didn't want to be here. He felt a gray detachment as though he were a ghost who'd once lived in this family, come back now to sit invisibly in the living room and listen to the sounds of the house.

Then Sharon reappeared suddenly and threw herself into the chair opposite him. She lit a cigarette. "God, it's a crime letting that child go out of the house dressed like that . . . but it seemed so warm."

"I know. It really was warm."

"But you never know in this crazy valley. It can be warm one minute and snowing the next."

"I know. I grew up here."

Lori was back, uniformed like her mother in jeans and a sweat shirt. She was barefoot. "Daddy's in the bathroom," she said.

"Go put something on your feet. . . . She's *impossible!* Well . . . so you and Al went to high school together?"

"Yeah. We went to Raysburg High."

"So did I. But that was after you were there, I guess. I graduated in sixty-five."

"Yeah, we graduated in sixty."

"You don't look that old. You don't look as old as Al. When you walked in, I thought you were more my age."

Evan shrugged. "I've been lucky, I guess." *She's really studying me,* he thought. *What is she looking for?*

"It doesn't seem so long ago, does it?" she said.

"What?"

"High school."

"Oh, I don't know. Sometimes it seems forever ago. And then

other times I'll have a dream that will take me back there . . . and then it seems as though I've never left . . . that I'm *still* going to Raysburg High." *On one of my bad nights,* he thought.

"Yeah," she said, shaking her head, "I know what you mean. Sometimes I really miss it."

BONK!: a loud mechanical bell in the kitchen. She stubbed out her cigarette, jumped to her feet. "Excuse me," she said, and then, with a coy smile over her shoulder: "No rest for the wicked." *Yeah, I'll bet you were the Queen of the Hop,* Evan thought. She had a delightfully pert little ass in those tight jeans.

He lay back in his chair and wondered why he was feeling so odd, not bad enough to merit the label *sick,* but an uneasiness was diffusing throughout his body. If he could talk to Dana, he'd be able to distance himself from all of this, find a way to handle it. He closed his eyes. *It's strange,* he thought, *how you need women when you've got them but you don't when you don't.* He could see Dana's face clearly in his mind, but he couldn't see Beth's. She was still his wife, on paper at least, but he didn't remember her very well. It really *was* strange. He could think of the words he'd use to describe Beth, but he couldn't see her face.

He opened his eyes and looked around the living room. He counted the empty cans lined up by the chair Alex had vacated. One, two, three, four, five, six.

The sound of the shower had stopped. Now he could hear Alex talking to Lori. Sharon called out, "Hey, I'm going to get Al Junior."

"Right."

"Where are the keys?"

"In my pants. Here." He threw them down the stairs.

"Don't let the casserole burn, okay?"

Door slamming. And immediately Alex appeared. He was whispering in an absurd conspiratorial voice: "Hey, Carlyle, come here. I want to show you something."

Evan followed Alex up the stairs and into the bedroom. "Don't let the casserole burn, she says. Shit, the only way I'd know if the casserole was burning was if the kitchen burst into flames." Lori was trailing after her father like a faithful dog. "You go and play now," he told her. "I want to have a private talk with my buddy Carlyle."

"Oh, Daddy!"

"Go on, now. We'll be out in a minute." He shut the bedroom door behind his daughter, reached onto the top shelf of the closet (so high that his wife would have had to stand on a chair to search there), and pulled down a pint of Jack Daniel's. He unscrewed the lid and offered it; Evan shook his head. Alex took a long pull, turned to a dresser, picked up a framed photograph, and handed it to Evan. The drapes, a drab blue, were shut in the bedroom; only one light by the bed, the small one with the plastic lace lampshade, was burning. The room was as murky as the bottom of a fishbowl. Evan, puzzled, looked at the photograph. It was the American Beauty Dream Girl, a pubescent Tuesday Weld, big-breasted but baby-faced, got up in a majorette's uniform, smiling glassily into the camera. The long, smooth legs—magnificent legs—under the tiny skirt were posed daintily; she held a baton. *What the hell?* Evan thought with an unpleasant swell of foreboding. Then he saw that it was Sharon.

"That's what she looked like when I met her," Alex said. "She was a senior in high school when I got out of the army. And I was as horny as six billy goats. Sweet Mother of Jesus, did she like to screw. Goddamn." He retrieved the photograph and set it on the dresser. "She really hates having that thing around," he said, grinning. He took another pull on the bottle, offered it again. Evan took it and drank off a good two ounces of whiskey at a gulp; it burned all the way down. Alex took the bottle out of Evan's hand, screwed the cap back on, and restored it to the top of the closet. Then, abruptly, he opened the door and walked out of the bedroom. Lori had been waiting by the door.

Chapter Three

Evan settled again into the chair in the living room. Outside the window snow was coming down harder now; it blotted out any possibilities of a view. In the kitchen Alex banged the oven door, jerked open the refrigerator, and popped open another beer can; Lori was talking, but Evan couldn't make out the words. And the diffuse, uneasy sickness that had been bothering him was turning now into genuine nausea. He knew he should have never come back to Raysburg, not even for a week. The picture of Sharon had made it all suddenly worse—and the light in the bedroom, that murky gloom. There was something unbearably nasty about that teen-age majorette with all her defects retouched away, kept framed on a bedside table by her husband years later, something that did indeed have to be chased with a shot from a bottle hidden on the back of a shelf.

The first thing he'd seen when he'd walked through the door to his parents' apartment had been a picture of himself, not either of the ones taken when he'd graduated from Raysburg High or from Ohio State, not the wedding picture he'd mailed back from California nor the shot taken with Dana he'd sent last summer; it was a tinted eight-by-ten of himself at age nine. He was dressed in striped silk pants and patent-leather shoes, holding a cane and a top hat, playing Yankee Doodle Dandy for the spring recital of the Mateski School of Dance, where his mother had sent him for the same reason she'd named him Evan instead of George, Bill, Tom, Frank, or Harry; for the same reason he'd been forced through ten years of piano lessons despite an ineptitude for music that bordered on tone deafness.

Evan had climbed the stairs to his parents' apartment accompanied the entire way by the hysterical barking of his mother's cocker spaniel, Mitzie. He walked through the door, set his suitcase down, hugged his mother and shook hands with his dad, and there staring him in the face, hanging directly over the mantel above the television set, was that idiotic picture. "Well," he said, "I see you've made some changes." His mother was much as he remembered her, small and round with her bright blue eyes and one of her standard blue dresses to set them off; her voice still went on in an unstoppable murmur, and she was still, even in her sixties, pretending that she didn't need glasses, wearing them hanging on a chain around her neck instead of on her face. But his father had grown impossibly old in the past five years. At eight o'clock in the evening he was dressed in pajamas, slippers, and a long brown bathrobe. He shuffled along supporting himself on the furniture. "How are you feeling, Dad?" Evan said.

"Oh, can't complain, can't complain." Although, of course, he had every right to complain. He was dying. "Well, how's Beth these days?" his father said.

"I don't really keep in very close touch with her."

"Evan's separated now," his mother said. "You remember that, dear."

"Oh, yes. That's right. That's right. You're seeing that other girl now, aren't you? You sent us her picture."

"That's right, Dad. . . . Dana."

"Oh, yes. Dana. That's right. Pretty girl."

The dog had become a round, stuffed sausage of fur with four tiny legs protruding ridiculously from the bottom; she was so fat that she couldn't jump onto the couch any longer but had to be helped. Any abrupt movement that Evan made could set her off; then she'd press herself against his mother's ankle, stare up at him with dim, hating eyes, and bark. "She just has to get used to you . . ." and his mother would bend to talk baby talk: "Don't you, honey? Yes, you do. After all these years. Yes, you do," she would say and pat the enormous lump of fur while Mitzie, her tiny paws braced on the carpet, her upper lip drawn back to show yellowed teeth, watched him and barked.

His mother had kept a dinner hot for him even though he'd told her on the phone that he'd grab a sandwich at the airport. He sat at the kitchen table and worked his way through instant mashed potatoes, hamburgers covered with a sauce he was sure had been made from the contents of a cardboard box, and "boughten" cookies as he'd forgotten his mother called them. His parents had eaten hours before, sat on the other side of the table drinking tea. Whenever he'd look up, he'd see his father watching him, his face showing nothing but tiredness, and his mother smiling that weak, strained, hopeful smile. He tried to talk, to make his voice sound cheerful, but he couldn't bring it off. They all went to bed right after the eleven o'clock news, and he couldn't sleep, not even with two capsules of Dalmane in him. He sat up and lit a cigarette. The bedsprings creaked under him and from across the hall, through two closed doors, from the foot of his mother's bed, came a single sharp bark. He finished the cigarette and walked into the bathroom; the dog went off like a string of firecrackers. His mother kept saying, "Shhh. It's all right, honey. It's all right. It's only Evan. You remember Evan." The bathroom was full of the paraphernalia of his father's illness: suppositories, ointments, pills, an enema bag hanging over the bathtub. Evan dressed as quickly as he could and fled.

He walked along the river, unable to think coherently because of the drug, fatigue dragging at his muscles, but he knew that sleep was totally impossible. There was a thermal inversion, his mother had told him; it had sat on the valley for three days now. "It happens sometimes, honey, you remember. But it seems to happen now more than it used to." The air was so thick with pollutants that he couldn't get a clear breath; he felt as though a rubber balloon had been pulled down over his head and chest. The lights of downtown Raysburg were reflected back in the river, smeary puddles of color, and high above on the hill the three red lights of the radio tower were reduced by the dense air into dull, luminous holes in the slate-black sky. That tower, which beamed out country-and-western tunes and mad gospel-preachers twenty-four hours a day, had been a beacon for him all the time he'd been growing up; he'd been fascinated even then with the magic of transmitting sound invisibly through the air. He used to imagine himself as an all-night disc jockey like Lee Moore, the Coffee-Drinking Nighthawk: "Well, howdy, friends and neighbors. Here we are bringing you the best in hill and country music—"

After the training conference, he'd called Dana from Toronto: "Christ, I met Colin McNaughton!"

"All right, Evan, let me in on it. Who the hell's Colin McNaughton?"

"He's only the vice-president for radio, English language division, for all of goddamned Canada, that's who he is. He came right up to me and said, 'I've heard about you.' I mean *he came to me*, right? He said, 'I've heard that you're doing really fine work out there in Vancouver.' I told you they were watching me."

"That's wonderful, Evan," she said, but her voice over the line to Vancouver didn't sound particularly delighted.

"I'm on my way, kid!" he yelled.

"Evan," she said dryly, "you've been on your way ever since I've known you."

Why did she have to do that? Why couldn't she just let him enjoy the pleasure of it? "They're going to bring me to Toronto ... or at least to Ottawa," he said. "I've got it made."

"Yeah, you probably do. You'll probably go right up in the corporation like a rocket. I suppose congratulations are in order."

"Dana, you know you could get work back east. You're good. You've had experience."

"Oh, Evan, for Christ's sake, don't start that again. I'm a B.C. girl. I hate Toronto."

But now it all seemed impossibly remote: Toronto, Vancouver, the CBC, Dana—Canada. Was it possible that he was really competent, a producer, holding down a goddamned real job and a demanding one at that? Was it possible that somebody somewhere really liked his work? West Virginia, as it always did, had eaten the heart right out of him the minute he stepped off the plane, had turned him instantly back into a dumb-punk asshole, a Raysburg boy. He walked along the river too tired, too spaced-out for something as simple as mere panic. Just trapped. Again. *Oh, Christ,* he thought, *if I can only get through Christmas. That's all, just through Christmas. It's only a few more days. Then I can get out of here and never come back, not ever, not for the old man's funeral, not for anything.*

Chapter Four

Evan woke up at noon the next day feeling groggy and stupid. He found that the air was clearing. It would never clear completely, of course, not in the Ohio Valley, but the inversion had lifted and a steady wind was blowing away some of the gray haze. If he smoked his mother's cigarettes instead of his own, he could get almost all the way to the charcoal filter without coughing. And the wind had also brought one of those freaky December warm spells; Christmas was only a week away and the thermometer outside the window told him that it was sixty-four degrees. His father was up and dressed, oddly enough in a gray three-piece suit. He was even wearing a necktie. The suit was too big; an inch of space gaped between his neck and the collar of his shirt. "I'm doing really well, Dad," Evan told him. "I'm almost certain to go on staff."

His father turned to look at him and Evan saw his own eyes in that collapsed face. "Do you know what that means?" he said.

"I won't be working from contract to contract . . . I'll be making more money."

"Good," his father said sharply, "that's good."

"They're probably going to transfer me to Toronto—"

"You know, Uncle Ed sold his plot," his father interrupted. His voice didn't sound old; it was still hard and clear.

"What?"

"He sold his plot out at Greenlawns. Some hunky and his wife are buried out there now."

"Oh?"

"Always been Carlyles buried out in that corner, but now there's some hunky and his wife. Not even at the side. Right in the middle."

"That's too bad."

"Your great-granddad's out there. Thomas Edward. That's how far back it goes. 'Don't sell the plot, Ed,' I told him. 'You can't tell who's going to buy it.' But he didn't pay any attention to me. Well, you probably don't care about it at all, do you? Probably doesn't matter to you." He levered himself to his feet. "Hand me my cane, will you? . . . Well, it shouldn't matter to you at your age, I guess. Never thought I'd be walking with a cane."

Evan's mother had appeared suddenly from the kitchen, a tea towel in her hands. "Tom, you're not going out today, are you? With Evan at home? He hasn't been home in years."

"I have to get out of the house." His voice was stubborn. "You know that, Grace. When I can't get out of the house, you might as well take me down to the riverbank and shoot me."

His mother shook her head. She said, exactly as though her husband weren't there to hear it: "He goes up to that bar every day and plays pinochle with that no-good Charlie Conners. He's going to fall one of these days, and then I don't know what I'm going to do. He doesn't appreciate anything I do for him. He doesn't know how hard it is for me."

"You'll be rid of me soon enough, Grace." There wasn't a sign of anger in his voice, just a bitter hardness, tired and determined. "But while I'm here, I've got to get out of the house."

"I'll help you down the stairs, Dad," Evan said.

In the afternoon his mother walked up to the corner store and Evan was left alone in the apartment. Smoking another one of her cigarettes, he wandered around and looked at all the familiar objects. The piano at which he'd suffered so many tedious hours was gone, but the bookcases with glass doors still held his high school texts and all of his mother's poetry: Keats, Shelley, Byron, and Wordsworth in expensive leather-bound editions. He remembered stupefyingly hot summer afternoons before he'd been old enough to go to school, lying on the floor, cranky and bored, kicking his toes into the rug, and the only thing his mother had thought to do about it was read aloud to him from those books of poetry. He hadn't understood a word. He still hated poetry.

But where were all the goddamned pictures? He walked into the back hall and began jerking cardboard cartons out of the closet and setting them down on the floor. Each carton was tied up with twine and labeled with his mother's neat librarian's handwriting: SUMMER CLOTHES, SUMMER SHOES, OLD FAMILY THINGS, and finally EVAN'S THINGS. He sat on the floor, his back to the wall, and sorted through the carton with his name on it. Right, that was where his mother had hidden all the pictures he'd sent back, the ones from Ohio, from California, from Vancouver. He was glad to see good old Dana from only last summer, posed in front of the Bloedel Conservatory in Wedgies and shorts, showing off her elegant legs. And Beth really had been a California hippie girl with her long, straight golden hair and wide eyes, wearing the unbleached cotton dress she'd made for their wedding. He pawed through a few more eight-by-tens and there, finally, was what he'd been looking for: his graduation picture. *Nineteen sixty and done, by God, with Raysburg High.* He was wearing a suit and tie, of course, but he was stubbornly refusing to smile. His hair was not quite long enough for a real D.A., but he wasn't exactly your clean-cut kid either. *On my way out of town,* he thought, pleased at that old image.

Underneath was more high school stuff. His one and only letter, a huge blue and white R that he'd never had sewn onto a sweater because of the smaller letter M at the bottom which would have blown it, told the world that he hadn't been an athlete but only a manager. He'd managed the track team his senior year so he could watch all the meets from down on the field, watch his friend Alex Warner break mile records.

His mother was home. "Do you want a sandwich, Evan?" she called to him. Strangely enough, she didn't walk on back to the hall.

"Yeah," he said, "I'll be right there. Just a minute." He was down to all the candid pictures he'd taken in high school with his father's Leica, Tri-X film, and available light. It was about time to stop and pack it all up again. No point of reminding himself what a little asshole he'd been in those days. But there was a rare shot of Alex, who hated to have his picture taken, slouched and scowling in front of Wolchak's garage with an enormous blond man by his side, some grinning guy who looked like a prizefighter. After a moment, he remembered. It was Frank Hospidarski, that small-time crook who used to work for Joe Patone. And then, more than memory, it was an icy spasm of fear in his stomach as vivid as if it had happened last week and not years before. *Good God*, he thought, *the night they got into that fight. The bartender with the gun. Christ, I must have been crazy to run around with those guys—we could have been shot!* And the last he'd heard, Hospidarski had been doing five-to-ten at Moundsville for armed robbery.

Absently he kept flipping through all the accumulated debris of the past. There was Elaine, of course. Everybody in the fifties had wanted a True Love, and he supposed she'd been his. She'd wanted to be an actress, and he'd shot a whole roll of her once when they'd both been seventeen, right out there in the living room while his parents were at work, a sheet thumbtacked to the wall for a backdrop. He'd taken all the dramatic shots she'd asked for, variations on the same theme: head and shoulders with a cigarette used as a prop, wisp of smoke curling up, her dark eyes focused into the distance, her young girl's face so heavily painted that he could barely associate the pictures with any memory of her. And there were a few more, the cheesecake that *he'd* wanted: Elaine in tight shorts, stretched out on the couch; Elaine posed behind the open umbrella arranged so that her swimsuit didn't show, trying to look naked except for her sexy high heels; but now, years later, she looked merely silly and sad—a gawky, long-legged kid with too much makeup standing stiffly behind a tacky black umbrella in old-fashioned shoes. Where was the picture of her at their graduation dance when she'd dressed herself up like Marilyn Monroe? Surely his mother couldn't have thrown it away. . . . Well, yeah, come to think of it, she could have.

But she hadn't thrown away Elaine's graduation picture, a five-by-seven in a cardboard frame. Her last year of high school she'd let her black hair grow out of that short boyish cut she'd always worn before; it just brushed her bare shoulders, and she'd set it for the occasion so that it swept away from her forehead in looping waves on either side, curled around to the front, and hid her ears. She'd plucked her heavy brows into those precise lines fashionable in 1960 and for once had put on just the right makeup. With her somber eyes staring straight into the camera and her full, sullen mouth carefully painted, she looked like a brooding Hollywood starlet from an old black and white movie. *Well,* he thought, *she finally did get the image right.*

He slid the picture out of the frame, turned it over, and found on the back, where his mother would never have seen it, Elaine's strangely abbreviated handwriting, the vowels strung out into straight lines, done not with a pen but with a dull, soft pencil. He'd remembered that something was written there but had forgotten what it was, that message from across thirteen years: "My dear, No matter how far apart we become some day, at least we'll always have the time we spent together. Love and French kisses. Elaine."

Chapter Five

Alex had rejoined Evan in the living room; he was popping open another beer. Evan had lost count, but he was sure that Alex was well into his second six-pack. Lori hung back at the far side of the room a moment, then trotted across the rug and climbed onto her father's lap. "Carlyle here's from Canada," Alex said. "Do you know where Canada is?" She nodded. "Yeah? Where is it?" She said nothing, stared at Evan with those disconcerting, pale-brown eyes. "Not talking today, huh? You should hear her sometimes, Carlyle. Sometimes she talks a blue streak."

The snow was still coming down just as steadily as it had been for the last couple of hours. *Talk*, Evan told himself. *Make conversation.* "Do you remember Elaine Isaac?" he said to Alex.

"Elly? Remember her? Shit, I've kept that old Ford of hers running for years now."

Evan said nothing. Out of the corner of his eye he could see that Alex was smiling slightly. "What?" Alex said. "Did you think I wouldn't remember her?"

The front door opened and closed. Sharon, with a small boy by the hand, passed in front of the archway that opened into the hall. "Get those shoes off, Al," she was saying.

Alex swiveled in his chair. "What do you say there, Crash?" he called out.

"Hi, Dad," the boy muttered, and followed his mother quickly through the living room toward the back of the house. He was eight or nine, built more like Sharon than like Alex, slight and small-boned, with straight black hair, much more of it than

Evan would have suspected for Raysburg; it hung over his face in a great, sloppy bang. In the boy's quick passage Evan had registered only a delicate, oval face made owlish by black-framed glasses.

Alex shook his head and grimaced. "That's old Crash Warner," he said. "He breaks his toes walking into furniture. He breaks his arm falling off his bicycle. He breaks the front window with a softball. He's a one-kid wrecking crew, that one. Haw!"

Evan shrugged. "They grow up," he said. "But how's she doing? Elaine?"

"Elly? . . . Oh, I think she's doing fine. Of course she hasn't been Elaine Isaac for a long time now. She's Elaine Jamieson."

"Oh . . . do I know him?"

"I doubt it. He was from Pennsylvania. They haven't lived together for years. Divorced. But she still uses his name."

"What kind of a guy was he?"

"Bill Jamieson? He wasn't worth a bucket of piss."

"What happened?"

"I don't know. She got sick of him, I guess. She left him."

Evan felt as though Alex were making him pull the information out, piece by piece, like nails out of a board. He closed his eyes and let his head fall back onto the chair. It was a comfortable chair, one of these fake-leather things that reclined. "She's got a little girl," Alex said. "Cute little thing. About Al Junior's age. Smart as a whip." Evan must have drunk too much beer on an empty stomach; he wanted to tilt the chair back and go to sleep in it.

Footsteps. Evan opened his eyes and saw that Sharon was joining them, somewhat breathlessly, throwing herself down on the couch. She'd found the time to brush her hair, put on lipstick, and change her clothes. She now wore tight black pants and a sweater with a circle cut out at the top to show off her cleavage. No doubt about it: she did have lovely breasts. "Well, dinner's about ready," she said levelly, looking at the empty beer cans, "and you guys look like you're about ready for it."

Alex turned to her and laughed. "Where's the boy wonder?" he asked her.

"He's in his room reading."

"Reading," Alex said, disgust in his voice.

Looking at Sharon, Evan finally understood why she'd been bothering him so much; he didn't know why it should have taken him so long to figure it out. Her intense black brooding eyes were like Elaine's. Her voice had that mixture of downstate slur with sharp immigrant edges you'd hear only in the Ohio Valley. And her manner— Well, she was a Raysburg girl, just an ordinary Raysburg girl. And it turned him on.

She had begun to pick the polish off her nails. "Alex," she said carefully, "when did you close the garage?"

"I don't know. Four thirty or five. Something like that. It was about then, wasn't it, Carlyle?"

"Yeah, about five." *Shit, he's already got me lying for him.*

"You know, Alex," she said slowly, "it's hard to make any money when you're not open."

"It's hard," Alex said, matching the slowness of her delivery, "to make any money when it's snowing like a son of a bitch."

"Watch your mouth in front of Lori, will you please?" She'd spoken quickly, her anger obvious. Now she seemed to regret it; her face colored. She dropped her eyes to her fingernails. Alex turned back to the window. Silence. Finally she said, a bit too brightly, "How is it up in Canada? . . . I mean, is there much of an oil shortage?"

"No. Not much. Not where I live anyway."

"That must be nice. . . . They say . . . people are saying . . . there's going to be a depression. Do you think so?"

"Haw!" Alex laughed. "What the hell do they think *this* is?"

"This isn't like the thirties," she said.

"How do we know? None of us were around then." He turned to Evan. "People care about their cars, you know that, Carlyle. As long as there's any money coming in, they'll usually take care of their cars. But when the squeeze comes, they've got to eat, and then they say, 'Well, screw it, I'll let it fall apart.'

And that hasn't just been since this energy crisis business, that's been for the last year. And of course the Ohio Valley has never been exactly the land of milk and honey, right? So I don't know how much more we've got to go before it's a depression. Haw! The truckers have the right idea. Go park their rigs in the middle of the road. The only way to get anywhere around here is to make trouble."

"Oh, Al," Sharon said. "Come on, let's eat."

Alex set his daughter on her feet and patted her roughly; she didn't seem to mind it. He was frowning. He looked at Evan, shook his head, and showed teeth in that grin that wasn't a grin, then abruptly walked into the dining room. Evan followed. Alex didn't sit down but stopped at the head of the table, pressed his hands down on the back of the chair and drummed on it with his fingers. He peered about as though he had misplaced something. "Where the hell is he?" Alex said, but he couldn't have been talking to Sharon; she was in the kitchen. Then, without warning, he shouted: "Hey, Crash! Soup's on."

Sharon's angry face appeared in the doorway to the kitchen: "You let him alone!"

"All right, all right," he said.

The boy came in immediately. He wore green corduroy pants and no shoes; the socks on his small feet were kelly green. He had brushed his great mass of hair up out of his face. He didn't look at his father. He sat down in his place at the side of the table. "Well, son," Alex said to him in a soft, deadly voice too low for Sharon to hear, "what did you break today?"

Evan looked at his friend and saw the marks of strain—white tension—around the eyes and mouth, something on that face he'd seen years before and had come to know. *He's drunk,* Evan thought, *and he's dangerous.*

They were all seated around the table. Sharon was trying to smile; her eyes—wide, full of message—were on Evan's face. *She's telling me something like this,* he thought: *You must know him too.* And Evan made a rapid search for a safe line of conversation, something he could toss off to make Alex laugh.

Sharon beat him: "Well, what do Canadians think of our president?" Her voice sounded forced, falsely cheerful.

"Probably the same thing you think of him down here," he said slowly.

"Haw!" Alex barked. "Everybody acts so damned surprised, it's ridiculous. The man's been so crooked all his life, when he dies they're going to have to screw him into the ground like a corkscrew."

"What's a corkscrew?" Lori asked.

"It's a thing you take corks out of bottles with," he told her. Then to Evan: "Of course they're all crooked. . . . What's this?"

Sharon was lifting the lid from a red ovenware dish. "It's a casserole," she said flatly. Evan saw noodles in a sauce with wieners and cheese.

"Great," Alex said. "Give the kid some of it. Pile up his plate. Got to put some meat on him."

"There's peas," Sharon said unhappily. "It's not much of a dinner, but I didn't know I'd have a guest."

"Oh, it's fine," Evan said. "Wonderful. Home cooking." *And she's laid out her best plates and silver for me,* he thought. *When did she have time to do it?* "So you voted for McGovern?" he asked Alex.

"Christ, no! I voted for Nixon . . . McGovern!"—he repeated the name as though it was an insult—"I'll tell you about him, Carlyle. He's a preacher and he's a dink. And he surrounded himself with a bunch of punk college kids who never did a damned thing in their lives but look around the world to see who they could screw out of something. I wouldn't vote for that man . . . not if he had Jesus Christ and the Twelve Apostles on the ticket with him."

Evan laughed. "I voted for McGovern," Sharon said, smiling. The children were giggling. Alex looked around the table; he grinned briefly, pleased with himself. "Give me half a chance, Carlyle, and I'll vote for old Georgie Wallace."

"Oh, Alex!" from Sharon.

Evan felt his stomach tighten. "Think you could find a better place for your vote," he said softly. "The Democrats will probably run a middle-of-the-roader next time."

"Yeah, well it doesn't matter much who they run. All this talk about an energy crisis . . . and a depression or a recession or some damned thing. And people going broke right and left. But it's a funny thing. There's always *somebody* making money. . . . Excuse me a minute." Alex pushed back his chair, walked out and up the stairs.

Sharon immediately began to chatter, asking Evan questions: Did he like Canada? How long had he been there? Did the valley seem changed? What did he do for a living? But her son interrupted her, saying: "Are there Eskimos in Canada?" His voice was so precise, it bordered on being dainty.

"Oh, sure," Evan said. "Up north."

"Do they live in igloos?"

"No, not much anymore." Then he saw that the boy wanted the Eskimos to live in igloos. "Well, some of them maybe."

"He's reading all the time," Sharon said.

Alex came back and seated himself heavily. The boy said, "Mom, may I be excused?"

"My God, kid, you haven't eaten a damned thing," Alex said.

"You're excused," Sharon said. The boy pushed back his chair and quietly left the room.

"He doesn't eat enough to keep a butterfly alive," Alex said.

"Maybe he's going to be a distance runner," Evan said.

"Are you kidding? He can't get off his ass long enough to walk around the block." They ate in silence.

After dinner Sharon cleared the table. From the kitchen, she called, "Hey, Al, bring that tray out, will you?"

"Yeah," he said, "yeah, yeah," got up, and carried it out to her. And even though she was whispering, Evan could hear every word: "Hon, don't go out tonight. The roads are too bad."

Alex didn't bother to lower his voice. "Shit, I haven't seen Carlyle in thirteen years."

"I know, Al. But you can stay home and drink. I won't get in your way."

"It's not the same thing."

Evan was embarrassed. He wanted to get out of there as fast as he could. Then he looked up and saw that Lori had been watching him with that peculiar Warner gaze. For an unpleasant second or two he wasn't sure what he was seeing; it was almost as though she were Alex. He smiled at her, but she didn't smile back.

Alex walked straight through the dining room without looking at either Evan or his daughter and disappeared up the stairs. Sharon sat down at the table. She laughed nervously. "Back in high school . . ." she said. Evan waited. "Well, back in high school you and Al must have been pretty good friends. He talks about you a lot."

He does? Evan thought. "I guess we were pretty close."

She started to say something, stopped. Then she looked directly at him. Her eyes were huge and black; again he felt the memory of Elaine like a sad tug from the past. "Look," she said finally, not caring if her daughter heard it, "try to keep him out of trouble, will you?"

He felt an immediate wave of sympathy for her, bittersweet and dangerous. He touched her hand quickly, careful that the gesture wouldn't carry a sexual overtone, and said, "I will."

Alex was back, sweating and grinning, his face drawn tight with strain. He threw a large gray overcoat at Evan. "Here, Carlyle, try this. Keep that goddamned fancy suit of yours dry."

Chapter Six

Evan shut the door, turned and looked down over the terraced hill. Consolidated's squat buildings had vanished. Fat snowflakes made shifting streaks in the streetlights as though lined out by a broad brush, and energy crisis or no energy crisis, many of the houses were strung with Christmas lights; all were shining cheerfully yellow from their windows. *It's what I always said about Raysburg,* he thought. *It's only beautiful at night.*

The cold was lovely, refreshing after the forced-air heat inside. The snow lay thick and wet, ideal for snowballs; three or four inches of it must have fallen since afternoon. He buttoned Alex's overcoat. *It's probably his best one,* he thought, *his dress coat. He probably never wears it.* Too big for Evan, it hung well below his knees, the sleeves to his fingertips; his shoulders, even in his suit jacket, didn't begin to fill it, but he was pleased, he was hidden. And he found himself smiling at the night, for the first time since he'd been back, glad to be in Raysburg. It felt like the old days, that tickle of excitement: he and Alex taking off into the possibility of danger, women left behind. Walking carefully in his expensive boots made for dry pavement, he edged down to the car. Alex had scraped the windows, started the engine. Evan slid into the passenger's seat.

Alex grinned wolfishly. He was pawing in his coat. He located a single key, unlocked the glove compartment, and pulled out a pint of Jack Daniel's. He offered it to Evan. Evan shook his head. Alex took a long drink.

"You think she doesn't know?" Evan asked him.

"What?"

"When the glove compartment's locked and the key to it isn't on the ring with the key to the ignition, do you think she doesn't know what's in the glove compartment?"

"Fuck," Alex said bleakly, "she knows." He locked the whiskey away, put the car in gear, and drove slowly toward the corner; there the road rose steeply to the left, fell away as steeply to the right. "Shit, we'll never get up," he said. Then: "Yes, we will," and he kicked the accelerator down. The tires spun in the wet snow, then took hold, and they shot forward, slid around the corner, taking up the entire road to do it, and started up the hill. Weaving from side to side, they rose to the intersection, still accelerating—Evan saw the stop sign sail by—and slid to a stop halfway across the road. "Fuck of a place for a stop sign," Alex said. He was laughing.

"Jesus, Alex! If there'd been a car coming—"

"Oh, fuck, no problem. You've just got to get a run on these hills." And they were off again, leaping up the next stage of the terrace. But instead of rising to the top, the car began to spin. Alex's foot was still pressing the accelerator down; he didn't react, he left it there.

"Alex!" Evan yelled. Alex lifted his foot; held it poised in the air, unsure whether to brake, and sat inert behind the steering wheel. *He doesn't know what to do!* Evan thought with a surge of panic, *Alex Warner, the guy I used to brag about: He was the best driver I ever knew in my life!* And Evan watched his friend sit stupidly as the car continued to spin. Houselights, Christmas lights, white snow: merry-go-round the window.

Finally Alex hauled the wheel over; they slid out of the spin, slid sideways. They were rocketing down the hill. He hauled the wheel the other way; they slid the other way. "Shit," he said, and sideways they continued down. Evan was braced against the dashboard, panting with fear. "Brake!" he yelled.

"We'll spin!" Alex yelled back. He straightened the car out. Evan saw that the speedometer had them at over sixty miles an hour. At each intersection they shot through the stop sign; at each stop sign Evan clenched his teeth for the crash that never came. And finally they were at the bottom of the hill. "Get down! Hang on!" Alex yelled. He hauled the car around; it slid sideways. He straightened it out and braked; it began to spin. He straightened it out and braked; it began to spin again. He straightened it out. But they were finally losing speed. And then the road curved, but the car didn't; they rode along the guard-rail to the sound of tearing metal. They were stopped.

"Jesus, Alex!" Evan yelled. "Maybe you want to die tonight, but I'm not ready!"

"Shit!" Alex jumped out of the car, slammed the door, walked around to look at the damage, walked back and got in. "Five or six hundred dollars worth of body work," he said. "Good thing I'm in the business. Haw!" He unlocked the glove compartment, jerked out the whiskey bottle.

"Just what you need, man, another drink!"

"Fuck off, Carlyle."

"Jesus, Alex, what the fuck you think you're doing? You're not eighteen anymore, you're fucking damn near thirty-two!"

"You don't need to tell me that." Alex drank, capped the bottle, and set it on the seat between them. "Well, looks like we go into town the back way after all." He put the car into gear and eased onto the road.

"Do you think you can drive?"

Alex kicked the brake so viciously that Evan was thrown forward in his seat. "Who the fuck you think you're talking to!" he yelled. "I'm Alex Warner! I can drive when I'm so drunk I can't *walk!*"

Evan saw that Alex had gone dead white. *Is he going to hit me?* Lips drawn back into a snarl, the gleam of teeth that now wasn't remotely like a grin, pale eyes ugly and strange. He'd seen Alex in action more than once. The worst time in an alley in center Raysburg. They'd had to pull him off. He'd not only sucker-punched the man and knocked him down—and not another boy, a grown man—but he'd kicked him senseless, kicked him bloody, kicked him until his face was like raw meat. All the time they'd been friends, Evan had been afraid of Alex. He discovered now, oddly enough, that he wasn't afraid of him any longer. "You keep believing that, man, and you won't live to see forty," he said.

Alex sat rigid, hanging onto the steering wheel. Then he exhaled explosively and said: "Shit!"

"Look," Evan said, "I know about drinking. A couple years ago I almost signed up with A.A. I know about the bottle in the desk, the bottle in the closet, the bottle in the glove compartment. Just how long have you been doing that? What the hell's going on? What's wrong with you?"

"Shit, Carlyle, it's all going to be gone by spring."

"Gone? What?"

"The business. The fucking goddamn business. I'm going to be wiped out by spring. I'm an independent. Naturally. What the fuck else would I be? And I can't get gas. We're getting squeezed out by the big companies. Jesus! I've got to buy gasoline for my own car from somebody else's goddamn garage! How do you like that? . . . And then what do I do after it's gone? Huh? Go to work for Raysburg Steel? Can you see me working at Raysburg Steel? Even if they was hiring . . . and they're not hiring, they're *laying off*."

"What is it, the oil shortage?"

"Shit, man, it's just the business, that's all. Just the fucking business. I'm not making a plugged nickel. I wasn't making a plugged nickel last year, but fuck, this energy crisis bullshit has got everybody sitting on their goddamned money like a bunch of hens . . . waiting to see what's going to happen. It's just the fucking last straw. The last fucking straw. I'm in debt up to my eye teeth."

Evan had run out of words.

"And naturally," Alex went on, "if you want to get some work done on your car, you're going to go where you can buy some gas to go with it, right? You're not going where some fucker's pumps are dry as a goddamned bone and say, 'All right, fix my transmission and then I'll drive her two blocks down the street to the Esso station and get her filled up.' Right? What a fucking piss-off." His voice was gradually dropping back into its standard flat, bitter tone. "I didn't even want to be in the fucking garage business, you know that, Carlyle? Shit, you know what I wanted to do? When I got out of the army?"

"No."

"I wanted to run a speed shop. That's a laugh isn't it? A little place where kids could come work on their cars. Something like Wolchak's used to be in the old days. Except for real. A real speed shop. Sheri told me I was nuts. She told me it was too risky. That's exactly what she said: 'It's too risky, Alex. You'll never make a dime. You'll go under in a year.' Well, shit, it's all over with."

"Maybe you could get a loan or something—"

"No, I don't mean the business. I mean cars . . . I fucking loved cars. And it's all over with. . . . It's never going to be like it was."

Evan picked up the bottle from the seat, unscrewed the lid, and drank. "Shit, you probably need that," Alex said.

"Yeah." He passed the bottle to Alex. "You too, eh?"

Alex took it and drank. "Well," he said, "you finally got your ride. . . . Here. Might as well kill it. About a shot left."

Oh, Christ, Evan thought, *he does remember!* His hand seemed to have reached out automatically to take the bottle. He drank the last of the whiskey. He sat silently, holding the empty bottle on his lap, staring straight ahead at the windshield, as Alex drove slowly through the snow around the back way toward center Raysburg.

Chapter Seven

"What are we stopping for?" Evan said. He couldn't see any reason for it, only deserted streets filling up with snow.

"Just thought you'd like to see it, that's all." Alex climbed out and slammed the door. Evan hesitated, then got out too.

There wasn't another car anywhere in sight and, except for their own tire tracks, the street and sidewalks were blank and white. And then Evan saw that Alex had parked in front of what used to be Isaac's restaurant; it was just an old weathered building now, leaning slightly out of plumb, with its windows boarded up. He stared directly across the street at what used to be Wolchak's garage; all of its windows were broken, even the one in the little upstairs room where Alex had lived for two years. The pumps were still there, but one of them was shattered and bent at a forty-five-degree angle as though someone had run a car into it. "I figured this was where you was going," Alex said, "when I bumped into you."

Yeah, Evan thought, *he's right. This is where I was going. Except that I didn't know it.* "Pretty bleak," he said.

"You bet your ass. . . . Come on," Alex said, crossing the street, "we can walk right in." He slammed his shoulder into the door, all two hundred pounds of him hurled against it, hard, and burst through with a crash, sound of splintering wood. "See," he said laughing, "they left it open for us." Evan followed him into the empty room where there had once been chairs, a Coke machine, a cash register, and a counter—a pile of those ridiculous calendars for the customers to take if they wanted them, naive fifties attempts at pornography: a farmgirl climbing a fence, her skirt caught on a post, staring back alarmed over one shoulder, showing her ass in shiny panties. Underneath in black lettering: WOLCHAK'S GARAGE—EXPERT AUTO REPAIRS.

Their footsteps echoed in the empty space. "We can even go upstairs if we're careful," Alex said. "The wood's kind of rotted out."

"I don't think I want to."

"Yeah, I guess I don't either." But Alex was staring up at the ceiling as though he could see right through it into the room where he used to live.

"Whatever happened to that old couch?" Evan said.

"I don't know."

"I'd like to have a dollar for every night I passed out on that couch."

"Yeah," Alex said, "and I'd like to have a dollar for every night I had to damn near carry you up those stairs." He walked away, into the back. The shelves that used to be stacked with auto parts were empty. Alex threw down his cigarette and ground it out on the cement floor.

"I always wondered where the hell old man Wolchak learned to work on cars," Evan said.

"I'll tell you a secret, Carlyle. He never did. That's why he hired me. Shit, he couldn't even speak English worth a damn. Everything was a 'fucker' with him. 'Hey, Alex,' he'd say, 'gimme dat fucker . . . yeah, dat fucker.' And he'd draw it in the air, open end wrench or whatever it was. 'Yeah, *dat* fucker!' He was a junkman before he opened the garage, you know that, and he stayed a junkman. Take away his torch, he couldn't have done a damned thing. But Jesus, that old guy had a heart as big as a barn. Five of his own and taking care of me too. Always giving me things. First truck I had, he give it to me. Just like that. 'You take dis fucker, Al. You run it.' He let me live upstairs and never charged me for it. Not a penny." Alex turned and walked abruptly away, through the empty building and out into the street.

This used to be a busy corner, Evan thought, looking out the shattered window at the snow. Kids with their fathers' cars, or their own cars, used to be in and out of the garage from late afternoon, when school let out, until closing time. Nobody would have used the word then, but it had been a kind of cooperative. Of course if you wanted to pay the full tariff, you could just drop the car off and come back for it a week later, but if you wanted to save money, you'd do most of the work yourself with Alex or Tony Wolchak giving you a hand. Old man Wolchak would sell you all the parts you needed; if you wanted something special, a racing cam or a blower, he'd order it for you. If you got hungry hanging out at the garage, you could walk across the street to Isaac's. You didn't really mind if John was so drunk that the ashes from the Chesterfields he chain-smoked ended up in your mashed potatoes. If you were over eighteen, or looked over eighteen, you could have a cold quart at J.R.'s two doors up; you could come back there on Saturday nights to dance polkas and obereks, sung and played by a huge fat woman on an accordion and her huge fat husband on washtub base. He was a wonder on the washtub, that old guy; people came from all over South Raysburg to hear him. Before he took up music, he'd worked in the mines right up to the day of the explosion that had put his eyes out. "What are they singing about?" Evan would say.

"It's a funny song," Pilsudski or Watinka would answer. "She's telling her daughter to watch out or she'll get knocked up. It's pretty funny. Don't know how you'd say it in English."

Good Christ, Evan thought, *what must it have been like for John Isaac and his family to move up from Carrysburg into center Raysburg? Must have been like settling down in Krakow.* "Dumb Polacks," John called them, even though J. R. Dutkiewicz, who owned the bar, was his best friend. *Glupi* the Poles called John and people like him, and the word had entered West Virginia English as *hoopy* meaning *hillbilly*, but in Polish it meant *fool*. Poor old John Isaac, crazy and mean and dangerous; as a young man he'd done a couple years at Moundsville for shooting a cousin of his in the stomach with a .38. But he could also be kind, almost gentle. He wasn't always a terrifying, round face which appeared suddenly over the side of the booth, hissing out of the corner of his mouth at Elaine: "There's customers in here, goddamn it! You move your butt, girl." It wasn't really that often he turned into an outright madman, a holy terror with Jesus whispering in his ear, telling him to blow his daughter's head off with a shotgun. Sometimes he'd sit just inside the door to the kitchen with his ten-dollar Stella guitar propped against the top of his belly and sing old country tunes in a faint, wheezing, but perfectly true voice.

There was one song that Evan hadn't been able to forget after all these years; it had been one of John's favorites, the story of a gambler who'd ruined his life with the cards. He's in a big game and he's losing; he's gambled away everything he owns except for one last possession. And when John came to that crucial line, he'd always look up, out at a nonexistent audience; his dark eyes would gleam for a moment from behind the fat gray pouches with a sad intensity just like Elaine's, and he'd sing the words slowly, half speaking them: "He took his dead mother's ring from his finger."

Evan followed Alex out into the street. "I guess Elaine's old man must be dead by now," he said.

"John Isaac?" Alex said. "Yeah, he's dead."

"He was crazy."

"You don't know the half of it, Carlyle. I had to take his shotgun off him once. Did I ever tell you that?"

"I don't remember. What happened?"

"Well, shit," Alex said, "I was working over there"—he jerked his head toward the garage—"and I heard a hell of a racket coming from across the street . . . screaming and things going crash. And here comes Elly out the door. She's running like she's going after the Valley quarter-mile record just getting her ass up to Twenty-first. And right behind her Big John waving his belt. He couldn't keep up with her, but he was giving it a damn good try. Red as a fucking sunset. And I talked him into J.R.'s and got him good and drunk, and he kept saying, 'She's got to come home sometime.' And after he was good and drunk, I said, 'You know, John, lots of break-ins going on these days. I sure would feel safer at night over at the garage if I had me a shotgun.' He knew what I was doing but he let me take it anyway. About a week later he come back all sheepish and asked for it back." Alex laughed. "I give it to him, but while I had it, I took the powder out of those two shells he kept in it."

"Christ," Evan said, "that's good."

They stood on the empty street, smoking. "Shit," Alex said, "we had some good times back in the old days, didn't we . . . when we didn't give a fuck?"

"Yeah, we did." Evan didn't want to remember all this, these old stories. He knew it would just make him sad, and if he got sad enough, he'd get drunk, and not merely drunk but hammered. But he didn't know how to stop it; he could almost hear the rhythm of Elaine's strained, tense voice, the short bursts of words with the long silences in between them. Her hands were never still; she was always fidgeting, jiggling, tapping her fingers on the tabletop. She never painted her nails red the way the girls did then because she never had much left to paint; she bit them down to the quick. Just like her dad, she chain-smoked, but only when John wasn't around.

"Well, Carlyle," Alex said, "you want to catch a drink?"

"Sure." Elaine had acted in every school production they'd staged in high school. Despite a downstate accent so pungent it could have been used to take the paint off the tabletops (as the old joke went), she tried out for all the leading roles. By the time she was a junior, she was getting them. When she was playing a part, she held back nothing, threw herself into it with pure, fiery, West Virginia craziness. Shakespeare was far too ambitious for Raysburg High, but on her own with no one to help her, she had memorized him by the yard. "Hey, Alex," Evan said, "do you remember how Elaine wanted to be an actress? How she used to act things out for us after her old man went up to the bar? After the restaurant was closed? Remember how she used to do Shakespeare?"

"Oh, yeah. She was good." He smiled slightly, looked over at the boarded-up restaurant as though he could still see her there. "She should have done something with it," he said. "She was fucking good. Remember that madwoman thing she did?"

"Lady Macbeth?"

"No, not that one. The other one."

"Oh, yeah ... Ophelia."

"That's it. I remember there was a whole bunch of us in there that night. You and me and Eddie Watinka and Pilsudski and I don't know who all. And she give each one of us a flower."

"I'd forgotten that." Evan had seen *Hamlet* staged several times since then, but he'd never seen an Ophelia even remotely like Elaine's. In Raysburg in the late fifties, she couldn't possibly have seen a production of the play, so she'd done it her own way without any notion of the tradition: not the wan and wistful, sweet and drooping mad girl, but more like something out of a modern West Virginia psycho ward from some horrible, gray hospital where they still performed lobotomies. Crouched like a cat, she had stalked up and down the restaurant between the booths and the counter—*real theater-in-the-round,* Evan thought—and had spat out the lines. It had been like watching someone in a trance; her black eyes had been perfectly insane. He'd been so nervous watching her that he'd held his breath, afraid for her, afraid that she'd forget the words and break the spell. But she hadn't. She'd given them each a flower from the imaginary bouquet she'd clutched in her left hand.

"That was really something," Alex said. "Shit, I'll never forget it. She give Pilsudski a daisy, I remember that. Do you remember what she give me?"

"Rue," Evan said flatly.

"What the hell's that?"

"I don't know. It's just a flower."

"What did she give you?"

"I don't remember. . . . Oh, shit, man, it's cold out here. Let's go get a drink." Evan climbed into the car and shut the door.

Alex slid into the driver's side and started the engine. "Well fuck, Carlyle," he said, "I don't know."

"Yeah," Evan said, "that makes two of us." Here he was lighting another cigarette and he'd told Dana months ago that he'd quit. Well, he *had* quit. Almost quit anyway; he'd been down to half a pack before the conference in Toronto. But now here he was in Raysburg, and this was the last one in the pack he'd bought that morning; he'd have to buy another one from a goddamned expensive machine in a bar. He watched the deserted buildings roll by as Alex eased the car out into the street and drove away toward the south end of town. He knew perfectly well what flower Elaine had given him. He'd copied out the line onto a scrap of paper and had carried it in his wallet until it had turned so old and torn that he'd thrown it away: "There's rosemary, that's for remembrance. Pray you, love, remember."

Chapter Eight

"Shit, it's still coming down," Alex said, "and it's still sticking too. Must be five inches of it. Going to have a fuck of a time getting back up the hill."

Evan glanced over at the speedometer and saw that they were moving at only twenty miles an hour; it had seemed faster. "Where you taking me?" he said.

"Thought we'd go down to the P.A.C." The Polish-American Club.

"That still there?"

"Yeah, but they remodeled it. You won't recognize the place. Looks like a cocktail lounge now."

The only way that Evan knew they were crossing the train tracks was by feeling the bump of them under the tires; the railway crossing sign was gone. "B 'n' O still run through here?" he said.

"Hasn't run through here for years," Alex said absently.

"Yeah . . . ?" The thought that the old B&O was gone made Evan feel immensely sad. "What are we going to the P.A.C. for?" he said. "You're not even Polish."

Alex gave him one of those brief, unreadable smiles. "Yeah, but I'm a member anyway." He stared ahead at the road. He didn't seem to want to talk.

Evan had been able to hear the whistle all the way up in the north end of town where he'd lived. Or, as his mother had kept saying, "where you eat and sleep"; he hadn't stayed home much when he'd been in high school. But he'd lain awake at night hearing that whistle come drifting all the way up from the railroad bridge into Ohio, and probably, just like thousands of other kids all over North America, it had filled him with an unbearable longing. *It's a cliché,* he thought, *but now even the cliché is getting to be obsolete.*

Of course when he'd been studying with Elaine (or pretending to study) in the end booth at the restaurant, the sound had been clear and close, the tracks only five blocks away. He'd look up from the lined paper covered with algebra or geometry or trig and hear that *ponk-ka-chick, ponk-ka-chick, ponk-ka-chick,* slow and deliberate. "I'm no angel," she used to say. It wasn't an ironic line; there was no way in hell either of them could have seen the Mae West movie then. She meant it, delivered it straight, deadpan. And later she'd say, "I'm no angel . . . and neither are you." That was the ultimate compliment for him in high school; he loved it when she said that. And—Jesus, how could he have forgotten the night they'd hopped the train?

It must have been early winter, probably November. That's the way the air felt: chilly and cold but not bitter. He'd stopped going to the pool hall every night. Instead he rode the bus down to 24th and got off at Wolchak's. His friendship with Alex was still new, and he was careful with it; he approached the garage each time as he would have approached a house with a dog behind the fence, a big dog that was known to be vicious. Old Man Wolchak and his son would have gone home; Alex would have been left in charge. There'd always be about half a dozen other boys hanging out: Watinka and Pilsudski, Gannister, Bud Clark, Billy Freedman, Pachinka, Witowicz, Francis Czyziwki. Alex seemed to like him, but Evan couldn't be sure. Alex seemed to accept his turning up every night along with the others, but he suspected that if he stopped turning up, Alex would accept that just as easily. And sometime between nine and ten Alex would say the same thing every time: "Let's close this fucker down." He'd lock up the garage and they'd cross the street to Isaac's for coffee and cheeseburgers.

Elaine was in their class, so Evan knew her, but it had never occurred to him to ask her out or even to talk to her; she was one of those badly dressed girls with "downstate" written all over her, "come up out of the hills at fourteen to buy her first pair of shoes," as they used to say. There was a strict dress code back then, and she seemed to keep tripping over it: sent home for wearing jeans, for a skirt that was too tight, for a thin cotton dress with no slip under it. Out of school she wore nothing but jeans and sweaters. Sometimes those white cowgirl boots that always embarrassed him: the absolute epitome of downstate, backwoods, hillbilly trashiness. She kept her black hair cut short with bangs in the front; ten years later it would be a fashionable style called a "Beatle," but in 1957 it just seemed plain and harsh compared to those set, poodle-dog fluffs the other girls were wearing. And she was as tall as he was, in heels three inches taller; he'd never thought he could take out a girl that tall. She'd bring the coffee and cheeseburgers to the booth and sit down with them. If her father had left, she'd steal a pack of Chesterfields or Camels out of the glass case and throw it down on the table. Alex always seemed to be in training for some sport or other and didn't smoke except for an occasional cigar, but the rest of them would drink coffee and puff away at the cigarettes until the pack was gone. And Evan would look over at Elaine and think: *She really is beautiful. She just doesn't do anything with it, that's all. If she'd set her hair and put on lipstick and learn how to dress so she didn't look like a farmgirl, she'd be a knockout.*

Yeah, it must have been November because it was chilly and cold, snowing lightly, but not yet bitter. The snow wasn't sticking. So he couldn't have known Elaine very long, but surely he must have kissed her at least once standing in that back alley behind the restaurant. They were walking along by the railroad tracks. Neither of them could have turned sixteen yet. "I see the way you look at me," she said. "I catch you all the time."

"How do I look at you?"

"Like you want to see how much of a girl I am . . . or how bad I am."

It was perfectly true. He didn't know what to say. They

walked along holding hands and heard, in the distance, down in South Raysburg, the train approaching, that slow and weighted slam-bang on the tracks. "You know something," she said, "I can scare people something wonderful sometimes. I bet you can't do it. All I have to do is look in their eyes. Give them a certain sort of look—" And she was doing it to him; those jet black eyes were totally crazy under the street light.

"Yeah, you would scare a lot of people doing that." *But not me,* he meant; he'd put that tone to it. Although he was afraid of her.

"I'm as much of a girl as anybody else," she said suddenly. Her mind seemed to make strange leaps; he couldn't always follow what she was thinking. She talked in short, explosive sentences with long pauses between them; everything she said, even something as ordinary as "Let's go for a walk" sounded deadly serious and painful. "Even though I'm not like Susie Galloway," she said. Not like the class fashion-plate, a majorette, a plump, spoiled little blonde whose father sold used cars and probably spent half his income on her.

"What are you talking about?" he said.

"Do you want to see how much of a girl I am?" she said and took his head between her hands, her fingers pressed hard on the back of his neck, and kissed him full on the mouth. She was the first girl he'd ever met who kissed with her mouth open, and her tongue always gave him an erection as quickly as if somebody had thrown a switch in him marked: SEX. He caught her around the waist; she slipped one of her legs between his. They stood kissing and swaying to the rhythm of the train that was rolling by on the tracks next to them. He couldn't get enough of kissing her; he loved the way her tongue slid so naturally and easily into his mouth.

Suddenly she broke away and said, "Hey, Evan . . . let's hop the train and ride it to Blantons Ferry."

"You're crazy."

"No, I'm not. I've done it hundreds of times. We'll ride it to Blantons Ferry and take the bus back."

"How the hell do you get on it?"

"You jump up on one of those ladders and hang on."

"You're crazy. The damn thing goes a million miles an hour when it gets going."

"Yeah, but it slows down again on the other side of the river. They have to go slow through towns. That's the law. . . . It'll be going just like this. Look at it now . . . how slow it's going." And without any warning she took off and began to run along next to the train. She was moving just as fast as it was. She caught a ladder on a boxcar as it passed and swung easily up and onto it. The train carried her ten yards down the track, and she swung off just as easily, landed, knees flexed, and ran a few steps with the momentum of it. He was out of breath when he caught up to her. "That's how easy it is," she said.

The high arches of her scuffed, white cowgirl boots had fit onto the rungs of the ladder so perfectly that they could have been designed for the job; his penny loafers would be slick as hell, clumsy and dangerous on the frosty metal. "You're crazy," he said.

"You're chicken," she said. "Coward!"

His mouth had gone totally dry. He knew he had to do it. If he ever wanted to stand in the alley behind the restaurant with his tongue in her mouth again, he had to do it. If he had time, he knew he could talk his way out of it, but there didn't seem to be any time left; it wasn't fair. "I'll get on first," she said and began to trot along next to the moving train. She knew as well as he did that he didn't have any choice. "Hurry up," she called back, "or it'll be going too fast."

He ran behind her, stumbling, nearly blind with fear. He couldn't think, could only follow behind her girl's ass moving so beautifully in her tight jeans; if she stopped suddenly, he'd run right into her. But she jumped and in a single, fluid motion swung herself up. Before he could hesitate, she caught his hand and pulled. He grabbed the ladder with his free hand and hung for a terrible moment with his feet pawing the air. Then he scrambled onto the ladder. The steel rung under his right hand was cold as ice.

They had joined the motion now, that roll and rattle; the ground was slipping away behind them, the streetlights were moving. Her boot-heels, made for stirrups, had nailed her safely in place; she hung there, her knees flexing with the motion, as easily as she would have stood on the sidewalk. His shoes had no grasp to them at all—*have to get some engineer boots like Alex wears,* he managed to think. His right arm was already beginning to cramp. Fear blurred his mind and sickened him. She let go of his hand, grabbed him around the waist, and gathered him in. "Hold onto me," she said. "You've got to hold on tight because we'll be doing damn near sixty when we hit the tunnel."

"Oh, Jesus Christ," he said. Her face was only inches away. Her eyes seemed black and endless as caves; he could fall right into them. He and Elaine Isaac, this strange girl he scarcely knew, were hanging onto the side of a boxcar together. They were wrapped around each other. They were French kissing. They were rolling along the B&O line through center Raysburg toward Ohio. He couldn't take it in. "This goes all the way to Cincinnati," she said.

He couldn't say anything.

"I want to ride it forever," she said. She had to yell above the gathering speed of the wheels. "I hear it in the night and I want to be on it . . . to Cincinnati . . . to Saint Louie. . . . I want to keep on moving and never stop. I want to drive down an endless stretch of smooth road. I want a Porsche Spyder like Jimmy's."

James Dean, she was talking about. "He got killed in that Porsche," Evan yelled back.

They must have been going over forty by now; the streetlights snapped by: *whisk, whisk, whisk.* He could see the speckle of snow falling in the yellow circles under the streetlights. The wind cutting back the side of the train was bitterly cold; it burnt his face, brought tears to his eyes. "He knew he was going to die," she said. He could barely hear the words. "You know, he had himself photographed in a coffin. I bet he was ready for it. I bet he knew all about it. . . . He knew he couldn't live any longer, that's all."

Then they were leaving the streetlights behind, moving through scrub and grass now, past vacant lots, past woods, toward the tunnel. They were going so fast that he couldn't look out anymore, so he looked at her instead. The wind was beating her hair into a black moving swirl around her face. And suddenly he forgot to be afraid; he felt elation soaring up in him as though he were roaring drunk. He'd never seen anything as beautiful as the way she looked to him then with her hair flying, her face shining with excitement, wind-tears streaming back from her black eyes. And said it: "You're beautiful. You're really beautiful."

The tunnel struck like fists in their ears, smashing assault of sound, thrust fast as a jet plane into total darkness. Their mouths struck together so hard that he'd find later he'd cut his lip on her teeth. The only warmth left in moving blackness, freezing cold, impossible roaring, was her mouth: her lips, her tongue. It wasn't enough that his legs were wrapped around hers; he wanted to be inside of her. What he wanted was impossible; to rush into her as fast as the train and vanish. They were kissing so hard it was like death chasing them down the tracks. And then, instantly, the sound was gone and they were sailing high, unbelievably high, above the city with the lights streaked out below in the dirty river that was only beautiful at night. His breath was torn away. The awful sound was gone, but his ears still rang with it. They were shot through the dark sky like bullets, must have been going damn near seventy miles an hour with Raysburg below them, the river below them, then sweeping down and across the bridge. "Oh, Jesus Christ," he yelled, "Jesus Christ!" He couldn't stop himself. "I love you," he yelled to her against the wind. "I love you."

"I love you," she yelled back.

She'd been right, the train did slow to a walk in Blantons Ferry, and she jumped off easily, running. The ground came up too fast for him; he would have fallen, but she caught him. They kept right on running fast and breathless into the nearest shadow, the square of darkness cast by the warehouse in the railroad yard. He unbuttoned her brother's hand-me-down Windbreaker, reached up under her sweater. She unfastened her bra in the back. He thrust his numb and icy hands into the rounded spaces around her small pointed breasts. She gasped, and a shiver went down her body. Snow was falling in their hair. Frantic against the wall of the building. He drove her against the wall of the building. Then for the first time with a girl, for the first time that wasn't alone in bed at night doing it into a clean, white athletic sock: that draining up from the guts, that wet jolting kick. He thought he'd never stop coming. He filled up his shorts. He stained his chinos. He thought he could never get enough of her.

Walking to the bus stop, she said, "Am I enough of a girl for you? . . . Am I bad enough for you?"

Evan saw that Alex had drifted the car into the parking lot at the P.A.C. He wouldn't have recognized it. The front of the building was new; the sign was new. *Jesus*, Evan thought, *what a fucking punk I was. What a fucking little asshole.* All those years were gone now; everything was changed. The years had covered over everything like the snow. "This is it," Alex said.

Chapter Nine

Well, Evan thought, *he warned me—now it's just another smooth plastic den with dim, recessed lighting, comfortable booths, a television set, and bottles of every damned thing you could possibly want lined up behind the bar.* He could even see a bottle of tequila. In the old days you had a choice of three drinks: beer, whiskey, or vodka. If you wanted a mixer, you got water. You sat on wooden folding chairs planted on a bare, sawdust-covered floor. The jukebox pumped out polkas, and you could barely hear yourself think for the sound of the cards slapping down on the tables and the huge laughing voices yelling in Polish. Now, listening carefully, Evan couldn't hear a word of Polish. All the members, even the old folks in the corner booth, were speaking English.

Alex had ordered a beer and a double shot for each of them; Evan was drinking the beer and Alex the whiskey. Neither of them seemed in a hurry to get drunk, neither had spoken much in the last ten minutes beyond a few stiff, dangling sentences. *Already sick of talking about the good old days,* Evan thought. *Probably don't have much left to say to each other.* But Alex looked up across the table with an expression of puzzlement and gloom. The twist to his lips was just deliberate enough that Evan knew Alex had chosen the expression, put it on like a mask. "That son of mine," he said, "you know, he isn't going to be worth a damn."

"What's wrong with him?"

"Shit, he's just a little crybaby, that's all. A momma's boy. And Sharon lets him get away with it. She babies him something awful. And . . . well, he never does a goddamned thing. He just sits in his room. You'd think a boy would want to go fuck around with his old man, right? Pass a football or some damn thing, right? But not him. Buy him a football and he never even has it out of the house."

"I don't think you ought to worry about it. I was exactly like that at his age."

"Yeah, Carlyle," Alex said with a slow smile, "and look at you. You're not worth a bucket of piss."

Evan laughed. "True enough. But seriously, Al, he's sure not going to be worth a bucket of piss if you keep telling him he's not."

"Do I do that?"

"You sure as hell do. 'Hey, Crash, what did you break today?' "

Alex laughed. "Yeah, but fuck, Carlyle, he's such a goddamned klutz. Lori was riding a two-wheeler before he was. She was five and a half and already going up and down the street like a bat out of hell, and he still had training wheels, for Christ's sake. And then when he does get it down so he can halfway stay on the goddamned bike, the first thing he does is break his arm. . . . Sometimes I think he does it on purpose."

"Oh, come on, man."

"I mean it, Carlyle. You really have to go some to break our goddamned front window with a softball. I mean you really have to work at it, right? And the coffee table—shit, glass-top coffee table—and what does he do but sit down on it." He shook his head. "He's howling like a dog and I come running in and there he is flat on his ass on the floor in the middle of the frame with his feet sticking straight up, broken glass all around him. If I'd been that way when I was a kid, I would have got crushed out like a bug. Between my crazy brother and the old man, I had to get strong fast or those bastards would have killed me."

"Yeah, I can remember sitting in bars with you telling me what a rotten son of a bitch your old man was. And if you're not careful, in ten years it's going to be your kid sitting in some bar telling his friends what a rotten son of a bitch *his* old man is."

"Well, I never hit him," Alex said quickly, "not once."

"Who said you did?"

"Not once," Alex repeated. "Although, goddamn, I've been tempted." He tilted back the rest of his shot. "Well, up yours, Carlyle," he said. "It's good to see you again, you worthless fucker."

"It's good to see you too."

Alex looked away, scowled, gestured to the bartender and pointed to his empty shot glass. "I like your daughter," Evan said. "She seems like a nice little kid." He hadn't particularly liked Lori, but it seemed the thing to say.

"Well," Alex said slowly, "you didn't really see her. Stranger in the house, she shuts right up. But she's . . . oh, fuck, Carlyle, it's in the blood, right? Not a thing you can do about it when it's in the blood. She's just like me, and God help her."

Evan didn't know what to say. "Al Junior doesn't have a drop of Warner in him," Alex went on after a moment. "Shit, Lori should have been the boy, and Allie should have been the girl." He stared at the table in front of him where his new double had arrived; he didn't touch it. "You know, Carlyle," he said, "I've been through things that should have turned my hair white. You know the way I used to drive, the things I used to do. And I was stationed up on the DMZ, right? And nothing happened much all the time I was there, but I was scared shitless the whole time anyway, waiting for those goddamned Chinese to come pouring down again. . . . I don't know. But the worst fucking two minutes I ever spent in my life was standing in my own living room looking out the window.

"I'm standing there drinking a beer, and Lori's out there with her bicycle and . . . well, you know that hill we slid down? How steep it is? Well, she gets up at the top, and she stands up on the seat, I mean she doesn't sit down on it, right? She gets up on the fucking seat, all bent over like a jockey, and away she goes. She must have been doing fifty by the time she hit the bottom. And you know what's at the bottom? There's a fucking blind curve at the bottom. Well, I walked outside and waited for her to push her bike back to the top, and I said, 'Hey, you know what would have happened if there'd been a car coming when you hit the bottom?' She just looks at me. I said, 'If there'd been a car coming, I'd be down there right this minute with a broom and a dustpan trying to find enough of you to bury.' And she just looks at me. Six years old, right? 'If I ever catch you pulling a stunt like that again,' I told her, 'you're not going to sit down for a week.' But it didn't do any good. I know it didn't. Fuck, you can't tell a Warner a goddamned thing."

Evan drank the last of his beer. "Sounds like you've already decided what your kids are going to be like," he said.

"I'll tell you, Carlyle, *you* don't decide what your kids are going to be like. Your kids are going to be like what they're going to be like, and you can go fly your ass like a kite for all the good it's going to do you. And Lori is going to be just like me. Except she's a girl. She's going to be like Elaine was, only worse."

Evan signaled the bartender for another beer. He'd had it with Raysburg and Alex; he was sick to the teeth with it. He wanted out, he wanted to be back in Canada. *Oh, fuck*, he thought, *I've got to ask him.* "Well, Elaine . . ." he said, "she turned out all right. Didn't she?"

"Oh, yeah, I suppose. Except for marrying that worthless piece of shit. Don't know what the fuck she saw in him. Only thing you could say for him is he dressed like a millionaire . . . even when he was drawing unemployment. Never saw such a goddamned dressed-up son of a bitch in my life."

He's jealous, Evan thought. *Good God, that's it!* He felt as though someone had dropped a hammer on his head. *That's why it's been so hard to get him to talk about her. They were lovers.* He was sure of it. He couldn't understand why the thought had never occurred to him before.

"Hi, Alex! How the hell are you?" Evan looked up to see a gross, drunken old man looming over the table: a huge figure in a shabby overcoat, well over six feet tall, bald, with a shiny, baggy face and great, battered nose. The man was resting one of his thick hands on the edge of the table and weaving slightly from side to side. There was something wrong with the hand; it was scarred, and the knuckles were swollen and misshapen.

"Sit down, buddy," Alex said gently, "and have a drink with us."

"Well, sure, Alex, sure. How, how, how are you? How's the wife and kids?" The man slowly unfolded himself into the booth, puffing and shaking. He was trying to smile. "Christ, Alex, I seem, I seem to be out of smokes. Do you have a smoke?" Alex took a pack of Camels out of his jacket and laid it on the table. The man reached for the pack and missed, knocked it to one side. He smiled sheepishly, tried again. His hand shook violently. He got the pack off the table, but dropped it immediately. Alex picked it up, tapped a cigarette out of it, placed it between the man's lips, and lit it for him.

"Thanks, Alex. Jesus, I got the shakes tonight. Shit, they been, they been getting better lately, but they just come back on me tonight." He bobbed his head up and down several times, dragged on the cigarette, took it out of his mouth, and immediately dropped it. Alex picked it up, pushed his half-drunk double whiskey across the table. The man smiled, inhaled, grabbed for the glass, got it into the air shaking, spilled it, got it to his mouth, and gulped. Much of the whiskey ran down his face. Alex pushed Evan's untouched glass toward him. This time the man bent forward so that his head was nearly resting on the table, took the glass between the palms of both hands and tilted it back. His fingers didn't seem to work right. He got most of the drink down, and then Alex handed him the cigarette. "Thanks, Alex. Jesus, fuck, but I got the shakes tonight. Shit, they been getting better lately, but they just come, they just come back on me tonight."

"Yeah," Alex said. "I know. But they'll be better tomorrow." He signaled the bartender: "Three more doubles and three beers."

"Well, how's the wife, Alex? How's the wife and kids?"

"Just fine. We're doing just fine."

"Well, that's good. Jesus, Alex. You know what? I got the shakes tonight. They just come back on me like that. I don't know—"

"Yeah," Alex said, and pushed another whiskey at him. Evan stared while the man downed it; his deformed hands were getting noticeably steadier. "You guys know each other," Alex said, "but I bet you don't remember."

"What's that, Alex?"

"I said you know this crazy fucker over here, but I bet you don't remember."

The man looked at Evan for the first time. His vast sagging face hung open in wonderment. "Eddie Watinka. It ain't Eddie Watinka, is it?"

"No," said Alex, "It ain't Eddie Watinka. Go back a few years. The first time you met him, he cleaned your ass shooting pool."

Evan was puzzled. He would have sworn he'd never seen this aged, fat drunk before in his life. The man stared at him, and Evan watched the wrecked face slowly spread into a wide moon-grin. "Shit, you cleaned my ass shooting pool. That's right, isn't it, Alex? And then we all got fucking drunk. That's it, isn't it, Alex? Shit, that was years ago, wasn't it, Alex? It was in the Ca . . . the Ca . . . the Cat's Eye—"

"That's right," Alex said. "You was setting up the house. You was buying drinks for everybody."

"Yeah, I was. I was buying drinks for everybody." The man's face was simple with delight. "I'd just . . . I'd, I'd just robbed . . . I'd just been . . . I'd just . . ." and he stopped speaking, but continued to grin. Then: "I'd fucking well just knocked over a store. That's it, isn't it, Alex? That's what happened, isn't it?"

Evan stared, fascinated. He didn't know this man. "This, this guy, this—" said the man. "This, this, this guy is—"

"Evan Carlyle," said Alex. "This guy is Evan Carlyle."

"Well, shit. Evan Carlyle! Fuckin' A. That's right." The man reached across the table. Evan took his hand and shook it. But he still didn't know him.

"Come on, Carlyle," said Alex. "You remember Frank Hospidarski."

Evan blinked. Something fractured inside his mind. "Sure," he said automatically, "I remember you. How are you, Frank?"

"We got, we got drunk, didn't we, Alex?" Frank said. "We got, we got, we got drunk, didn't we? Jesus. We, we sure got drunk—"

"It's all right, Frank," said Alex, and slid his whiskey at the man. Frank downed it immediately.

"Jesus, Alex. How are you? How's the wife and kids?"

"Fine, Frank."

Evan stood. "Got to piss," he said. He walked quickly back to the men's room. He locked himself in the stall, leaned against the wall, and cried. He was astonished at himself; it had come upon him with no warning. After a moment he stopped, blew his nose. He lit a cigarette, smoked half of it, threw it in the toilet, and returned to the booth.

Hospidarski was still there; he'd appropriated all of the drinks. Alex was leaning against the bar. He'd just bought two cases of beer. "What, what, what's your hurry, Alex?" Frank was saying. "You just got here."

"No, Frank," said Alex, "*you* just got here."

"That's right. I just got here."

Alex handed a ten-dollar bill to the bartender. "This is for Frank," he said under his breath.

"Hey, hey," said Hospidarski. "You ain't going, are you?"

"Yeah, got to get back to the wife," said Alex. "You know how it is, Frank."

"Yeah. Yeah. I know how it is." Hospidarski's face had folded in on itself. He stared at the beer and whiskey in front of him. Then he looked up, grinned, and called after them. "Hey, you. Hey, what's-your-name. I'm glad to see you again!"

"Yeah, me too," said Evan.

Out on the street Evan said, "Jesus, Alex, what's happened to him!"

"Fuck."

"Jesus, he can't be much over forty!"

"Yeah, he's forty-two or three. He's about ten years older than us."

"What the fuck happened to him?"

"They broke him the last time. They really fucking broke him."

"What?"

"He's been in and out of prison for years. The last time they fucking well broke him. He's never been the same. He just drinks now. That's all he does." Alex turned away, walked to the car, opened the door, and set the two cases of beer on the backseat. "Some nights I can take him, some nights I can't," he said. He stood and inspected the crumpled right side of the automobile. "Fucking fine tin they make cars out of these days," he said.

"Jesus, Alex," Evan said, still stuck there staring at his friend, "he was such a hell of a guy!"

"Yeah, I know."

"Christ, and now he's a total wreck!"

"Oh, shut the fuck up, Carlyle!" Alex said. "Haven't you ever seen a drunk before? Jesus! It's just what happens to people." He climbed into the car and slammed the door angrily. After a moment Evan got in the other side. "Well, Carlyle," Alex said bleakly, "why don't we drive down to the farm?"

"The farm?"

"Sure. I thought you might like to see it again. It would be really great now with all the snow."

"Christ, man, it'd take us all night to get there. The roads must be—"

"No it wouldn't. We'd be there in a couple hours. There are still beds in the place. We could make a big fire, get hammered. Drive into Harrod tomorrow and have breakfast. Drive back. Shit, the snow will be beautiful down there."

"Don't you think your wife would—"

"Look, Carlyle. I haven't seen you in thirteen years. And the way things are going, it's going to be a fuck of a long time before I see you again. Let's go down to the farm . . . just forget all the bullshit and go down to the farm like the old days and get drunk."

Alex was staring straight ahead out the windshield; Evan looked at the impassive profile but could find nothing on it. "All right," he said finally. "Sure."

Alex put the car in gear and drove out of the parking lot. "It's just what happens to people," he'd said. *Yeah*, Evan thought, *people who stay here. Happen to you too, buddy*, he told Alex silently, *if you don't watch your ass*. And Evan couldn't go on trying to pretend it didn't matter to him. He'd nearly forgotten how angry he used to get, but now that old, hopeless fury was burning in his blood again, and just as always there was nothing to do for it but get drunk. *Go ahead*—this time he was talking to himself—*be reckless and irresponsible, turn right back into a total West Virginia asshole. So what if he did fuck Elaine? You were the asshole in the old days, and now the two of you can be assholes together.*

The only possible place to be was riding along with Alex, headed straight out of town at ten o'clock on a night that wasn't fit for a dog. Down the river road past the steel mills all the way to Carreysburg, then turn southeast and follow those insane, twisting mountain roads all the way back in to Harrod. Then you've got the drive out to the farm to look forward to, on a mud-and-gravel road so narrow that if another car's coming, one of you has got to stop and let the other go by. Yeah, the only place to be was driving south with Alex through six inches of new, wet snow like a goddamned fool.

Chapter Ten

It's the fall of 1957, late September, cold enough for a jacket. Football season. Raysburg High's already played three or four games. In the pool hall Evan is waiting for a table. He looks up and sees Alex Warner walk through the door. Eyes like that yellow stone in one of his mother's rings. Black hair damn near as curly as a Negro's, cut off short all over his head, but long sideburns. And lean, high cheekbones, narrow hips, thin wrists with black hair on them and veins like wires. Always looks like he's disgusted with something, hesitates inside the door, scowling, shoulders hunched, rubs his hands together and blows on them.

There's a man with Warner; Evan has never seen him before.

Not a boy, but a grown man, six feet four if he's an inch, shoulders in that blue Windbreaker like Boulder Dam, great mass of blond hair greased back, ear-to-ear grin and bright-blue eyes. The man's chewing gum; his jaws working it steadily. He drops a hand lightly onto Alex's shoulder, then lets it fall: hand large enough to palm a basketball. He's so big that Alex almost seems like a little kid next to him—so massive, so full-grown out to thick muscle and sheer solidness that he seems to have come from another world, the one where the adults live. Men. They drive their own cars, work at jobs, get drunk on Saturday night, get laid. They can walk into any bar and get served, can knock on the doors in the back alleys of center Raysburg and somebody will let them in. Solid and grown, money in their jeans. Warner and the man walk on back into the pool hall. "Somebody want to shoot a game?" the man says.

"Yeah," Evan says before he can stop to think. "Yeah, I'll shoot a game with you." He's so nervous that his hands are shaking; he shoves them into the pockets of his khaki chinos. He realizes suddenly that he looks like a punk. He's got on an Ivy League shirt with a button-down collar, white socks and penny loafers. His chinos are pushed down on his hips and riding on a half-inch black belt buckled on the left side. As soon as he'd left the house, he'd unbuttoned his shirt all the way down to his navel, but there's no hair to show off yet. He hasn't got much of a D.A. because his father won't let him. But the man looks at him, and his face doesn't say "punk"; he's grinning. "Sure. All right. Let's see if we can get a table."

"I'm Evan Carlyle," he says, more to Alex than to the man.

Alex scowls and looks away. "I know who you are," he says, his voice flat. "This is Frank Hospidarski."

"Oh, you guys know each other, huh?"

"Yeah, we go to school together," Evan says.

Alex says nothing.

"What the hell did you say your name was?" Frank says. "I didn't get it."

"Carlyle. Evan Carlyle." Hating the name.

Hospidarski repeats it as though he's trying to memorize it: "Evan Carlyle. Evan Carlyle. Shit, that's a good one. Well, pleased to meetcha," and takes Evan's hand in a monstrous, grinding grip.

"Hey, you can have this table, Frank," somebody's yelling.

"Oh, yeah? Are you sure? Are you done?"

"Yeah, Frank. You go ahead."

They're afraid of him. Evan looks around and sees it. He's not menacing, he's not pushing anybody, he's just standing there and grinning, his jaws working up and down with the gum, and they're afraid of him. Someone's bringing him a beer he didn't pay for. "Hey, thanks," Hospidarski says, raises the glass, and toasts the entire pool hall.

"What do you say, Frank?" somebody yells.

Hospidarski winks. "Horseshit," he calls back, laughing. "That's what I say. Horseshit." And turning to Evan: "You want to break?"

"Why don't we flip for it?" Evan's hands are still in his pockets, his elbows pressed into his sides, so the shaking won't show. His voice sounds like a little kid's, breaking, too high. He's sweating like a pig.

Hospidarski smiles at him; he's strangely gentle for such a big man. He's shaking his head. "Naw. You go ahead, kid." He pats Evan on the shoulder. "Or do you want to play wit him?" he says to Alex.

Warner's lips draw back a moment showing teeth, more of a grimace than a smile. "You know I don't play this fucking game, Frank."

"All right," Hospidarski says, hands Alex the beer, and takes up a pool cue. Chalks it.

Evan's already got a cue out and chalked. It's like trying to move in a dream; he's so terrified that he's numb, feels like slow motion. The Greek has come over and has cleared away the record of the old games from the wire above their heads, has moved the little metal disks with a cue, setting it all back to zero. Alex has slumped down on the bench that runs along the wall. He's already drunk half Frank's free beer. He's watching. He's got on a leather jacket, not black and shiny and new like the one Evan bought with his birthday money, keeps hidden from his parents, hasn't yet dared to wear out of the house, but brown and old and worn, stained with grease, the right elbow torn clean away.

Evan knows all the stories about Alex Warner. He collects them. Alex is a real farmboy, comes from down back of Harrod, and he's mean as a dog. He comes up to Raysburg High and his first year out for track, runs a five-minute mile. He's only a sophomore, only weighs a hundred and forty pounds, and he's already playing first string. Yeah, left half. And he's fast as fucking lightning. He's a street fighter, a dirty fighter. He steals cars. No, they've never caught him. They can't get anything on him. He's too smart. He loafs with some guy who works for Big Joe Patone. He don't go out with girls; he hangs out in the whorehouses down in South Raysburg.

Evan doesn't give a shit for football, but he hasn't missed a game yet this year. He's sat in the bleachers and watched Alex on the field, the way he moves. He's incredible, can skip through a broken field like a dancer, elusive as a ghost. Against Carreysburg, where he used to go to school, he's vicious, a monster on the field, out for blood. He intercepts a pass in the end zone and runs with it ninety-five fucking yards for a touchdown, flips the ball back to the ref, and grins up at the screaming crowd. Evan would never have told anybody why he wants to get to know Alex Warner, why he wants to be his friend, but it's simple. He wants to be friends with the meanest son of a bitch in the class.

He's tried to talk to Alex half a dozen times, but Alex never has a thing to say to him. Why should he? Evan Carlyle is a punk. Evan Carlyle doesn't try out for a single fucking sport. The only girls who'll go out with him are the losers. He isn't even good in school; he fights for every C, does his book reports out of Classics Comics. Every day after school he walks straight to Main Street Billiards and stays there till dinner time. After dinner he tells his mother, "Hey, I'm going over to Johnny Pilsudski's and do my homework, okay?" and then grabs the bus straight back to Main Street Billiards. That's what he's been doing since the eighth grade, and he isn't fooling anybody. His father says to him, "Evan, are you going to spend your whole life on the fat end of a pool cue?" But he gets five dollars a week allowance and makes twenty or thirty more on the fat end of a pool cue.

The Greek has racked the balls. "Dollar a game?" Hospidarski says.

"We don't have to play for money."

"Oh, you don't want to, huh?"

"It doesn't matter. Whatever you want."

Hospidarski seems puzzled. He looks over at Alex, then back at Evan. "Dollar a game?" he says again.

"Sure." Evan chalks the cue. He's already chalked it half a dozen times. He stares down the length of the green felt. His hands are shaking. His legs are shaking. But when he bends to the table, the shaking stops. He's keyed up, charged and ready to go, electricity in every pore. The break's clean with two in, and the leave's perfect. He knows if he stops to think, his nerves will fuck him up. Shooting as fast as he can, he runs the table.

"Well, fuck me!" Hospidarski says. "Hey, rack!"

Evan breaks again, one in and a fair-to-middling leave. Other people have stopped playing and come around to watch. They're all looking at Hospidarski to see how he's taking it. Hospidarski is rubbing the back of his neck and looking at Evan. Evan wipes the sweat off the palms of his hands. He's never been so frightened in his life. He sinks one and draws the cue ball back beautifully right where he wants it: that sharp clean snap of the cue flashing in and out like a whip. Makes the next shot, but the leave is horrible, it's a disaster. Can he massé it? Sometimes he can do it and sometimes he can't. He bends, holds the cue straight up above the ball, vertical to the table. The silence around him is unbearable. Cue down sharp: *snap*. Bang on the top of the ball. Cue ball spirals off lazily, makes a perfect half circle around the eight ball to strike the object ball on the side: *tap*. Slow as poured honey, the object ball oozes toward the corner pocket, hangs a moment, undecided, and then goes in with a plop. The leave couldn't be better.

Hospidarski starts to laugh. "Well, fuck me!" he says, then to Alex, "I told you we should stay out of this end of town."

"You never said anything of the kind, Frank," Alex says, his voice dry. But Evan thinks he can hear a hint of laughter in it.

Hospidarski rolls back, all six feet four of him, head pointed at the ceiling, and laughs. "Fuck me! I didn't want to shoot pool tonight anyway." He reaches in his jeans and hauls out his wallet. It's stuffed with inches of money. Unless all the bills are ones, he's got hundreds of dollars in his wallet. He pulls out some of the green paper, doesn't hesitate, doesn't count it, just makes a random grab between thumb and index finger and shoves it at Evan. "Here, have some of this," he says.

Evan looks at Alex. There is an expression of some sort on Alex's face, but Evan doesn't know what it is. "Take it," Alex says just loud enough for Evan to hear him.

Evan takes the money. Later that night, closed away behind his bedroom door, he'll count out a hundred and forty-seven dollars, small bills, none larger than a ten. But now he just shoves it into his pants. "A fucking shark!" Hospidarski says to Evan. "A goddamned fucking shark. Jesus man, fuck me. Standing there sweating and shaking like he's going to drop dead any minute. 'Oh, shit,' he says, 'I don't care if we play for money.' Like the Pope ain't Catholic, he don't." He reaches out, grabs Evan behind the neck, and shakes him gently. "You hauled my ass, you little fart. You slipped it right in on me. Well, now you're going to get drunk wit me, right? You bet your ass you are. We're going to get so fucking drunk, they're going to have to roll us home like fucking beer barrels."

Walking out of the pool hall and onto the street, Alex speaks directly to Evan for the first time: "You could have hustled him."

"What? You think I'm out of my mind?"

Alex laughs.

Frank drives a gray Chevy, chopped and channeled. "Well, how do you like the Gray Ghost, kid?" Telling Evan he's got a blown engine, racing cam, cutoffs. Jerks a switch under the dash to show off and the engine roars back like an animal. Evan doesn't know what he's talking about. He's jammed into the middle of the front seat stiff as a board, Hospidarski enormous on his left, Alex a lean, coiled spring on his right. They're driving south through center Raysburg passing back and forth a pint of Jack Daniel's. Evan's never drunk anything stronger than beer before, but he takes a careful gulp each time the bottle passes. The whiskey burns like fire. And how the hell is he going to get these guys to like him? The only thing he knows is that he's got to make them laugh. "You don't drive this thing, Frank," he says, keeping his voice flat, imitating Alex's delivery, "you just aim it."

"Right, kid."

"Bet you don't park it either . . . you just abandon it."

Hospidarski does laugh. "You're all right, Carlyle."

Back-alley bar called Pulaski's, all the way down on 41st Street, Polack town. Bartender's a little guy, bald in the front. They don't sit down at the bar but at a table in the back, wait for the bartender to come to them. "Sorry, Frank. These guys ain't old enough."

"What do you mean they ain't old enough? They're jockeys. Work over at the Downs." Big, friendly grin on Frank's face.

"Sorry, Frank."

"Just in from Pennsylvania, both of them. Fucking wonderful riders, you ought to see them."

"Sorry, Frank. I'm just trying to run a clean place, all right? You know how it is." Then he says something in Polish. The other customers have stopped talking. Some of them glance over curiously, but when they see it's Frank Hospidarski, they look back at their drinks.

"Oh, sure, I know how it is." Hospidarski stands up lazily,

stretches himself. Then without any warning, he's got the bartender by the throat. He lifts him into the air with one hand, hoists him right up; Frank uncoils slowly and pushes until his right arm is extended straight up and the little man is against the ceiling, kicking, trying to yell, but can only squawk like a chicken. Then Frank lets him fall down with a crash. The little man's on his feet instantly, scrambling. Hospidarski sends Alex a look, just a quick nod toward the bar, and Alex is already moving; he's in between the little man and the bar, he fakes right and then left just like in football, then punches twice, hands blurring out to nothing in the air. The bartender's head snaps back, twice, and he sits down on the floor. "For Christ's sake, Frank!" he yells. He jerks his head around to Hospidarski and yells something else. Polish.

"Oh, Jerry, Jerry," Frank says sadly. "We know how it is. We all know how it is." He picks up a full pitcher of beer from the next table and very slowly begins to pour it onto the bartender's head. "Now you was going for your gun, Jerry," Frank says. "I just want to tell you one thing, Jerry. If you go pulling a gun on Frank Hospidarski, you're a dead man. That's all." And empties out the last of the beer. The bartender sits on the floor, not moving a muscle, and lets the beer run over his head and down his face. Frank holds the empty pitcher in his hand, bouncing it, testing the weight of it.

"Don't do that, Frank."

"You was going for your gun, Jerry." Deliberately, with all his body behind it, Frank throws the pitcher across the bar and into the mirror. "Now you just sit there, man. Because if I see you move before I get in my car, I'm going to come back in here and kill you." Alex has got the pistol from behind the bar. "Throw it out in the street," Frank tells him.

They're moving again, too fast, engine roaring, back north toward center Raysburg. Evan can't remember when he's ever had to piss so bad. "I don't know, boys," Frank says, "fucking dumb Polacks. Can't even do something for one of their own. Shit, have we drunk up that whiskey? . . . Goddamn, he used to loaf wit my old man, can you believe it? I thought he was one of my uncles, he was around the house so much, and see how he treats me? Jesus, I just can't believe it. Well, fuckin' A, man, we got to get drunk tonight, that's all I know . . . We'll try old man Witowicz. He knows me." Evan can't say a word.

Another bar, across the B&O tracks down by the river: the Cat's Eye. The back room is jammed with people, mill workers, women, old folks, even little kids. The jukebox is blaring and Frank is suddenly happy again. "Hey!" he's yelling, "set up the bar. Set up the whole bar. Give everybody a drink. It's on me. It's all on me. *Frank Hospidarski!*" Nobody's asking their ages now; the beer's coming to the table faster than they can keep up with it, shots of whiskey are coming and going; the bartender, an old fat man, waits until they drink and then carries away the glasses. It's illegal to sell whiskey by the drink in West Virginia. The Everly Brothers are whining away on the jukebox, then Del Shannon, then Chuck Berry pounding out rock 'n' roll. Frank has turned up the volume knob on the back of the jukebox as loud as he can get it. Evan has got his voice back; he's telling Frank the one about the midget standing on the box in the pisser. Hospidarski's laughing. He yells, "Hey, Carlyle. You're okay. I like you." He buys packs of Camel cigarettes and throws them down on the table in front of Evan, he buys Dutch Masters cigars and throws them to Alex, he buys pretzels, potato chips, dried hot sausages, pickled eggs. He tells the bartender to turn the grill back on and fry up some hamburgers. "Hey, it's on me. It's all on me. *Frank Hospidarski!*" People are yelling, "Hey, Frank. Thanks. Thanks, Frank." Evan is plastered; the alcohol has pounded his brains to mush. There's so much Polish all around him, he can almost convince himself he can understand it. He's trying to think of more jokes. "Hey, give them kids a drink," Frank yells, pointing at the next table. Some of them can't be much older than twelve.

"Oh, come on, Frank," the bartender says and adds something in Polish.

Evan holds his breath, but Hospidarski's all good nature and laughs now: "Well, give them some more Cokes then. Give them some potato chips. Here," he says, shoving all of his silver at the old man, "give them this for the jukebox." A woman has somehow joined them at their table. She seems immensely old to Evan with her eye makeup and red lipstick, her skintight skirt and spike heels. She has to be at least thirty. "Hey, it's Betty Kupla," Frank's yelling. "How the hell are you, Betty? What are you drinking? How the hell are you?"

"Can't complain, Frank."

And only Alex seems unchanged, his face closed off, his eyes watchful. He doesn't drink everything that comes to the table as fast as he can the way Hospidarski does; he drinks slowly, deliberately, like someone who's set out to walk a hundred miles and knows he's got to pace himself or he'll never get there. And Alex will talk, Evan discovers, if asked a direct question: "Well, it *was* a damn good play, but sheer luck. I was just there, that's all. Hole in the fucking line, and I went through it, and that was the right place to be, that's all."

Evan is drunk enough to ask Hospidarski: "Where'd you get all that money, Frank?"

Quietly, out of the side of his mouth, he says, "Knocked over a store," and then he winks.

Evan has run out of jokes. He's got to do something. They've got to remember him. He looks across to the other side of the room. There's a little girl, can't be older than twelve, wearing a dress that used to be pink. She's filthy, her knees skinned, her bare legs already hairy, cracked, old white sandals on her feet. Straw-brown hair hanging down in two braids, small oval face pointed at the chin, and blue eyes, clear and beautiful as a Siamese cat's. Little Polish kid, he's sure; Saint Christopher medal around her neck. She's sitting with some round, red-faced women. Will they think it's funny or only dumb? They'll probably think it's funny. He stands, lurches to her table, says, "Dance?"

The little girl rises without the least sign of hesitation and Evan's jitterbugging with her to Chuck Berry. Only two things

Evan *can* do, shoot pool and dance; alcohol has freed him from anything that might hold him back. He's spinning the little kid around, he's lifting her into the air to send her skirt flying, he's driving himself to the music like a madman, he's pushing until the sweat is streaming down into his eyes. The little kid is laughing and so's Frank. Evan spins her fast to swirl her skirt so she's bare for a split second all the way to her white cotton panties. Frank's laughing and pounding the table: "Hey, go there, Carlyle, go you crazy fucker!" Evan ends the dance by falling onto one knee. Giggling, the child curtsies to him, and with that gesture instantly transforms herself from a budding rock 'n' roller into a little Polish peasant; she flees back to her laughing mother.

Evan stumbles deliberately, pretends he's drunker than he really is, and Frank supports him with one big hand. "You're all right, Carlyle."

And the beer keeps coming to the table, more beer than Evan could imagine drinking at one time, but he seems to be drinking it. He was supposed to be home by eleven thirty and it's already one in the morning. The kids have gone home, the old folks have gone home, the front of the bar is shut down and the door locked, but the back room still goes on rocking away to the jukebox as Frank throws money down on the table. Frank's gathered half a dozen more people around them now; he's pulled the tables together, and he doesn't look like he's ready to stop, looks more like he's just getting started. The people who are left seem to be Frank's age, adults but young; they seem hard and unpleasant to Evan, they have loud voices, all English now, not a word of Polish left. Evan is so drunk and exhausted he can hardly sit up; he's not having fun anymore. Betty Kupla teeters off to the can in her immensely high heels and Frank says to Alex: "I think I'll be going home wit the young lady. Here, take the car," and hands him the keys.

"Fuck, Frank, how you going to get home?"

"Take a cab, dumb shit."

"We're only six blocks from the garage. I'll walk over and get the truck."

"You sure?"

"Sure I'm sure." Alex stands. "Come on," he says to Evan under his breath.

Alex and Evan walk back toward 24th Street in the crisp fall night. Evan is so drunk that he can feel every footstep all the way up into his hip joints. " 'Young lady,' he says." Alex's voice is dry and flat. "Shit, that's a good one." It won't be until the next morning that Evan will understand what he meant. "You sure can shoot pool," Alex says. "I never could do it worth a shit. Fuck, I'm as likely to tear the goddamned felt off the table as anything else."

Evan has run out of stories, talk, jokes, anything. All he wants to do is get home and sleep. They're at Wolchak's garage. Alex unlocks the door of a three-quarter-ton Chevy pickup truck. "Where do you live?" he says.

"North Raysburg . . . Hey, you got your license already?"

"No," Alex says with one of his rare smiles, a grin that suddenly transforms his lean face, makes it pleasant for a moment, almost friendly. "Get in, man. I'll take you home."

Two

Chapter One

Alex drove south through center Raysburg. The light had just turned red at the corner of 35th; he lifted his foot from the gas and let the car drift on its own, losing momentum, down the white street. Evan saw that five boys or men were standing huddled together at the edge of a vacant lot. They seemed to range from middle teens to late twenties, but he couldn't be sure; their faces were oddly unfocused and ageless. They were all wearing what appeared to be policemen's hats—blue, peaked caps with badges—too small, balanced precariously on the very tops of their heads like saucers. When they saw the car, they began to wave furiously and blow on traffic-cop whistles. One of them, the smallest, jumped up and down. Another began to direct invisible traffic around the snow-covered lot. Alex gave them an army salute, tapped his horn. The light changed and he pulled away. He said to Evan in his flattest voice, "The Hackett boys . . . Their folks have been fishing in the gene pool too long."

Evan couldn't stop laughing. "What's the matter, Carlyle?" Alex said in the same wry tone, the humor carefully concealed, "Haven't you ever seen idiots before?"

"Christ," Evan said, "when I go back up to Canada and tell people about seeing a bunch of idiots standing in the snow at ten o'clock at night at the corner of nowhere, they're going to think I made it up. Oh, Jesus fucking Christ, Warner, this state is incredible!" He reached into the backseat for the beer, opened two cans, handed one to Alex. "People who didn't grow up here just don't understand it. Especially the jokes. I tell West Virginia jokes and people look at me like I've lost my mind. Like that old downstate story about the kid who shoots his bride. You know that one, don't you?"

"Yeah, probably. But I don't remember."

"Well, the kid goes in the shack and his old man says, 'Where's your bride, son?'

"He says, 'Had to shoot her, Paw.'

" 'Oh, why'd you have to do that, son?'

" 'Well, paw, she was a virgin.'

" 'That's right son,' the old man says. 'You done the right thing. If she weren't good enough for her own folks, she sure ain't good enough for ours.' "

Alex laughed. "Yeah," he said, "I have heard it. It's old as the hills."

"When I told that story at a dinner party in Vancouver, people looked at me like I'd just dropped a turd in the middle of the table."

Alex drove south past the mills, past the mill workers' homes. Evan smoked and stared out at the unrolling, snow-covered streets. *If you lose your sense of humor in this goddamned place,* he thought, *you're done for. Yeah, got to hang on to all the jokes you can even if they are black as a coal miner's lungs.* "Raysburg Steel hiring?" he said.

"Are you kidding?"

Evan laughed. As long as he could remember, Raysburg Steel had never been hiring. Oh, they might send out a call now and then for a few shit workers, might need fifty of them, and they'd have five hundred fully grown men show up for the jobs. But no, Raysburg Steel had never been hiring, and Consolidated had never been hiring, and Continental had never been hiring, and Allied had never been hiring. The best you could ask was that they weren't laying off. But Alex had been right too, at dinner, when he'd said, "Somebody's making money."

"Hey," Evan said, "you ever hear about the flood parties at the McClain?"

"What's that?"

"Something Susie Galloway told me in high school. Whenever we'd have a flood, a bunch of steel executives' wives would rent out a suite on the top floor of the McClain Hotel so they could sit up there and watch the show."

"Haw! That's good."

"Isn't it? Just wonderful. I can imagine all those ladies sipping their Scotch and sodas and watching the peasants getting flooded out of their homes on the Island."

Alex drove south through the Polish ghetto, through Millwood, toward Scottsbog and the long chain of enormous chemical plants and steel mills. "Still run open-hearth furnaces?" Evan said.

"Naw. Not much anymore."

"That's too bad. I was kind of looking forward to it . . . all those flames in the middle of the night."

"Well, the open hearths may be gone, but the stink sure ain't. All the way down the river it smells like a goddamned gob pile. Worse than it ever was. Sometimes white crud comes down out of the sky thick as that fucking snow out there."

"What happened to all the pollution-control laws I keep hearing about?"

"Oh, fuck, Carlyle, what do you think? Some of them just blow their stacks out at night when nobody's around to see it. You know what those assholes at Allied did? The federal government come in and said, 'Hey, you're way off the guidelines. You're laying out shit by the goddamned ton.' The management said, 'Oh, that's too bad. But if we have to put in all these antipollution devices, we'll lose money, so I guess we'll just shut her down.' Then the workers got together and sent a petition in to the government. Said, 'Oh, please don't shut the plant down. We'll all be out of jobs.' Ain't that a joke? So they give them another five years . . . to work down there and galvanize their fucking livers."

"Jesus." Evan laughed.

"Yeah. The union endorsed it. . . . Those fucking assholes are dead already and they don't even know it."

So would I be if I'd stayed here, Evan thought: *just another zombie, just another bitter Raysburg asshole trying to make sure he doesn't get laid off.*

Maybe he could do a show on it, go interview the guys at Allied and ask them what it felt like to be working at a place that was not only poisoning the whole goddamned valley but was poisoning *them* too, just a little bit faster than everybody else. But no, that was a ridiculous idea; who in Canada would give a shit? Canada had her own problems. You could find the same damned thing in Quebec. It reminded him of that book that had come out that year, the one by that Atwood woman. He couldn't remember the name of it. And he hadn't read it, of course; he never read anything but newspapers and summaries from his research assistant (good old Dana), but he'd done a couple of items on it. Canada was supposed to be the land of victims and failures, that's what it had said, something like that. But he wished he could take all of his Canadian friends—the people who thought of the States as big cars and color TVs and glossy homes full of gadgets—wished he could pack them all up and take them on a quick tour of West Virginia. Dana in particular. Right. He should have brought her along so she could see for herself the idiots standing on the corner, so she could smell the stench from the chemical plants and meet Hospidarski, see what a real West Virginia wreck looks like. Maybe then she'd stop riding his ass all the time: "Evan, you don't have to be a spy for Toronto, you know. It's not part of the contract, eh?

You don't have to jump every time Toronto whistles. You're getting a reputation around here, you know that, don't you?" *Well, to hell with her. Where does she get off with that shit? What does she know?*

If he'd ever done anything in his life except fuck up, there was a simple reason for it: since the day he'd packed his bags and left for Ohio State at the end of the summer of 1960, he'd been afraid that if he didn't learn to do *something* right, he'd have to go back to West Virginia. He still had that boy buried down inside him who was just like any of those other poor fuckers he'd met in the old days, just come down out of the hills with too much hair, in Levi's before it was hip to wear Levi's, drawn to dreams of motorcycles or big cars, to the painted ladies of Raysburg's whorehouses, walking the gray streets with "born to lose" tattooed on their souls. West Virginia: his friends turning into drunks and falling apart; black lung disease; small farmers going broke; the state government screwing everybody straight up the ass; and somebody was always making money but it was never anybody you knew. No accident that John Henry had busted his heart here, that Hank Williams had picked the state to die in, that the very first prefrontal lobotomies were performed down at Weston, that Charlie Manson had spent his formative years in West Virginia.

God help me, Evan thought, *and it's no wonder that I'm never comfortable in this stylish suit Dana talked me into, that I can never wear it the way she wears her crazy outfits, with that self-assured go-to-hell verve. Christ, it's still just amazing enough that they let me walk around loose anywhere but Raysburg. . . .* Oh, he had a pretty good life these days—a woman who liked him a lot, his own goddamned radio show. They liked his work in Toronto. They were going to put him on staff, move him back east. He was going to be a success if it killed him. But inside of him the West Virginia boy was still there, and every few months he'd wake up from that nightmare, the same one he'd had for years. He'd wake up to the sound of his own screaming voice. If Dana had stayed over, she'd pat him and say, "Evan, it's all right. It's all right." He'd grab for a cigarette, turn on the radio, pace up and down his apartment and look at all the things he owned, the objects that would bring him back to the present. Or maybe he'd stare out at English Bay, which didn't look a thing like the Ohio River. Anything to forget the total horror of the old crystal-clear dream: that he'd never left, that he was still going to Raysburg High School.

Chapter Two

Alex drove steadily, his right leg relaxed on the accelerator, holding the speed right where he wanted it. They'd left the last of South Raysburg behind, were out in open country now, moving through long stretches of trees and scrub between the chemical plants. With all the snow, it was like driving over a white carpet. They'd stopped talking, and Alex was using the silence to try to sort out his thoughts. He'd always known that Evan Carlyle would have to turn up back in town someday, but still it had been a shock seeing him on the street like that.

One thing you'd have to say about him, he thought. *Carlyle was just about the only guy you ever knew you could really talk to, and he was right more often than not.* Now Alex was wondering if Carlyle was right about Al Junior too. He could see it in his mind, the kid grown up into some slick young asshole like on the Johnny Carson show—his glasses, a suit and tie and long hair, a good talker. He's sitting in a bar . . . no, not a bar, some fucking lounge with leather everywhere, drinking a martini, and he's saying: "You wouldn't believe my old man. Ignorant, mean, red-necked hillbilly." It wasn't funny, but that picture made Alex smile. *Me and Archie Bunker,* he thought.

Well, Al Junior could make his own way, and the farm would go to Lori. When she got a little older, he'd take her down there and walk her around it, give her a feel of it, get her out of the fucking valley and let her smell some clean air for a change. Maybe there'd be a storm so she could hear the thunder echoing off all the hills, rolling in like doomsday, see the way the sky piles up. Alex glanced over at Carlyle, who was watching the river out the window. *In spite of everything that happened,* he thought, *it is good to see him again.*

But all the old memories were coming back, and Alex never knew what to do with them. He'd have dreams sometimes, wake up and lay in bed thinking it could be last week instead of years ago. He'd remember how it was when he was Al Junior's age, the hot quiet of the summer, nothing easy about it, but pressing down, and the way the sky would feel heavy, moving along. Remember sitting on top of the hill looking down at the farmhouse, next to him that old dog named George, the Bluetick coonhound. When Alex sits down, George sits down. When Alex walks, George walks. "Goina rain," Alex says to the dog. For miles in any direction the locusts are singing in the trees, and they'll keep buzzing away until the fall. Alex will be in the sixth grade in the school at Harrod. Sometimes his mother goes in there and substitutes when one of the teachers is off sick. Then he's got to pretend he doesn't know her.

Brother Bob's laying on the front porch drinking a Coke and reading a comic book. The Coke bottle glints green in the sun. The day's hotter than the holy hinges; he's wishing it'd rain and get it over with, hoping it's going to thunder and lightning, and fire-fork down the sky. He wouldn't mind if it stormed like that all day and all night. Then they'd all be inside yelling at each other and he'd take off up the hollow, go stay with his grandfather, sit out on the porch where they could see the lightning the whole way down the run, and the old man would say, "Now ain't that a show?" Once they'd seen a tree blown to smithereens. The next day they'd gone to look at it, and it was just like something his old man had hit with a stick of dynamite.

But no rain now, just the push of it in the air. Alex jumps up and takes off down the hill with the dog trotting next to him. He makes a big circle around the house and comes in the kitchen door. "You stay," he says to George, and the dog sits down, *thump.* Alex doesn't bang the screen door. Everybody else lets it bang on the spring, but he eases it shut. His mother's in the bedroom putting on a black hat. "My God, Allie," she says, "you scared me out of seven years' growth."

He sits down on the bed. "Where you going, Maw?"

"I'm going into Harrod as you know perfectly well." She settles the hat on her head. He don't know what she's doing wearing a hat in the summertime anyway. "If I didn't do it, I don't know who would around this place, and that's a fact. The Lord knows where your father's gone to by now. He's over to Stacey Yoho's right this very minute more than likely, and I won't see hide nor hair of him until eight or nine tonight, and then he'll come in wanting his dinner." She pats the hat, turns and looks at Alex with her hands on her hips. "Well, it's goina rain, son. Goina rain pitchforks and hammer handles before it's through. So why don't you just come along with me into Harrod now?"

He shakes his head.

She's looking at him hard. He knows what she's thinking. "You just come along with me, son. I'll buy you a soda in at Froelich's." She's thinking if he stays here, Bob's going to be picking on him again, but that's not the way it's going to be. Bob's not going to see him. He shakes his head again. "All the Warners is stubborn as mules," she says.

"I ain't goina get in trouble. I'm going up to Grandpaw's."

"You ought to let that old man alone. He's got troubles enough."

"I ain't no trouble."

"Just like I said, you can't tell a Warner a thing. You're all alike, the whole bunch of you. You got your own ways, and if the world don't like it, then that's just too bad." Alex slides off the bed. "You eat something now. You're no bigger than a minute."

In the kitchen he smears two slices of boughten bread with peanut butter. He shoves one slice in his mouth, opens the screen door and offers the other to the dog. George reaches up with his muzzle and takes the bread easy as he would have picked up a bird. "My God, Allie, don't be feeding that dog peanut butter. Sometimes I don't think you got good sense."

Alex walks slowly up toward the barn. The peanut butter's sticking to the roof of his mouth. He turns and looks back down to where his mother's climbing into the pickup truck. The road's dusty. Bob's still laying on the porch. "Don't you be picking on your little brother," Mrs. Warner yells from the driver's seat.

Bob don't even look up. "I ain't seen him, Maw."

"You just listen to me, Robert Warner. You touch that little boy, and I'll hit you alongside the head with a skillet, and you just see if I don't. Did you hear what I just said?"

"I heard you."

"All right, then." The truck goes rattling away up the dusty ruts. Knock in the engine. When he gets older, he's going to learn to fix things like that. Maybe he'll go over to Yoho's and get Stacey to show him how to fix trucks. You can make money fixing trucks.

The peanut butter's left his mouth all thick and gummy. "Should have brought us some water," he says to the dog. "Well, he ain't goina hear us. You be real quiet now."

He sneaks back down to the kitchen door, stands there a minute listening. Can't hear a thing but the locusts. He takes down a Mason jar from the shelf and starts filling it up at the tap. There's a slam-bang, and Bob's off the front porch. Alex waits holding the jar of water in his hands. He doesn't know which way to go, out the front door or the back one. He knows his brother's thinking the same thing, standing out there in the dust trying to outguess him. Probably figuring he's going to cut out the back way same as he come in. But no, he's probably one jump ahead, figuring that Alex would be thinking about it and go out the front way. Alex runs out the back door and straight into his brother. Bob was dumber than he thought.

Bob's got Alex's arm jammed up between his shoulders, the

water's spilling all over the porch. The dog growls and Bob kicks at him. "Where the hell you going in such a hurry, squirt?"

With his free arm, Alex throws the rest of the water into Bob's face. "You little cocksucker. Jesus." Bob jerks up Alex's arm higher. It hurts something awful. "You go telling Maw, and I'm goina sharpen your head down with a hatchet and drive you into the ground like a tent peg. You hear me, you little prick?"

"That ain't your joke," Alex says, "that's Stacey Yoho's joke."

"It ain't goina be nobody's joke when I get done with you."

Jesus, the bastard's going to break his arm. Alex twists around and kicks his brother's shins. "You really want it, don't you, you little prick?" Bob slaps Alex in the face a couple times. "Cry and I'll let you go."

Alex spits in his brother's eye. Bob jams him up against the porch railing and bends him backwards, leans all his weight on him. "You're goina cry, you little fucker. I'm goina make you cry. You just see if I don't." Bob shoves a finger up Alex's nose, up the left side. He shoves it up deep and works it around. Alex can feel tears burning his eyes. He hears a sound in his ears like locusts, only louder. "Cry, you fucker." Alex grinds his teeth together.

Bob pulls his finger out. Blood comes pouring down all over Alex's face, all down his shirt. Bob laughs. "Now the other side. And when I get done with that one, I'm goina twist your ears off. How's that?"

Bob's not paying enough attention. He's really dumb. He's dumb as a post. If Alex can just twist around a bit more, he can get a good kick in, and Bob won't even see it coming. Bob's holding his index finger up, waving it in the air. Long nail with dirt under it. Blood all over it. "Now the other side," he says. "You ready? I'm goina dig right into your brains."

Alex twists and kicks, gets Bob a good one right in the balls. Bob bends over and lets go. Alex is off the porch and running.

Bob don't chase him because he knows better. "You gotta come back sometime," he yells, "and when you come back, I'm goina cut your pecker off with a knife."

Alex runs up the hollow. He knows every tree and stump, every twist and turn of it. He runs as hard as he can, sweat pouring down him in the heat, until he feels a pain in his side big as a baseball. He slows down to a walk. There's nobody to see him now and so he can cry all he wants. He hears his own voice howling like a dog. *Stop it, you baby,* he tells himself. But he can't stop it. He walks along crying and yelling. The sun darts along above his head peeking in and out of the tree tops. He wipes his face with his bare forearm. It comes away all covered with blood and snot. "I'm goina grow up and kill him," he says to the dog. "You just see if I don't."

Way back in the woods Alex has got his paint can buried. He digs it up with his jackknife, pries the lid off. The can's full of all the money he's saved since he was a little kid. He started hiding it back up the hollow after his old man busted open his bank once. He leans up against a tree and counts it, has to do it twice to make sure he hasn't made a mistake. There's twenty-seven dollars in that can, all of it in silver money. He hammers the lid on and walks away with it. Feels good how heavy that can's got to be.

His grandfather's truck is right where he knew he'd find it, pulled off to the side of the road, but there's no sign of the old man. Alex climbs a tree to wait, hangs his paint can on a branch. The dog sits at the base of the tree and looks up. "You want to come up here too?" Alex says. The dog wags his tail. Alex climbs back down, picks up the dog, throws him over one shoulder, and works his way back up. It's hard going. He sits on a strong branch with the dog on his lap. "Don't worry," he says, "I ain't going to drop you."

Through the high tops of the trees he can see storm clouds starting to move in, white on the top but black and thick on the bottom. Now a little bit of breeze is cutting the heat. The dog's shivering. "Don't worry," Alex tells him, "you ain't going to fall." His nose hurts something awful. He pushes his face into the dog's warm coat.

The old man's coming. He's crashing and banging down the

side of the hill out of the woods, swearing to himself. He gets to the bottom, leans against the side of the truck, and mops his neck. He sees Alex looking down at him. "Good God Almighty, son, what the hell you doing with that dog up a tree? You just get him down out of there now. Give him to me. In all my born days, I never seen a dog up a tree. It ain't natural."

Alex hands the dog down to his grandfather. "There now, that's where dogs belong. On the ground. Maybe somebody told you he was a bird dog, is that it? Well, it just ain't natural. What the hell happened to your face?"

"Fell down."

"Looks to me like you got one of them nosebleeds. You come down here, son, and let me look at it." Alex grabs his paint can and slides down to the ground. His grandfather hunkers down on his heels and dabs at Alex's face with his big checked handkerchief. "Well, it ain't bleeding anymore. You're all right. What have you got there, son?"

"That's my life savings."

"Well, you got to be careful then if it's your life savings. What do you do, keep it buried out in the woods? You're a smart boy, that's for sure. Already know better than to trust them banks. I've buried me a few things back in the woods in my time too. Here, you need a drink of water." The old man keeps water in a pint whiskey bottle in his overalls. The water tastes warm and stale. "It's goina rain to beat hell." The old man's got a long white beard halfway down his chest but no hair on his head at all. He wears an old slouch hat to keep his head from getting sunburnt. He spits a brown stream off to one side. His moustache's stained yellow with tobacco juice. "Wish you was a little bigger," he says. "You could help me tote them bags." He jerks his head toward the truck. The tarp's drawn back, and the whole bed is stacked with hundred-pound bags. "Used to tote two of them at one time. Can only tote one now. But Jesus, at my age, that's doing all right. Senile. That's what they're saying about me. 'The old man's senile.' Well shit, boy, you show me some other eighty-two-year-old man can tote hundred-pound bags of sugar. That don't sound like senile to me, does it to you? What you goina do with that life savings of yours?"

"I don't know. Been thinking about it."

"Well, that's a good thing. Serious business. How much you got there?"

"Twenty-seven dollars."

"Well, that really is serious business. Same as what I'm doing's serious business. You don't tell nobody about what your grandpa does, do you?"

"Naw, I don't tell nobody."

"That's good. You just keep it that way. What I do back here's nobody's business. You understand, boy?"

"Yeah, I understand."

"That's good. Yeah, I know you understand. I done told you about King Washington. Do we pay that whiskey tax?"

"No, we don't pay no whiskey tax."

"Did we ever pay it?" the old man yells.

Alex has played this game before. He never gets tired of playing it. "Never," he yells back. "We never paid no whiskey tax."

"And when we goina start paying it?"

"Never," Alex says, laughing. "We're never goina pay no whiskey tax."

The old man winks. "That's right. And don't you forget it. Here, let me give you a quarter. You can throw it in there with the rest of your life's savings. Now tell me what you're goina spend it on."

"I'm either goina buy me an Enfield rifle or I'm goina study that Charles Atlas course, one."

The old man hunkers down in the dirt. "Well now," he says, "that's sure a serious decision to have to make. Just what Charles Atlas course is that?"

Alex takes the page of the comic book out of his jeans and unfolds it. It's getting pretty torn and wrinkled by now. His grandfather takes out his store glasses from his overalls, puts them on, and then holds the paper out as far away from him as he can get it. When he reads, his lips move. "Now what's this?" he says. " 'Fear no man . . . dynamic muscles . . .' Seems to me this is a little bit like them things you can buy on that radio station. You know the one, boy? They'll sell you anything. I remember they was advertising once for the world's best coat hangers, five for a dollar. And you sent in your dollar and what you got back was five big nails about the size of railroad spikes. The thing about mail order is you don't know what you're going to get." He folds up his glasses and puts them away. "And you don't know who you're dealing with neither. Now instead of this here Charles Atlas business, I'd get me a set of barbells."

Alex thinks about that. He'd like to have a set of barbells.

"How'd you say you got that blood on you again?" his grandfather asks him.

"Fell down."

The old man rests on his heels and pulls at his beard like he's thinking about something. Finally he says, "You recollect that Bible story about Cain and Abel?"

"A little bit."

"Well, let me tell it to you again. Cain and Abel was brothers, you know, and Cain was a pretty straight fellow, but Abel he was as crooked as a dog's hind leg, and Cain he had a short temper just like us Warners and he figured his brother had done him wrong. Which more than likely his brother had. So he rose up and slew him."

"How'd he do it?"

"Shit, I don't rightly remember."

"Did he shoot him?"

"No, they didn't have guns back then. I don't remember how he done it. Maybe he hit him in the head with a shovel, I don't know. But you know what happened to Cain, don't you? He got driven out of his home and had to wander around in foreign lands for the rest of his natural days, and that's a terrible thing to happen to a man. He had no people, he had no land, he was just like an old drummer selling soap, always on the road with nothing to call his own."

Alex has the funny feeling that his grandfather can tell what he's thinking. He stands there, and his grandfather sits there on his heels, and the dog lies there on the ground, and the sky's rolling along over their heads with the storm blowing in. He's wishing it'd start to rain. Maybe then he'd feel better. "The thing about a gun," the old man says, "is that somebody can always take it away from you. But if you get real strong, nobody can take that away from you. Now if I was you, I'd take that life savings of yours up to Harrod and go in that Sears store there and order down a set of barbells from Raysburg. The thing with the Sears Roebuck people is, they always give you good value."

A hundred and fifty-five pounds, and to an eleven-year-old kid it seemed like a ton, but by the time he was fourteen it was too light and he had to get a couple more twenty-five-pound plates. That damned old pile of iron, rusty from being kept out in the barn, he'd gone back for it in Tony Wolchak's pickup truck. He worked with it in the garage until he found out he could walk six blocks up the street to the Y and they had all the pounds he'd ever need. *Shit*, Alex thought, *wonder what ever happened to that old set of barbells?*

Chapter Three

Evan watched the river roll by on his right. The American beer tasted too thin to him, watery, and he was beginning to feel let down. He couldn't think of a thing to say. Glancing at the speedometer, he saw that Alex was holding them at an unvarying forty miles an hour. *A damn sight slower than we used to do it*, Evan thought. But it was a dangerous night with all the snow. They were approaching the outskirts of Scottsbog. Not much of a town; if you didn't already know it was there, you might miss it. "You know something, Carlyle," Alex said without taking his eyes from the road. "I should have been a coach. I'm ignorant enough for the job. Football in the fall, wrestling in the winter, and track in the spring . . . and usually they let you teach something easy like geography. Give you the summers to fuck off. The pay ain't bad."

So that's what he's been thinking about for the last ten minutes. "You would have been a good coach," Evan said.

"Damned straight. I would have taken it seriously . . . not like old man Rurak, who just left us alone to train ourselves. I would have turned out some damn good milers. And shit, I could have done it, you know? I had that scholarship down at WVU, and there I was in the dorm and everything. All I had to do was play ball, run, take in a few classes. . . . They would have given me the piece of paper."

"Why didn't you?" Evan had heard that Alex had dropped out. He'd never understood it.

Alex didn't answer. After a moment, Evan glanced over just in time to see that Alex had been looking at him. Now Alex was again staring straight ahead through the windshield. "You talked me into going down there," he said. "Shit, I should have listened to you."

Evan laughed. "Why didn't you?"

"Oh, you know the bullshit they give you in the recruiting office: 'Well, come on in, son. Sign up and we'll teach you a trade.' And that's right, they do . . . if you want to learn it. And I wanted to learn it. It was either sports or cars for me, right? So I learned everything I could, and I'm a fucking good mechanic now . . . not just a blacksmith like I used to be in the old days. And I thought that's all I'd ever need. Nobody ever told me the oil was going to run out."

"Well, it hasn't run out yet . . . and maybe you could do something else."

"Oh, fuck me, man! What the hell else am I going to do at thirty-two with a wife and a couple kids and a fucking mortgage on a cardboard box sitting on top of a hill?"

Good question, Evan thought. Alex rubbed the back of his neck. "Shit," he said, "I keep drinking these fucking beers like soda pop. You want to open me another one? . . . Thanks. . . . It must have been Hospidarski. That must have been what it was."

"What?"

"The reason I dropped out of school. When they got him, it just kind of took the heart right out of me."

"I never heard how it happened. Heard it was armed robbery, but—"

"Yeah. Armed robbery. The goddamned asshole! I don't know why it hit me as hard as it did, but it did. I guess the amazing thing was that they hadn't got him sooner. He worked for Joe Patone, you know that."

"Yeah." Evan had never known Frank Hospidarski very well, but he'd collected every one of his stories to retell for the shock value and the reflected glory. He'd loved seeing the expressions on the faces of the guys in his class when he'd talked about Frank. They had to be thinking: "Carlyle must be all right if he can hang out with a bad-ass like that." And what Joe Patone had used Frank for had been his little jokes. Not his big ones; for those, the boys would come down from New York and a body would turn up in the trunk of a stolen car in Covington or Pittsburgh. But if it was a little joke, he'd call in Frank and say, "I think this fellow needs a talking to."

So maybe when you were at work one day, Frank would go through your house with a fifty-pound sledge and a couple of cans of paint. Or he might go down to the dump, shoot a dozen rats, and leave them in your car. Maybe he'd pour a little valve-grinding compound in your oil, or, if you were known to take a drink, you might run into him and he'd be buying you shots, laughing and slapping you on the back, and then you'd wake up the next morning with the worst hangover of your life in a fleabag hotel in Zanesville with not a stitch of clothes to your name and your head shaved. And if you didn't get the point of these little jokes, the next time you ran into Frank, he might be tapping your kneecaps with a baseball bat.

"You know, when Frank and I were stealing all them cars," Alex said, "I used to tell him all the time, 'Frank, I'm indestructible.' I believed it too. Now I don't know what the fuck I was thinking about. . . . But the things we did just got crazier and crazier, right? And the time we run McCarthy off the road was kind of the last straw for me. I knew I had to straighten my ass out or I'd really fuck up, so I quit loafing with him. But he kept right on going, and then he'd come around and say it back to me: 'I'm indestructible. They'll never get me. Nobody can touch me.' Used to bother the shit out of me when he said that. And then he had to go and get himself that fucking gun.

"Frank didn't need a gun, but he used to get a kick out of carrying it around, pretending he was on television or some damn thing. And finally I guess he just had to use it. Oh, Jesus, Carlyle, it was just so fucking dumb! He walked into a grocery store on Twenty-ninth Street with a handkerchief over his face, walked out with the money, and the police was there waiting for him. He didn't even get a chance to shoot one of them. And I was over at Morgantown trying to be a goddamned college student. Jesus!

"See, there was a little kid in the store. A little boy about nine years old. Frank didn't even notice him. And he was a clever little fucker, I'll give him that. I mean he must have been watching television too. So he snaked out the back way. And it just happened there was a cop car at the foot of the hill. You know those Raysburg cops . . . like the old joke, 'always working on a case and it's usually Black Label.' Well, they put down their beer and drove up and met Frank at the front door. It was all very friendly. They all called him 'Frank.' They was really happy; they'd been waiting for years to get him on something. And he knew them, of course. They went down to the station having a nice little talk, like old friends. There wasn't much he could say. They'd got him dead to rights.

"It didn't make any sense. After everything Frank had done . . . shit, I mean Frank and I had done enough together to go to the chair nine times . . . and then they got him for this little chickenshit thing. But old Patone didn't think it was very funny. He didn't like the joke at all. 'What's the matter?' he said, 'I don't pay you enough?' So he just threw Frank to the wolves. Wouldn't have done it if it had been one of his own, but to him Frank was just a dumb Polack. I think he even put the word out: get this son of a bitch, take him down a notch or two. And by Christ, they got him. They give him shit the first time he was in, but then when he got out, Patone wouldn't have anything more to do with him, and Frank couldn't get a job anywhere, so naturally he was back in again within six months. And the next time they really broke him.

"They kept him in the hole fucking weeks at a time. They put out the word he was an informer, right? So the other prisoners wouldn't have anything to do with him. They beat him up. Shit, I don't know what all they did to him. They broke his hands."

"What?" Evan said.

"You heard me. They fucking broke his hands. Load of steel rods in the yard. They had to move them into the shop. You've got to see it, right? Two- or three-inch steel rods about ten feet long all stacked up in a pyramid. Each rod must weigh god-damn several hundred pounds. So here's Frank reaching in to pick up his end, and there's supposed to be another guy picking up the other end . . . except that all of a sudden that other guy ain't there, and somebody else is moving the pile down on him. When those steel rods start to roll, they motherfucking roll. And Frank was tired. He didn't see it coming. He didn't get his hands out in time, that's all. And then they threw him in the hole for a couple days before they let him see the doctor. Shit, he can't even drive a car."

Evan hadn't noticed that they'd passed through Scottsbog. They were turning into a parking lot. "There it is," Alex said: the bar where they had always stopped in the old days. It was open.

"You knew he was going to come in there," Evan said, "didn't you? . . . Into the P.A.C.?"

"Yeah. He loafs in there every night."

"Christ, man, what did you take me in there for?"

Alex turned off the ignition. "I just wanted you to see him, that's all."

Chapter Four

The only time before that Evan had ridden south with Alex all the way to the farm, it had been at the tag end of one of those long, viciously hot summer afternoons when the humidity rises to a hundred percent without a sign of rain—August of 1960. Alex and Evan had graduated from Raysburg High that spring. Alex hadn't run in competition since the regionals in Columbus; he had, as he'd been constantly complaining, picked up five pounds since then, but Evan couldn't see where those pounds could have gone. Alex was still lean as a hound. You might almost take him for fragile as long as he had a shirt on and you couldn't see the deep cuts of the musculature built by years of weights and wrestling and football. Evan always thought of his friend as ugly, but an ugliness that was interesting and pleasant as with certain kinds of dogs—bassets, English bulls, mastiffs. As they bounced along in the pickup truck, Alex said suddenly with no warning at all, "You've been drinking too much."

"Yeah?" Evan said tentatively.

"Yeah, you have. And your system can't handle it, man. Do you know what I mean? You don't do anything. When you're training at something, you can really abuse yourself, and your system can handle it. You work it off. But you don't do a fucking thing. Most exercise you get is hanging out at the end of a pool cue. You should train at something, take up weights or something . . . or you're going to go to pot what with all the fucking beer you put away."

Evan laughed uneasily. "Yeah, sure," he said.

"Me too," Alex said. "Happens to me every time I start loafing with Hospidarski. Shit, we go on many more benders like last weekend, we're not even going to be fit to bury. Have to pour us in the ground. . . . Well, you'll like it down on the farm. We'll run some, lift some weights. . . . Take you over to the pool hall in Harrod, let you show them hillbillies how to shoot."

"Really been four years since you've seen your brother?"

"Yeah," Alex said, "at least. Let's see . . . I'd just got out of the eighth grade when we had that big fight. That's when I come up to Millwood and moved in with my Uncle Gladney. . . . Yeah, so it's been four years. He's been home on leave before, but that was the first time he come to see me. I sure as hell wasn't going to go see *him*, the son of a bitch."

Last Saturday Evan had been sitting on an oil drum, smoking a cigarette, waiting for Alex to finish whatever the hell he'd been doing under Pilsudski's Chevy. Gannister's pickup truck had been on the lift, so Alex had the Chevy jacked up a couple feet under the front bumper. "Should have put the fucker on the lift," Alex kept muttering to himself, "knew I should have put the fucker on the lift," and banged metal. There was nothing to see of him but his engineer boots sticking out from under the side of the car. It was already past closing time; Evan knew that Elaine was already getting pissed off waiting for them. "Shit," he said, "I better go across the street a minute." But then an ancient, battered Pontiac with a crumpled right fender pulled up by the gas pumps.

"Hey," Alex said, "sell that fucker some gas, will you?" But a man had already climbed out of the car and was walking over to them. He was built along the lines of a Sherman tank, short and squat with huge round shoulders; his hair was cut off into a half inch of curly black burr. "Al Warner here?" he said.

In one quick motion Alex shot the creeper out from under the Chevy and sprang to his feet, lit like a cat, knees bent and crouched slightly forward. He held an open-end wrench in his right hand. The man had stopped a few feet away, stood stiffly, his arms at his sides. Neither he nor Alex moved; they stared into each other's faces. "Well, hello, Bob," Alex said slowly.

"Hi, Al," the man said. "You've growed up some."

"Yeah, so they tell me."

"Been hearing things about you. Hearing you been burning the cinders off the track."

"Yeah, burned off a cinder or two. . . . So what the fuck you doing, Bob? Your hitch over?"

"Naw, signed up again. Just home on leave. Going to stay in awhile, I guess." He laughed slightly, a thick sound, like a cough. "Shit, maybe stay in forever and draw that pension. It ain't a bad life. . . . Fuck, so you're out of high school now? Can't hardly believe it." And with a slow and very careful motion, he extended his hand.

Alex hesitated, then shifted the wrench to his left hand, stepped forward, and reached out. They shook: formal, careful, not testing each other's strength, just the arms pumped up and down in the air a moment and then dropped. Evan already knew that this had to be Alex's older brother, Bob, who was in the marines; he'd never heard Alex say a good word about him. "Thought I'd look you up," Bob Warner said. "Thought it was about time."

"Seen the old man?"

"Yeah, just come up from the farm. He said I ought to look you up. Said there weren't no point in letting it run on any longer. . . . You're my fucking brother, right? So why don't we just forget it?"

"Sure, Bob, that's fine with me."

"I mean your people's your people, right? What the fuck are you going to do?"

"Sure. Yeah. Can I buy you a drink?"

"Well, fuck. I wouldn't mind that at all."

"Let me clean up." Alex turned to Evan. "This here's my brother, Bob," he said. "This is Evan Carlyle. He's a good buddy of mine. You want to shoot pool with him, he'll take your ass any day of the week."

"Pleased to meetcha," Bob Warner said and shook Evan's hand. He didn't look at Evan's face but instead away at the sky. He was now obviously Alex's brother, but he was a good two inches shorter and sixty pounds heavier than Alex. He didn't seem to have any neck at all, just a blunt bullet-shaped head resting directly on hunched, round shoulders. On Bob, the Warner features weren't the least bit attractive; he seemed to Evan merely ugly: double chin, sagging cheeks, pouches under the eyes, hair receding in the front into a sharp widow's peak. "Shit," Bob said turning back to Alex, "I bet you know where to get laid in this town. I bet you know all the good cathouses."

"Know a few."

Bob laughed and slapped Alex on the arm. "Shit, you can't fool me . . . you're a fucking Warner through and through. . . . Hey, I got my bonus in my pants. Why don't we go see if we can spend it?"

"Well, I'll do you one better, Bob. You remember Hospidarski?"

"Yeah, I met him once. Boxer, wasn't he? Boxed Golden Gloves?"

"Yeah, that's him. Well, he's working for Joe Patone now. We'll go look up Hospidarski and get laid tonight on Joe Patone, how's that?"

Within an hour all three of them had already managed to get pretty well hammered, riding around town in Alex's truck, passing a fifth of that fine George Dickel sipping whiskey. They'd finally located Hospidarski out at Leonti's, on Route 88, across the county line. He'd been in the back room playing poker, losing of course, so it hadn't taken much to persuade him to leave with them. They were walking across the parking lot minding their own business when a green open-topped sports car came careening in off the highway headed straight at them. Evan jumped back, but Alex turned deliberately to face the oncoming car; it slid to a stop only a few feet away from him, spraying gravel. "Why the fuck don't you watch where you're going?" the driver yelled. He looked like a high school kid, but he was big. So was the other boy riding with him. They were both wearing sunglasses even though twilight was already settling over the valley.

"Why don't you watch where you're driving?" Alex said in a conversational tone, neither friendly nor unfriendly.

A second car pulled into the lot; there were six guys in it. "What the fuck is this?" said Bob Warner.

"Looks like half the Canden High football team," Alex said.

"You guys wouldn't be looking for trouble, would you?" the driver of the sports car said.

Hospidarski laughed. "Naw, not us," Alex said, and walked away toward his truck.

"Fucking punk!" Bob Warner said.

"Forget it, Bob," Alex said.

"Hey," the driver of the sports car yelled, "I know you. Al Warner, right? Shit, the last time I saw you was in the crapper at the McClain. . . . Down on your knees like you were saying your prayers."

Alex turned back slowly and smiled. "Only way I'd be on my knees to you, honey," he said, "was if you was on your elbows."

The boy sprang out of the car and Bob Warner kicked him in the balls. Alex and Hospidarski ran straight for Bob to try to pull him off; Alex got an arm bar around his brother's neck. "Shit," Alex yelled, "stop it. You'll kill him. Jesus!" Bob was kicking the prone boy in the ribs and head, with each kick yelling, "Punk! Fucking punk! Punk!"

"Watch it!" Evan yelled.

The other kid, the one from the passenger's side, had jumped Alex from behind. Alex let go of his brother, twisted, grabbed, got a wrestling hold on the boy, and flipped him. "Fuck," he said to Evan, "let's get out of here."

But the other kids were already piling out of their car. "Polacks!" one of them yelled, "South Raysburg Polacks!"

"Oh yeah?" Hospidarski said, laughing. "Come and get yours, you little fucker."

Jimmy Leonti had burst through the door of the bar and was

sprinting toward them across the lot. He was an ex-boxer; he ran the bar for Joe Patone. "What the fuck's going on here?"

"Nothing much," Frank said, "just some out-the-pike punks making trouble."

Bob Warner swung at Leonti's head. Leonti dodged the blow easily and hit Bob square on the mouth. Bob's head jerked back, but he didn't seem particularly bothered. He punched again; Leonti slipped the blow and countered, fist in Bob's stomach. Bob grunted and kept on coming. "That's my fucking brother," Alex yelled to Hospidarski. Frank dodged between the two men, blocked Bob low and knocked him down, shoved Leonti back a few feet. Bob scrambled up and swung a wild haymaker at Frank's head. "Alex," Frank yelled, "call the fucker off."

Bob hauled back with his right; Alex grabbed him by the bicep and yelled in his ear: "He's a friend. Friend. Hospidarski."

Evan didn't know where all the people were coming from, seemed like hundreds pouring out of the bar. Must have thought it was a raid or some damn thing. Somebody hit him in the back of the head, and he went down on all fours, scraping elbows and knees, face in the gravel. He looked up, stunned, saw that Bob had gotten away from Alex and was punching at some of the Canden High kids; Leonti, with Hospidarski hanging onto his shoulder, was still after Bob. Evan scrambled to his feet and a fist came out of nowhere and caught him on the cheekbone; he sat down flat on his ass. He decided to stay where he was. Hospidarski had given up on trying to hold Leonti; he turned, picked the first person he saw, and knocked him sprawling ten feet. "Jimmy!" he yelled. "Just let us get out of here, all right? Just let us get the fuck out of here."

Evan wasn't safe sitting on the gravel either; somebody kicked him in the back of the neck. He jumped up and ran for the truck, heard footsteps running behind him. He got his hand on the door handle, turned and saw that Alex had intercepted one of the Canden High kids. For the first time Alex looked angry; his face had gone clean white, and his lips were drawn back into a snarl. Fast as a dancer, he feinted: right, left, left again. The Canden High kid couldn't find anything to hit, stopped, panting, and Alex booted him in the balls, fired his kick into that moment of hesitation. The kid went down and barfed. Deliberately, as carefully as if the boy's head were a football he was going to ram on home through the goalposts, Alex set himself up and kicked again, caught the drooping head dead in the teeth. The boy's entire body was ripped straight up into the air then fell back slack on the gravel. Alex ran for the truck, threw Evan into it bodily, yelled back to his brother: "Bob! Move your fucking ass."

Hospidarski was on the running board. "Your brother's in the back," he said. "Move it!"

Alex accelerated out of the lot. There was an enormous crash as Bob toppled over into the bed of the truck. "Shit," Alex said, "that goddamned fucking animal."

When they finally pulled up in the alley outside the door to Harriet Axford's house, Hospidarski turned to look at Bob Warner. "No rough stuff in here now, Warner. You hear me?" Frank's blue eyes glittered like ice cubes in a tall glass.

"Yeah, yeah," Bob said.

"I mean it, Warner. I'm serious."

"Shit, Hospidarski, I just want to get my ashes hauled, that's all."

"Well, you'll get them hauled. You'll get them signed, sealed, and delivered. But no rough stuff. And I'm not going to tell you again."

Bob grinned weakly. His shifty eyes tried Frank's face for a moment and then settled on looking at his own feet. "Yeah," he said, "I heard you once, Frank."

Hospidarski had called ahead from the bar, and Harriet Axford herself met them at the door. "Well, hi, boys. Nice to see you tonight." She looked just like one of the ladies who worked with Evan's mother at the library; in fact, she looked a lot like Evan's mother. Her dark hair, streaked with silver, had been permed. She wore a conservative blue suit and glasses with blue frames set with rhinestones. Evan had never seen her up close before and he sat uneasily in one of the fat stuffed chairs, sipped the drink that had appeared mysteriously on an end table next to his right hand, and peered over at her out of the corner of his eye. Half a dozen times he'd been walking somewhere with Alex and had seen Harriet drift by in her white Cadillac. Alex would yell, "Hey, Harriet!" and wave. She'd always keep right on going, looking neither to the right nor the left, and then just about the time when Evan was sure that she hadn't noticed a thing, she'd tap lightly on her horn, twice: *beep beep*. Local legend had it that Harriet had opened her first house at the time when Joe Patone had been taking over the rackets in Raysburg. He'd wanted to be sure that she knew exactly who was running things in town. He'd invited her to a party, taken a crap in his hat, handed it to her, and told her to eat it. She'd eaten it, so the story went, and since then she and Joe had been the best of friends.

Harriet's living room looked just like anybody else's living room: blue drapes closed over the window, doilies on the arms of the chairs, a painting of a cow standing in a field under a blue sky with fluffy white clouds, and a Philco record player going in the corner, softly spinning out light classical music. They were drinking something or other in tall glasses with mint and lots of ice. "Hot day today, ain't it, boys?" Harriet said. She must have been reading the *Raysburg Times* when they'd come in; the paper was still lying next to her on the couch.

"Sure is," Frank said. "Seen the bank sign this afternoon. It was ninety-six."

"Where are the girls?" Bob Warner said. He hauled out his wallet and began throwing money down on the floor.

Hospidarski looked at Alex. Alex shrugged. Frank turned on Bob Warner a look of pure, focused disgust. "Keep your money, Warner," he said. Bob's eyes bounced around the room. He gathered up his money and shoved it back into his pants.

"Paper says it's going to be just as bad tomorrow," Harriet said, as though she hadn't seen a thing.

"Well, Harriet," Frank said, "it's West Virginia and it's summer, right? What are you going to do?"

Evan's mind was racing; he was trying to figure out how he was going to get out of having to attempt his first act of intercourse with one of Harriet Axford's whores. He remembered the one he'd tried in the upstairs room above the Caravan. She'd been a perfectly nice girl it had turned out, but not exactly pretty, a skinny little thing in halter, shorts, and bedroom slippers who'd told him right off that a straight lay was three dollars. He'd been drunk and scared and totally lacking in erection. She'd taken his money anyway and said: "Don't let this give you no complexes, honey. Come back and see me when you're sober." But that one attempt had cured him of trying it with whores. Elaine had let him do everything he wanted with her except stick his prick in; he was sure that by the end of the summer, she'd let him do that too. And that's how he wanted it to be the first time, with Elaine some afternoon when his folks were off at work and not with a painted stranger, and more than likely Alex and his brother and Hospidarski watching. But the only way he could get out of it was to get so drunk he'd pass right out. He drained his glass down to the last tinkling ice cube. "Care for another, son?" Harriet said.

"Sure. Thanks." *Christ*, he thought, *and Hospidarski's really going to do it right. Naturally. He hates Bob Warner's guts so he's going to spend money like water just to show him. How many whores were there going to be? Six? Ten? A hundred?*

But when the party moved into the big bedroom at the back of the house, only two girls showed up. The names they were using were Candy and Laverne; they both had downstate accents strong enough to drive nails. Candy was a slender bleach-blonde in white baby doll pajamas and pink ballet slippers. Laverne's hair was dyed so black that the highlights in it were crackling electric blue; she had enormous tits, wore a long black negligee all the way to the floor, black-lace panties, a garter belt, black stockings, and silver high-heeled slippers with black feather-puffs at the toes. Both girls were painted up to required Raysburg whore standards: fiery lips, long blood-red nails, great bug eyes with black lashes thick and stiff as bristles on a hairbrush. "Hey, fuckin' A right!" Bob Warner yelled when the girls walked in. Evan knocked back the last of his drink. The third drink, or maybe the fourth; he'd lost track. Whatever the stuff was, vodka or gin, it went down easy as 7-Up. He was drunk, but he still wasn't drunk enough.

There were two double beds in the room, a coffee table with bottles and ice, and not much else. Alex had kicked off his boots, fallen back on one of the beds, and lit a cigar. He seemed totally uninterested in the whores, was blowing smoke rings at the ceiling. Hospidarski was sitting on the edge of the other bed; he'd taken Laverne onto his lap, was kissing her on the ear. She was giggling. Evan made straight for the bottle. Candy intercepted him, took the glass from his hand, said, "Here, let me do that for you, honey," and gave him a wide, toothy smile. "You're really cute, honey," she said. "I bet you've got lots of girl friends." His tongue seemed thick as a rug.

Evan didn't know where to go. He didn't want to sit on the floor and he certainly didn't want to lie down on the bed next to Alex. He retreated to the corner, leaned against the wall, and gulped at the gin. Or maybe it was vodka. Bob Warner already had his pants off. He grabbed Candy by the shoulders and shoved her down to her knees. His uncircumcised cock was short and blunt; it seemed damn near thick as a man's wrist. He stuck it into Candy's mouth, grabbed her head with both hands, and hauled her in. "Gobble it up, baby," he said. Her stretched red lips disappeared in his curly pubic hair. Her chest was heaving up and down under the sheer white nylon; she tried to pull her head back, but Bob held on to it, big hand over each of her ears, dragged her in to him. She was gagging. "Christ, Bob," Alex said, "let the poor girl breathe, will you?" Bob's fat ass was jerking steadily, slamming away. Sweat was running down into his face; his pale blank eyes were focused on the wallpaper.

Candy was making loud, retching noises, trying to pull away. Bob's forearms knotted, holding her; his knuckles went white. Alex stood up.

"Ah . . . fucking Jesus!" Bob gasped and let go. The girl jerked her head back and Bob's cock fell out of her mouth, bounced a moment in the air, and then dropped, trailing a dribble of come. Evan thought he was going to throw up.

Bob walked away from the girl, poured himself a straight shot of whatever the hell it was they were drinking, and knocked it back. "Ah, Jesus," he said.

Alex helped Candy to her feet. She was panting, rubbing her neck and the side of her face. Thin lines of tears had run down both of her cheeks. "You all right?" Alex said.

"Jesus," she said, "thought he was going to choke me there for a minute." She tried to smile. "Well, I guess it takes all kinds."

"Hey, Warner," Hospidarski said, "you're really an animal, you know that?"

Bob seemed to think it was a compliment; he laughed. Evan threw some ice cubes into his glass, dumped it full of vodka—he saw by the label that it was vodka—and drank it. To hell with the mixer. The alcohol was hammering away behind his eyes; he was sweating. He lay down on the bed where Alex had been. Yeah, he was really going to manage to do it. Pass right out.

There was a dim, dreamlike memory of the bed squeaking. He was wedged in next to the wall, his face a few inches from the partially drawn window blind. He turned his head and was swept away a moment by a fast, swirling downdraft, fell a million miles, and arrived right where he'd started, flat on his back. The room was dark, but he saw a long white arm and a hand with painted nails. The hand kept opening and closing. Alex was fucking Candy on the same bed with him.

The next thing he knew was blinding, horrible, disastrous, searing light. He sat straight up yelling: "Turn off the light! Turn off the light! Turn off the light!" Hospidarski was snoring on the other bed. The girls were gone. Alex and Bob Warner had found two chairs, were sitting opposite each other on either side of the coffee table. Alex looked over at him very slowly and said, his voice thick: "The light? . . . Carlyle, you simple shit . . . it's the sun."

It was the worst hangover he'd ever had in his life: Evan's head was shattering with an unrelenting steam hammer. He saw an impossible, dazzling bar of white sunlight right where his face had been lying; it must have been falling directly onto his closed eyes. He stumbled up and out into the hall, found a bathroom—luckily the door was open—and threw up. When he came back, Hospidarski was getting dressed. "Jesus, Carlyle," he said, "you look like something the cat dragged home."

"I feel like shit."

"Well, you just relax, Carlyle. I'll go get us a pick-me-up." He jerked his head toward the Warners. "Them assholes ain't even been to sleep yet."

"Me and . . . Bob here," Alex said, forcing the words out carefully a few at a time, "we just been . . . talking about . . . old times." Bob's head had fallen forward and was hanging slackly; his eyes were closed. "Right, Bob!" Alex said, reached across the table and slapped his brother's face.

Bob sat straight up. "Fuck," he said.

"You'll have another one . . . won't you . . . Robert?" The ice had melted long ago. Somebody had brought in a case of beer and a fifth of bourbon. Alex reached for the bottle, got his hand around it, and slowly poured himself and his brother a shot. Half the bourbon was already gone.

"Fuck," Bob said. He reached out, found the glass, and drank. Alex drank.

"You guys is nuts," Hospidarski said, and walked out of the room. Evan fell back on the bed and tried a cigarette; he didn't make it. He ran out and down the hall, threw up again. He stayed in the bathroom a long time, splashing water on his face. When he came back, he found that Frank had returned with a tray: two glasses of Alka-Seltzer, two glasses of red stuff with ice cubes, toast and jam. "Old Polack hangover cure. Learned it from my grandmaw." Frank winked. "Drink her right down, Carlyle."

"How about . . . another beer, Robert?" Alex was saying to his brother. His speech was barely comprehensible. He looked over in the general direction of Evan and Hospidarski, his eyes unfocused and red. "We just been talking about . . . the good old days . . . Robert!"

Bob sat up with a jerk. "Fuck," he said.

"Beer?" Alex yelled at him.

"Beer? Yeah . . . another fucking beer." Bob began to talk, a long, monotonous mumble of words, but Evan couldn't understand any of them. Saliva was dribbling down Bob's chin; he picked up the bottle of beer and drank.

"What the fuck you trying to prove, Al?" Frank said.

Alex squinted. "Shit," he said. "Just talking . . . to my brother." He peered around the room, shook his head. "Right, Bob?" he snarled.

"Huh? . . . Yeah . . . right . . . fuck."

"Drink up, Robert." Alex tilted up his beer bottle and began to gulp, his Adam's apple bobbing. His brother stared at him stupidly, picked up his own bottle, and began to drink again. "That's the way . . . Robert," Alex said. "And now a couple shots, right?" Bob's head had fallen forward, and he'd begun to snore. Alex reached over and shook him. "Hey buddy, old buddy, come on!" he yelled. "Got a drink here, buddy." Alex's lips were drawn back showing teeth. Bob's eyelids were at half mast; he muttered something. "Drink!" shouted Alex.

Bob's hand wandered across the table, picked up the glass, and tilted the shot down. "Beer!" yelled Alex. Bob took a long gulp. The bottle slid out of his hand. Alex caught it before it spilled. Bob fell out of the chair and onto the floor.

"Robert?" Alex yelled, "are you crapping out on me? *Robert!*" Bob didn't stir. Alex poured the bottle of beer on him.

"Kick him," suggested Frank.

"Good idea." Alex stood up with considerable difficulty, supported himself on the wall, and kicked his brother in the ribs.

Bob grunted; he tried to say something, but all that came out was a wet gurgle.

"What's that, fuckhead? You say you'll have another one? Good." He made a loose gesture to Frank. "He says he . . . wants a double."

Frank laughed and poured the whiskey. Alex knelt next to Bob's body, tilted his head back, and began pouring the whiskey down his throat. Bob spluttered, shook his head. "You're not . . . crapping out on me . . . are you, pissface?" Alex yelled. He hauled Bob into a sitting position, tilted his head back against the wall, pushed his nose up with the heel of his hand, and poured down the rest of the double. Bob began to choke.

"What's that?" Alex said. "You want a chaser? . . . He says he wants a chaser." Frank laughed, opened another beer, and handed it to him. Alex took Bob's nose between his thumb and index finger, hauled his face open, and dumped the beer on him. Some of it must have gone down his throat; Bob was choking and gagging. Alex managed to get clear before Bob threw up. Alex giggled. In the three years he'd known him, Evan had never heard Alex giggle, but he was giggling now. He leaned down, grabbed Bob by the ear, yanked his head up, and screamed into his face: "*Bob . . . did you crap out?*"

Alex straightened up, leaned against the wall, and announced in a grave voice, "He crapped out." He began to laugh. He laughed until tears ran down his face.

"Shit," Hospidarski said to Evan, "let's try to get them to the garage, all right?"

Outside on the street at two in the afternoon, ninety-some degrees and the sun blazing down, Hospidarski and Evan dragged the dead weight of Bob Warner's totally unconscious body. Alex lurched down the sidewalk in front of them, waving his arms in the air and chanting: "Fucker crapped out, fucker crapped out, fucker crapped out." Alex fell to one knee, jumped immediately up and took off in a loose shambling run. "Fucker crapped out!" he yelled to the amazed people on the street. "Fucker crapped out. Fucker crapped out. Fucker crapped out."

Chapter Five

Alex was driving through Scottsbog in that little bit of calm between afternoon and night. "My fucking brother," he said to Carlyle. "Well, you seen him, right? Stupid? My God! And mean? Oh, Jesus." *Try having a brother like that,* he thought, *when you're ten and he's fifteen.* And there, on the outskirts of town, was the little bar where they always stopped. Alex wheeled the truck into the parking lot and said, "Let's get a beer." He turned off the ignition, jumped out onto the gravel, listened to the sound of the engine as it died. It needed a little work. He looked up at the sky; cloudless, the smeared blue was fading away to gray. The day had started to cool off; the locusts sounded like stones rubbed together, Alex thought, like old women talking to each other. He pushed through the screen door and into the bar. Evan was right behind him.

They sat at a table in the back, ordered beer and cheese-burgers. "You know what's funny?" Evan said. "I'll bet your brother thought he'd had a good time."

Alex laughed. "Yeah, he did. He even thanked me for it, the dumb fuck." Alex peeled the cellophane off a Marsh stogie, bit the end off, licked it, and lit it. He didn't want to talk anymore, just wanted to sit there. He was thinking how crazy it was that strangers were better to you sometimes than your own people. His own father and brother would have killed him if they could have got away with it, but old man Wolchak had given him a job, a place to live, given him the first truck, lent him money, and even had him over at Christmas a few times, given him a present and everything just like he'd been one of the family.

And then there'd been Hospidarski. He'd been more of a brother to Alex than Bob ever had.

"Hey, Al," Evan said. "Why'd you quit your job?"

Alex had known that Carlyle was going to ask him that. He had an answer all prepared. "If I stayed on there working at Wolchak's, I'd end up loafing with Hospidarski again, and every night would be just like last weekend. And shit, if I really am going down to WVU on that sports scholarship, I've got to be in shape." *That's close enough to the truth,* Alex thought, *but goddamn Elly Isaac anyway.* He hated the thought that he was running away from something, but that's exactly what he was doing. "Can't stay in town and not loaf with Frank. Tried it once before after we run McCarthy off the road, and he just can't understand it. His feelings get hurt, you know?" Evan was looking at him. *Smart son of a bitch, he won't miss a trick.* "Known Frank for years," Alex said, "met him when he was the bouncer upstairs at the Caravan."

"The whorehouse?" Carlyle was grinning, and Alex knew that he'd already said too much. Now Carlyle would want to hear a big story about it, and he didn't feel like telling him.

Alex drew the thick blue smoke from the cigar into his mouth, let it trickle out slowly. "I'd just come up from the farm," he said. "I'd been working awhile and I had all this money I hadn't spent. It wasn't nothing, but I thought I was rich. Fourteen years old, right? I really wanted to get laid."

Hospidarski's big hand had come out of the dark right onto Alex's shoulder. "Hey kid, if you're eighteen, then I'm Grand-maw Moses." Not being mean about it, smile all over his face, and Alex gave him that old joke, "I'm a jockey from Pennsylvania." Frank must not have heard it before because he laughed his ass off, said, "You're all right. You can stay."

Guys were sitting there by the dozen waiting their turn, nervous, not looking at each other. Farmers, businessmen, high school kids, mill workers, everybody you could think of. The girls usually didn't even get a minute to rest before they were snagged up by another customer. They were mostly young, not really pretty but not ugly either. They looked like a bunch of waitresses. "Not class like Harriet's place," Alex told Carlyle. "It was a real assembly line."

Alex picked the one who looked the youngest. She wasn't very pretty, and a lot of the guys didn't seem to want her. She was so skinny, all her ribs stuck out, and she didn't have any tits at all. "Lark" was what she called herself. She led Alex down the hall to a little room with nothing in it but a bed, and he began to think he'd made the wrong choice because she had a bad cough, but he didn't want to tell Carlyle that. "You know how they look at your wong to make sure it ain't rotting off you with disease?" he said. "And then they get a bowl of water and some soap and wash it off, right? And Jesus, Carlyle, I was so excited, I come right in her hand. Well, as far as she was concerned, I'd already had my three dollars' worth, but I just had to get laid. You know how it is when you've never had it. So I give her a bunch of money, and she started in on me, sucking me off and everything. And I finally got it in her and started pumping away."

For most of the next year Alex had gone to see Lark every week or two to get laid. Sometimes he'd even visit her on Sunday afternoons when she wasn't working, and they'd sit on the fire escape in back of the whorehouse and just talk. She was a farmgirl from Polderoy, and her father had screwed her when she was twelve, so she figured she'd go up to Raysburg and charge for it. And it wasn't any of Carlyle's business that she had TB so bad, she finally died from it. "I didn't think I'd ever come," Alex said. "I thought I was going to be there still working away on top of her when the sun come up. But then finally I made it, and she says, 'Well, kid, no cherry now, huh?' I mean she had my number right off the bat." Alex laughed, pushed back his chair and stood up. "Come on, Carlyle, let's grab some more beer and move it down the road."

Alex put one case in the back of the truck, the other in the front seat. Evan was already sitting in the cab ready to go, but Alex stood there a minute in the parking lot looking at the sky.

It was twilight now, and something about it hurt him inside his chest. It was funny how there were some things you could never forget. That first time he'd been with a woman, when he'd been pumping away at Lark and so fucking scared that he might not be able to do it, she'd smiled at him from right there flat on her back. "Slow down, kid," she'd said. "You're only human."

Chapter Six

They drove south along the river toward Carreysburg. They were out in the country now. Wind was whipping in the windows, and the temperature was dropping off. Alex had fallen silent. Evan smoked and drank his beer. He was thinking how easy everything was for Alex. The lucky bastard had gotten himself laid at fourteen, just like that, and Evan was still cherry as a schoolgirl. He still couldn't understand why Elaine wouldn't let him do it, and ever since the prom they'd had so many fights, he was almost glad he'd be leaving her behind in Raysburg. The worst time had been that Sunday afternoon back in July. When Evan had walked into the restaurant, he'd thought for a moment that it was empty; then, as the sun-dazzle had cleared from his eyes, he'd seen Elaine waiting at the back in their booth. "It took you long enough," she'd said, and he'd thought: *Christ no, I can't stand it!* He'd crossed the room slowly, walked toward her cautiously, hoping to be able to talk her down, deflect the explosion. The venetian blinds were drawn, and the sunlight was cut into a series of blinding white slices on the old linoleum.

"Sorry," he said. "I stopped in at the Main Street and shot a game with Pilsudski."

"Oh, great . . . Well, at least you bothered to come at all. At least you didn't just go off again and get drunk with Alex."

"He doesn't drink in the daytime, you know that," he said and sat down in the booth with her. The corners of her eyes had that revealing, pinched tension to them: she was probably suffering with one of her headaches, those migraines that could flatten her to nothing, like a landed and twitching fish. Her mother got them too; occasionally they'd both get one at the same time. Then the two women would be laid out upstairs each in her own bedroom with a cold cloth while John Isaac fumed over the grill below: "Good fucking Christ! Women!"

"Headache?" Evan said.

"Just the beginning of one. It's not bad. I feel about half sick. . . . It's too damned hot. . . . But more than anything else, it's just the constant *boredom.*" She was wearing lipstick, lots of it, and against her pale and sweaty face, her lips stood out like fresh blood. She lifted one hand, swung the car keys around on her index finger with a flourish. "I want to drive down to Carreysburg," she said, "the back way." Not straight down the river road which was the quickest way to get there, but over Route 88, twenty-five miles of ass-kissing hairpin curves through the hills.

"What for?" he said.

"For the drive," she answered, as though explaining something obvious to the village idiot, stood up, uncoiled from the booth like a big animal—he could see the vibrating tension in her entire body—grabbed her purse from the table, and banged away in that rangy, hip-swinging gait she had when she wore heels, half awkward, half sexy. She helped herself to a pack of cigarettes from the glass case, shoved them into her purse. She was wearing a white blouse and tight, very brief blue shorts, her legs bare. She must have shaved that morning because her black hair grew in faster than his beard and her calves were usually dotted with stubble, but now they were sleek, smooth, and brown. He followed her out into the street. "Don't say a word," she said.

"Who was going to say anything?" He spread his hands in the air, open, palms up, and shrugged.

"I can read you like a book. I can see right through you," she said, snapping at him. Her dark eyes had that desolate, bleak stare to them; she was obviously furious. He shouldn't have stopped off at the Main Street; he should have come right over when she'd called. "I'll dress any way I damn well please," she said. "I don't care if people think I look like trash. They can think anything they want." She reversed the sign in the front so it read CLOSED, slammed the door hard, and locked it.

"Who was going to say anything?" he said again. Although at another time when she'd been in a better mood, he *would* have said she looked like a 23rd Street whore.

"Don't worry," she said, "I'm not going to drag you into a bar or anything like that. You're not going to have to be *seen* with me."

He followed the metallic click of her heels half a block down to her father's beaten brown Dodge. "Where's the old man?" he said.

"He never came home. He's sleeping it off somewhere. He'll come crawling in tonight or tomorrow and then there's going to be hell to pay. I wish he'd die. I wish he'd drop dead." She unlocked the driver's side and slid into it, bent across the seat to flip up the button so he could get in. The inside of the car was like an oven. He rolled down his window. She pulled out into the deserted Sunday street, made an illegal U-turn, and drifted into Wolchak's. Tapped on the horn: shave and a haircut. The garage had a vacant look to it: glassy and shimmering in the sun. "The fat old bastard doesn't take the car anymore when he goes on a bender," she said. "Three of them he's run off the road . . ." She was spitting out angry explosions of words, pebbles thrown against a hard wall. "Old lady's got a migraine. . . . I'll be damned if I'll keep the restaurant open . . . for two or three kids to come in and buy Cokes. . . . I'll be damned if I'll keep it open for that . . . make three dollars in the whole afternoon . . . to hell with all of them."

Nobody seemed to be stirring in Wolchak's; Evan was sure that Alex hadn't made it home. The last he'd seen of him had been at three thirty in the morning at the Pines. Evan was sure that he and Hospidarski were still sleeping it off in a cathouse somewhere on Frank's money. "Looks closed," he said.

"He's in there. I saw him come in." He jerked around in the seat to stare at her. "I couldn't sleep," she said without looking at him. "I saw him come in . . . four or five in the morning."

"What were you doing up that late?"

"I told you: I couldn't sleep! I was just listening to the radio. I was bored." And she gave his own look right back to him: direct and angry. Her eyes said: Where the hell were you?

"I'm sorry I didn't call."

"The hell you are. You were in the pool hall." He said nothing. He hadn't been at the pool hall; he'd been at the Cat's Eye, the P.A.C., and the Pines. "I had a migraine," she said. "I couldn't sleep." She jerked her purse open and pulled out a pair of white-framed sunglasses. The frames curved up sharply at the corners, made her look like a huge cat with blank, green eyes. She tore open the Chesterfields, pounded one out for herself, and threw the pack into his lap. She punched the lighter on the dashboard.

Alex in sneakers and jeans, bare to the waist, came drifting out of the front of the garage and over to the car. "You look like death," Elaine told him through the window.

"Fuck," he said. He leaned against the car, nodded in to Evan. "What time is it?"

"Almost two." Evan said.

"Fuck," Alex said. His eyes were bloodshot, the rims reddened.

Elaine lit her cigarette, then Evan's. "Want to ride down to Carreysburg?" she said to Alex.

"Can't. Wolchak's coming in." He yawned, then kicked himself into motion: unscrewed the gas cap from the car, shoved the nozzle from the pump into it. "Goina quit this bullshit," he said to no one in particular. "Goina take my ass back down to the farm one of these days." The musculature of Alex's bare torso, Evan saw with a stab of pure, hot envy, was magnificent. The deltoids were as sharply defined as if cut out with a knife, the pectorals were powerful slabs, the broad shoulders tapered down in a dramatic V to a waist damn near as small as Elaine's but scored all the way to the low-riding jeans with parallel, washboard ridges of muscle. And all of him was evenly tanned, dark as a buckeye from working in the sun.

Alex fell against the side of the car and leaned there staring in the window with his expressionless, hung-over eyes. "Got to quit loafing with Hospidarski," he said across Elaine to Evan. "Couldn't run a mile these days if they set the fucking dogs on me." He yawned again. "Which way you going?" he said to Elaine. "Out the back way?"

"Yeah."

"Well, if you lose it, give me a call, and I'll send the tow truck down." The gas pump clicked off and he pushed himself abruptly back, jerked the nozzle out and hung it on the pump, screwed the gas cap back on the car, and walked away, leaving them with a short, jerky wave tossed over one shoulder. "Stop in if you make it," he called.

"He didn't charge you!" Evan said, surprised.

Elaine didn't answer. She started the engine, jerked the shift into low, and kicked down on the accelerator. Screaming like a shot animal, the Dodge catapulted out of the lot and onto the street. She laid rubber all the way up to 21st. "For Christ's sake, Elaine," Evan said. She ran the red light, pushed the car up to fifty on Main Street. Evan braced himself on the dashboard. "Goddamn it," he yelled at her, "you'll get stopped. You're right in the center of town."

"Yeah," she said. "Sorry." She lifted her foot and let the speed fall off, stopping at the next red light. She pulled off her shiny black heels and threw them into the backseat. "Can't drive with these on," she said. The light changed and she pulled out slowly, well under the speed limit. "Maybe he got killed this time," she said. "That'd be a joke! Maybe somebody got sick of

him and shot him. If we'd stayed down in Carreysburg, somebody would have done it by now, I know damn well they would
have. People shoot each other down there all the time. I couldn't
cry if either one of them died. My mother says I'm giving her a
nervous breakdown. She says I'm hurting her more than I realize. Oh, you should have seen her this morning; she could
have beaten me to death with a chair. I could tell by the way
she was looking at me. 'Elaine,' she says, 'you're never going to
be any good. You're just trash. You're just like your father's
people, nothing but trash. It's in your blood. Half your father's
people are down at Moundsville, you know that, so many of
them in the pen they've got their own damn club. . . .' Here,
light another one, will you?" She handed him the last inch of
her cigarette, hot red lip-prints on the white paper.

Pounding along in second, she ran the old six-cylinder Dodge
up Raysburg Hill. "He locked me in the closet once," she said.
"Did I ever tell you that?"

"No," he said, although he certainly must have heard that
story—along with the hundreds of other horror stories of what
her father had done to her. But he knew that when she was in
one of these moods, the less he said, the better; the thing to do
was let her talk until she blew off all the anger.

"Yeah, he did. I guess I was thirteen. We'd just come up
from Carreysburg. I can't even remember what I did. He locked
me in that upstairs closet with all the coats and boots. It was
hotter than hell in there, you wouldn't believe how hot it got in
there. I thought I was going to die, I really did. I knew if I
yelled or cried or something, he'd let me out, but I wouldn't do
it. I wouldn't give him the satisfaction, the son of a bitch. I
didn't make a sound. I just waited and he just waited. I could
hear my mother saying, 'My God, John, you can't leave her in
there, she'll die of heat prostration in there.' He said, 'You
touch that door, woman, I'll slap you down.' I was sweating like
a pig. I had a dress on, I remember that, and I took it off. I just
sat there naked with all the damn coats and shoes and waited. I
really did think I was going to die, but I thought I'd rather die
than make a sound. I thought it'd really be something wonderful

if he'd open up the door and find me there with all my clothes off . . . dead. You know, Evan, he left me in there until dark. He left me in there all damn day."

"Slow down, Elaine. We're still in town."

"When he let me out, I was sick as a dog. I had to go and throw up. But I'd beat him and he knew it. He couldn't even look at me. He went off on a bender and he didn't come back for a week. You know what I said to him? Oh, it was wonderful what I said to him. I'd planned it all the time I was sitting in there in the dark. I said: 'What do you think Jesus thinks of you for doing this to your daughter?' He couldn't even answer me. He couldn't even look at me."

They'd turned off past Tommy's Drive-In and were drifting out the shady, tree-lined roads past the big houses where the fucking rich kids lived, toward Waverly Park and then open country, hill country. She was relaxing a little; he could see it in her shoulders. Driving always calmed her down. "Hey, light me another cigarette, will you?"

"You just smoked two of them."

"Well, I'm going to smoke another one, do you mind? You're just like my mother sometimes, Evan. . . . I don't think there is any Jesus. If there was, I'd hate him. . . . Oh, God, I'm in oblivion . . . just this constant boredom. . . . I feel like I'm still stuck inside that goddamned closet, like I never got out of it."

At the turnoff to Route 88, she pulled over to the side of the road and flicked off the ignition. The engine continued to rattle and knock for a minute or two, then fell silent; the hot summer day was full of the heavy buzzing of locusts. *We've only got another month and a half together,* Evan thought, *so why the hell can't it just be fun, like the prom? Why can't we just have a good time? Why the hell does she have to get like this?*

"I've got a terrible headache," she said. "Maybe you should drive." But she didn't make a move to get out of the car, and he didn't either.

"Will you take those goddamned sunglasses off?" he said. "I can't tell what you're thinking."

Angrily she tore the glasses off then threw them down on the seat. Her black eyes were pinched and bleak; all they said was *pain*. She stared at him. "I never thought I was very feminine . . . like other girls," she said. He didn't have the remotest idea where that particular train of thought had come from. "To hell with Susie Galloway," she said. "I never wanted to loaf with that crowd of girls. They can all go to hell."

Now he knew where her mind had gone. "Well, look, Elaine, what did you expect? I mean—"

"Oh, shut up. Don't tell me any more about it. I've heard plenty about it." At one of the graduation parties during the last weeks of the school year, a picnic out at Waverly Park, Elaine had come in a black mood and a pair of the tightest shorts she'd been able to get over her ass. She'd sat most of the evening with her back against a tree, her face closed off, thinking her own thoughts—had sat with her legs spread wide open, absolutely oblivious to the fact that anybody who walked by could see the precise outline of her pussy and the soft tufts of dark pubic hair sticking out from below the shorts. The next day it had been all over the school. Evan had been sure she'd done it on purpose to get even with him for something; he wasn't sure what, but she'd sworn that it had never crossed her mind: "Christ, you must be crazy. I never even thought about it, that's all. I never thought anybody would care about how I sat down."

She grabbed up the sunglasses and shoved them back on. He could tell that she wasn't used to how long her hair had grown, and it bothered her: she shook it violently back out of her face. "Well, when I walk in a room, I think: Now these people are going to get a taste of me!" she said. She started the engine and put the car in gear. "Yeah, these people are really going to get a taste of me." She pulled out onto Route 88, pressed the accelerator to the floor with her bare foot, and ran them up to sixty on the straightaway. The first curve was coming up, the first of dozens of sharp curves they'd have to negotiate before they got to Carreysburg.

"I thought you wanted me to drive," he said. She accelerated into the curve, hauled the wheel over, and held it as the tires screamed. "Elaine!" he yelled and grabbed for the dash. She kept the gas pedal pressed to the floor even though they were riding just at the edge of the brim over a twenty-foot drop-off. She spun the wheel back as the road snaked the other way, took the curve sideways, sliding, and shot the car like a rocket at the next straightaway. She still hadn't touched the brake once. She threw her cigarette out the window, and he saw her jaws tighten like a vise. They were doing eighty.

"Elaine!" he yelled. She wasn't paying any attention to him. She goosed the car up to ninety in the dip, but the speed fell off mercifully as the grade rose. With the sound of ripping metal, she jammed the shift into second, ghosted around the blind curve at the top of the hill, shifted into third, and kicked the accelerator down. He'd seen a brief flash of the road ahead for several miles before they blazed down the hill: sliced-off rock face on their right, sheer murderous drop-off on their left, and straight ahead for a couple of miles, not another car on the road. She must have seen that clear road too; she didn't let up a hair, and they approached the next reverse curve at over a hundred miles an hour.

He didn't know which would be worse, to go on yelling at her or to keep his mouth shut. He pawed a cigarette out and lit it; he braced himself and hung on; sweat was pouring down his face in torrents. *She's going to kill us!* he thought. *She's going to run us fucking well right off the road. John Isaac's old clunker Dodge with its bald tires, she's going to blow those bastards, and we're going off the road, no doubt about it. She's just fucking well going to kill us.* "Elaine!" he yelled at her.

"Shut up," she said. He hung on miserably. She covered the first ten miles of that insane, twisting road in less than ten minutes by the clock on the dash. She pulled over at the top of a hill into a semicircle of gravel set aside for some damned historical marker, slid the car to a stop, the brakes locked up and screaming like cats.

"Who the hell do you think you are?" he yelled at her, "Alex Warner?"

She scrambled over the front seat to retrieve her shoes, jammed her bare feet into them, got out and walked away, hips swinging, leaving the car door open and the engine running. He turned off the engine and followed. She was standing at the edge of the fence, legs spread and four inches taller than he was in her spike heels, staring down into the quiet green valley full of humming locusts. Without looking at him, she yelled: "I'm just a stepping-stone for you, aren't I? Just a stepping-stone in your goddamned life."

"What the hell do you want me to do?" he yelled back. "Stay in Raysburg?"

"If you hadn't copied my homework for three goddamned years, you wouldn't even have got into Ohio State."

"For Christ's sake, Elaine! And if you hadn't been such a troublemaker, you would have got better grades. How the hell many times did they expel you anyway? Five? Six?"

"Yeah, I should have been a suckhole like you," she said, spitting out the words.

"Oh, for God's sake, it isn't— If you want anything in this world, you've got to be nice to people. It isn't— Oh, Christ, you can't just go around telling teachers to shove it and— Oh, Jesus, Elaine!"

"I'm just as smart as you are, and they almost didn't let me graduate. But I didn't go around to every single one of them and kiss their ass the way you did. Well, to hell with all of them. I'm out. Good-bye, Raysburg High School. They can all go to hell."

"Look, you could go over to WVU. Anybody can go down to WVU."

"On what? The money the old man makes. That's a joke. . . . I'll be damned if I'm going to go on being a waitress forever . . . and that's what I'd be in Morgantown, just another goddamned waitress. . . . I'm not just as smart as you, *I'm smarter than you!*"

She still hadn't looked in his direction. "Well, what the hell do you want to do?" he yelled at her.

"You know what the hell I want to do."

"Well, take some theater classes, for Christ's sake. Take some classes out at Raysburg College."

"Yeah, damn little piss-ass Raysburg College, that's where I belong, right? 'Take some night classes.' That's exactly how your mind works; I can see right through you. . . . You're going off and be a hot shit, but Elaine, well, just get her calmed down. Say anything at all to her, it doesn't matter what, just get her out of your hair. Tell her to go to night school, take some theater classes . . . maybe that'll do it. . . . Well, you can't act by taking night classes or reading books about it. You've got to do it by doing it. You've got to *feel* it. Jimmy didn't take any god-damned night classes."

"Oh come on, he took acting classes. He was at the Actors Studio for Christ's sake."

"Oh yeah. Sure. . . . But he wouldn't have gone to any little piss-ass Raysburg College."

"Jesus, Elaine, he was from some little hick town in Indiana. He was in the school drama club in some little piss-ass high school same as you were."

"I know where he was from!"

"Well, get the hell out of Raysburg then. Go to Hollywood. Go to New York."

"Maybe I will."

"Why the hell don't you?"

"You'd like that, wouldn't you?"

"Elaine, for Christ's sake, what the hell are you doing? What the hell's the matter with you?"

"I don't love you!" she yelled at him. She was still staring out into the valley. "I'm sorry I ever said it. You don't need it."

"Elaine . . . come on, now . . . Jesus."

"Don't talk to me in that goddamned voice . . . 'Calm down, Elaine. Calm down, Elaine.' . . . Well, fuck you!"

He was shocked and horrified. He'd never before heard a girl say "fuck," let alone "fuck you," directly to him. He felt a total blinding fury so absolute, it struck him numb and speechless.

She went on spitting out those short, sharp sentences: "I

don't love you. The more I see you, the more I know it's true. . . . There's nothing between us. . . . Our lives are miles apart. . . . We don't think alike, we don't look at anything alike. . . . We're not meant to be together. . . . You've got your whole life planned right into the future. I'm just a stepping-stone for you." *Christ,* he thought, *it sounds just like she rehearsed it in front of the mirror on her vanity table.*

"I understand you," she went on in that same hard voice. "You don't need love. It's the last thing you want. You're just going to go on with your plans. You'll use anybody you have to. . . . But it doesn't matter at all to me . . . I'm not going to live that long anyway. There's no use to fear it. My life is just too mixed up, too unanswered to go on much longer." He said nothing. "Give me back my necklace!" she suddenly screamed at him.

He'd worn it for over a year: a chain with a gold disc embossed with her astrological sign. He'd worn it to bed, worn it in the shower; in fact hadn't taken it off since she'd given it to him. Now he thought that the gold figure on the disc really was just like her: a coiled, murderous scorpion. Without a word he slipped it off and handed it to her. She dropped it over her head and swept her hair out of the way so it could settle onto her neck. "What do you expect me to do?" she said. "Cry?"

Banging her heels on the gravel, she strode back to the car. She jerked the keys out of the ignition and threw them at his head. He ducked and they brushed his hair, sailed five feet away into the dust. "You drive!" she yelled at him. "Take me back to Raysburg."

He still couldn't tell if she was really as angry as she seemed or if she was acting. He knew that she was perfectly capable of planning it all, sitting up alone in her room working it out until five in the morning. But if she was acting, she was damned good. Well, he'd always known she was damned good. His own anger had fallen away as quickly as it had come, and now he felt only a wretched, hangdog misery. *Oh, poor Elaine,* he thought, with her Shakespeare and Edgar Allan Poe and her sad, impossible ambitions. If there had been any way he could have done it, he should have left the day after the prom, then all his memories would have been good ones. He picked the keys out of the dust, walked to the car, and slid into the driver's seat. Her face was like a pale, sweaty mask behind those green, blank cat's eyes. He turned the car around and began to drive slowly back toward town.

They rode along in silence. "We could get our swimsuits and go out to the park," he said.

"That's a joke."

"We could pull over to the side of the road and make out," he said.

He'd calculated his tone very carefully, hoping she'd laugh. It worked. "You've got a one-track mind," she said.

"What do you expect when you dress like that?"

"I expect exactly what I get."

He glanced quickly over at her. "Please take off those goddamned sunglasses," he said.

She took them off, shook out her hair. She'd been crying. "Oh, Elaine," he said sadly, "for Christ's sake."

"Turn off here," she said, pointing. He turned off. Neither of them had to say a word. He drove about a mile down some poor dirt road on its way to nowhere, rural route something-or-other leading to nothing but crapped-out farmhouses. He shut off the engine. She slipped her arms around him and her tongue into his mouth. "You taste like sweat," she said. "I like it."

"You scared me half to death with your driving."

"Yeah, I shouldn't drive like that with somebody else in the car." It was odd, unpleasant, to hear her say that; it was Alex's line.

"You shouldn't drive like that at all."

"Oh, it doesn't matter."

"Yeah, it does. It matters to me."

She slipped the necklace off and handed it to him. "I do love you. I was lying. I do love you."

Was that real or still part of the performance? "Yeah, I love you too," he said uneasily.

"Do you?"

"Yeah."

"You love me right now. . . . I believe that. . . . Well, that's all right with me."

Cars passed by occasionally on Route 88. Through the rolled-down window of the backseat, he could see a bird so high that it was only a tiny moving speck circling slowly in the hazy blue sky. *Probably a hawk,* he thought. The locusts hummed in the trees, a rising and falling vibration that never stopped, as though the day were breathing. She lay on her side, panting with sex and summer heat, her ribs rising and falling with the sound of the locusts; he could count every rib if he wanted to, all the way down to the last one that curved up toward her breastbone. He squeezed the muscles in the hard deep cave of her stomach, stroked the beige nipples on her small breasts until they were pointed and hard as acorns. As always, she'd let him strip off her blouse and bra but wouldn't let him undo even the snap on her skintight shorts. She'd left her shiny black shoes on because she knew he liked them; she was too long for the seat and her knees were drawn up, her sharp heels digging into the uphol-stery. Oh, Christ, yes; he loved the way she dressed, sure he did: her trashy shorts, her lipstick, her long bare legs and whore's shoes—just as long as he didn't have to walk around town with her when she looked like that. But for the backseat, she was perfect. He liked her just fine. He felt wonderful. He came all over her bare brown thighs.

She sat up and reached for her bra. "It's always over before I want it to be," she said. Her voice had that sullen, smoky tone it always got when they'd been making out. "I could go on for hours." Her eyes seemed black, deep, and as dangerous as mine shafts.

Driving back to town, she said with a laugh that didn't quite work, "I bet they've got waitresses in Columbus."

He knew exactly what she meant, but he didn't answer her.

Chapter Seven

At four in the morning, Alex slipped into Wolchak's lot and stepped out of the truck. He was drunk, could feel it when he walked. He unlocked the garage, climbed the narrow stairs to his room, sat down on the edge of the bed, and lit a cigar. He wasn't ready for sleep, although he'd run himself half to death all over town looking for it, loafing with Carlyle, loafing with Frank in the Cat's Eye, the P.A.C., and to end it all a little run out the back way, a bit of a scramble on the curves. If he closed his eyes, he could see the road unwinding in front of him. *What the fuck are you doing, Warner*, he asked himself. *Waiting? Yeah, and fucking up.* And then there was a tap at the door downstairs, and he knew that he really had been waiting and so had she—sitting up there in her window watching for him to come in. He went down and opened the door for her. "What's the matter, Elly, can't sleep?"

"Not a prayer." She was wearing shorts and a halter top, barefoot. "Do you mind, Al?"

The streetlight was behind her; he couldn't see her eyes, just two dark holes looking at him. "Oh, hell, no," he said, "I never mind. Come on up."

It wasn't something they had to talk about, but they never lit a light. From his bedroom window they could look right across the street to her bedroom window and right next to it the window where her old man was asleep. "One of these nights he's going to catch you and shoot us both," Alex said. "You want a beer?"

"Sure."

She sat in the only chair; that wasn't something they had to talk about either. He sat on the edge of the bed. "Were you with Evan?" she asked him.

"Yeah, for a while."

"Jesus, sometimes I think you guys ought to get married."

He laughed. "I don't tie a rope around his neck and drag him along with me, you know."

"Yeah, I know you don't. Damn him anyway. I'm supposed to be waiting for him when he gets around to me, and when he's doing something else, I'm not supposed to care."

Alex didn't say what he was thinking: *What do you see in him anyway?* He'd never say something like that. For one thing it wasn't any of his business, and for another he already knew what she saw in Evan. And besides, if he said that, she might say, "So what do you see in Susie Galloway?" so all he could find to say was, "Figured out what you're going to do yet, Elly?"

"Are you kidding? I keep thinking that there must be millions of girls out there in Hollywood trying to get into the movies, and I'd just be another one of them. I'm not even that pretty."

"The hell you ain't."

"I know what I look like, Al. I'm pretty enough for Raysburg, but I'm not pretty-pretty, you know, like what's her name . . . Sandra Dee. . . . I've got something else though, and I bet there's not a hell of a lot of those girls who have it. But I'm not so dumb that I think it'd be easy. Damn, it just seems like a silly little kid's dream sometimes." She lit a cigarette. "I've got a downstate accent as thick as molasses," she said.

He had to laugh at that. "Well, sure you do. So do I."

"One time I borrowed Evan's tape recorder, and when nobody was around, I read into it. I played it back, and I kept thinking: 'Elaine, how the hell do you expect to do Shakespeare with a voice like that?' It really made me sick. And I'd been trying really hard too. Do you remember old Miss Crawford?"

"Of course I remember her, that old bag."

"Well, our freshman year—I haven't told anybody else this,

not even Evan—I went to see her. She opened the door and she looked like she was going to drop dead right there. I know she was thinking, 'What's Elly Isaac doing here at my house on a Sunday afternoon . . . little white-trash girl from Carreysburg?' And I was scared to death, so I just came out with it: 'I want to learn to talk good English.' She just looked at me. You know how stiff she was, like she'd break? And then she said, 'All right, Elaine, we'll begin right now. You want to learn to *speak proper English*.' And so I'd go and visit her every week or two, and we'd just drink tea and talk, and she'd correct me. And you know what's funny? I got to like her. She didn't seem like an old bitch anymore, she just seemed like a poor old-maid lady who's been teaching school too long. . . . And I can speak proper English now as long as I'm thinking about it, but damn, I've still got an accent." She fell back in the chair and covered her eyes with her hand.

"Headache?"

"Yeah. It's too hot. It's always too hot in the summer. When I was a little kid, I never minded it somehow. It was just the way things were. Like my daddy being in the pen or Earl Bob preaching at the tabernacle."

She's going to talk for hours, Alex thought, and there was nothing he could do but listen to her. Just sit there until the sun started to come up and she went home. "It's funny about Earl Bob," she said. "He was always nice to me, but I didn't even know it. I didn't even know how much I liked him until after he left. He used to protect me a lot from the old man, and I didn't know that either . . . until he wasn't around to do it anymore."

"So how's Big John doing these days?"

"He'll go on another binge in a month or so. Oh, Jesus, Alex, you know I wanted to like him so much. I wanted him to like me. I just tried and tried for years no matter what he did to me, and then I guess I ran out of trying. Now when he's being nice to me, I couldn't be nice back, not if it killed me. The other day he took all the money out of the cash drawer and gave it to me and said, 'Buy yourself a dress or something, Elly,' and I couldn't even thank him. The words stuck in my throat. And one time he said to me, 'You've had a dog's life, haven't you, Elly?' and he called me 'baby,' which he'd never done before. And I couldn't even answer him. I just walked on by him. I know he's trying now, but I kept thinking, 'Where the hell were you when I was just a little kid and needed a father?' I don't know, Al, I've got to get out of here."

"Yeah."

"Maybe we should have stayed down at Carreysburg. I'd probably be married by now and have a couple of kids."

"No, you wouldn't."

"You're right. I wouldn't. I would have run away. I'd probably be over at Harriet Axford's getting paid at three dollars a fuck." She laughed. "You're the only one I can talk to, you know. Really talk to. I can't tell Evan this stuff. He doesn't even like me to swear. 'Girls don't swear,' he says, and that just stops me right there." Alex didn't say anything and knew he didn't need to. She just had to talk it out, and then she'd be able to sleep. "You know, it's true," she said, "just like all the jokes. I never did wear shoes in the summer. I used to get a layer of callus on my feet damned near an inch thick. Sometimes now I look at my feet and they're all white and tender and I'm proud of them, and then other times I wish they were all callused up again. . . ."

Alex didn't know how many more nights he could sit up with her like this. It wasn't that he minded doing it, not even as tired and drunk as he was right now. It was that he'd come to look forward to it, and the nights when she didn't show up, he was the one who couldn't sleep. Drinking too much, pissing away his life in bars, how the fuck was he supposed to go away in the fall and run cross-country? She was leaning back in the chair with her eyes shut and her long legs stretched out in front of her, legs that looked white as milk from the streetlight outside. He'd never touched her. He goddamned well better go back down to the farm.

Now Elly was talking about how, right after her father got

out of the pen, the whole family went down to the tabernacle. "It's not like the regular Baptist church," she said, "it's just a little house with a stove in it, and folding chairs, and a picture of Jesus on the wall." Alex closed his eyes so he could listen better. She was such a good storyteller that he felt like he was right back there with her.

The preacher comes in and shakes everybody's hand. He's not wearing a suit like the Baptist preacher, he's wearing overalls like a farmer. He's an old man with a skinny neck, and he calls the men *brother* and the women *sister*. He's toting a burlap bag with him, and when he puts it down, it wiggles.

The preacher's name is the Reverend Jimmy Mathews. He stands up and talks about Jesus, and then Earl Bob stands up and he talks about Jesus too. Everybody listens when Earl Bob talks, and Elly thinks: *That's my brother up there, and everybody's listening to him.* Her daddy's sitting in the very front row with his head bowed down. The Reverend Jimmy Mathews plays on his guitar and sings, and all the people clap their hands and sing and sway back and forth. Elly sees that some of the women are starting to shake all over, and in the back somebody makes a funny sound. It's like, *Ohhh, ohhh, ohhh.* Then the reverend sings out: "The Holy Spirit come down!" and he fetches up his burlap bag. "And he said unto them, I beheld Satan fallen as lightning from heaven." Elly feels a shiver go down her back, because she can see it like that, Satan coming down like lightning from heaven. "As lightning from heaven," the reverend says. "Behold, I have given you authority to tread upon serpents and scorpions, and over all the power of the enemy, and nothing shall in any wise hurt you."

Everybody says amen. Elly knows all the people there. They're farm people mostly. The Atkins people are there. "And these signs shall follow them that believe," the reverend says. "In my name shall they cast out devils. They shall speak with new tongues. They shall take up serpents." And he lifts up the burlap bag.

Now he's talking to her daddy. "John Isaac, step forward."

And her daddy stands up slow and steps up to the front. "John Isaac, do you accept the Lord Jesus Christ as your personal Lord and Savior?"

"I do."

"Do you know Jesus?"

"I do."

His voice is real gentle. "Tell us all about it, John. How long have you knowed Jesus?"

Her daddy turns around to face all the people, but he looks down at the floor. She can't see his blue eyes. "I was up there in the Moundsville Pen," he says real quiet. "You all know what I done. I done shot my cousin Davis in the belly with a thirty-eight. Right out there on the street I done it. I done it because I was deep in sin, and I didn't know Jesus. I was drinking hard liquor and fornicating and committing abominations and I took it into my head that my cousin Davis done me wrong, so I shot him in the belly with a thirty-eight, and they done sent me to the Moundsville Pen for it. Well, I was up there in that pen and my heart was like a stone inside me and I couldn't see no light. And my own son he come up there time after time and he tried to tell me about Jesus, and I wouldn't listen to him, not even my own son. And I was just mean like an old dog. And then one night I was laying in my cell, and I didn't think a man could go no lower, and I said, 'John Isaac, your whole life's been nothing but a sin and a waste and you ain't fit to live,' and I busted out crying right there, and I ain't never been a man to cry much, not my whole life. And Jesus in his mercy sent his grace to me right then and there and He said to me, 'John Isaac, you turn to me and I'll take up that load from off your back. I'll take your sinful life and wash it clean as snow. I died for you, you poor fool,' He said to me, just as plain as day. 'My blood was shed for you, and all you got to do is let me into your heart.' So I opened up my heart to Him, and a great peace come over me."

Her daddy stops talking, but there's tears on his face. It makes her cry too, seeing his tears like that. And the people are all saying, "Amen" and "The Lord be praised!" and swaying and clapping and making sounds like the wind in the trees, and the Reverend Jimmy Mathews takes her daddy by the shoulder and turns him around and reaches in that burlap bag and pulls out a rattlesnake and gives it to him. She knows it's a rattlesnake because it's got rattles on its tail.

"Praise the Lord!" says the Reverend Jimmy Mathews, and Elly's daddy holds the snake in his big hands like he's surprised and just looks at it, and then he passes it back to the reverend. The reverend gives it to Earl Bob, and he holds it a minute, and then he gives it to somebody else. The people that want to hold the snake come up and reach out. Not everybody gets to hold the snake, just the people that come up. Everybody's clapping and moaning and lots of people are shaking all over. Billy Atkins's mama falls right down on the floor, and she's shaking all over. Earl Bob bends over her and pats her head and says something in her ear. And now Elly's shaking all over. She jumps up and runs before her mama can grab her. "Elly, Elly," her mama's calling.

She's right there in front of the Reverend Jimmy Mathews, right there next to her daddy. People are reaching to pull her back, but the reverend yells out: "Let her be. The Holy Spirit's on her." He's got a big smile just like sunshine. He hunkers down so he's looking right in her face, and he says, "You're John Isaac's little girl, ain't you?"

"Yes sir."

"What's your name?"

"Elly."

"Do you know Jesus, Elly?"

"Yes sir, I know Jesus."

Her daddy's looking down at her. His face is all scrunched up, and he just stands there looking down at her. Somebody in the back says, "She's just a child," and all the people are talking, making noise, scraping their feet.

The Reverend Jimmy Mathews keeps on smiling and he sings out: "A little child shall lead them," and he fetches back the snake and gives it to her. It's not slimy. It's dry and funny like her mama's purse, and it's got little bitty eyes that go straight up and down. She holds it real careful so she won't drop it, and its tongue goes in and out, tongue with a fork at the end. It's got two big teeth in the front curving down. She wishes it'd rattle its tail, but it won't do it. And then the reverend takes it from her and puts it away in the bag. They all sing a hymn and then the reverend says, "The Lord bless thee and keep thee. The Lord make his face to shine upon thee and be gracious unto thee. The Lord lift up his countenance upon thee and give thee peace," and they all walk out into the sunshine.

There's food laid out on the tables there in the sunshine, cakes and pies and ham and tongue and potato salad. There's cookies and bread and cider, and the sun's bright and hot, shining down on everybody, and the people are all laughing and talking at once, and her daddy's a big tall man with the sun shining in his face, and she says to Billy Atkins, "That's my daddy there who just got out of the Moundsville Pen."

But later on he took to drinking corn liquor again, and then he'd come home and walk around the house like he didn't know where he was. He caught her one time and held her head up, held her under the chin and pulled her head up so it hurt her, and she cried. He let her go, and he said, "Them ain't Isaac eyes."

Chapter Eight

Except for the addition of a color TV set that hung noisily from the ceiling, the bar outside Scottsbog looked much the same as it had thirteen years before. But it was strangely crowded for a weekday night: young men. They wore mustaches and long hair, jeans and cowboy boots. *What,* Evan thought, *West Virginia hippies? No—they're probably just all out of work.* As he and Alex stamped the snow off their feet and pushed their way through the people back to the corner by the jukebox, Richard Nixon's face, drawn and tired, appeared briefly on the TV screen; specterlike, the colors wrong, it hung suspended behind the news commentator. "I hope they tear him to shreds," Alex said, showing teeth.

"Yeah, me too," Evan said. "He'll probably go down. . . . They can smell the blood."

"I hope they don't leave nothing of him but a fucking wreck," Alex said.

Evan studied the selections on the jukebox. Some country music was still listed, but now Alice Cooper as well, the Rolling Stones and revived fifties rock. Evan was glad to have Alex's overcoat to hide in; his suit would have focused every eye in the bar on him. "Four beers," Alex told the waitress. She wore a short skirt and platform heels. "Nice legs," Alex said, watching her walk away.

"Yeah, they are," Evan said automatically, not really noticing. He sat down at the table, stared up at the TV, and tried to hear the words of the news broadcast, but it was too noisy in the bar. "Hey," he said, "did you mean that about voting for George Wallace?"

"I just said that to piss off Sharon," Alex said. "She still thinks the sun rose and set in John Kennedy's asshole. . . . You still shoot pool?" he asked, jerking his head toward the pool table.

"No, not much."

"That's too bad."

Evan was surprised by the remark. "Why?" he said.

Alex shrugged. "Because you were so fucking good at it."

"Well, it was something I seemed to have needed in West Virginia . . . and I guess I just didn't need it after I left."

Alex smiled broadly at the girl when she brought the beer to the table. "Goddamn, Carlyle," he said, staring after her retreating legs, "some of this young stuff is really fine, you know that? Jesus, the girls are sure screwing more now than they used to when we was in high school. Some fucking wild kids now. Shit, you should see some of the girls that come in the garage."

"Well, fuck, Warner, we're getting old. Cheers." He tilted back the beer. He was beginning to feel that old compulsive binge coming on: drink and talk and to hell with everything. His unbelievably sober life in Vancouver, getting up every day at goddamned four or four thirty in the morning, going to bed every night by nine, seemed remote and dreamlike. Now he was beginning to feel as though he'd never left West Virginia at all, that he'd never done anything at all but lay around Raysburg and drink.

"Maybe I'm going to turn into one of these dirty old men chasing the girls around the schoolyard," Alex said. "I always figured that if I didn't watch my ass, that's how I'd end up." He stared at his bottle of beer. He was peeling the label off with his thumbnail. "Just so long as I don't end up like Frank, that's all." Then, before Evan could find anything to say: "Shit, you should have seen Sharon when I met her. What a fucking knockout!"

"She's a damn fine-looking woman now."

"Oh, yeah, she sure is. Fuck, you'd never know she had a couple kids, just looking at her. Yeah, she's okay. But she's a pusher, that one. . . ." He ran his hand through his short curly hair.

"A pusher?"

"Yeah, she climbs right on my ass. I wouldn't have done one quarter of what I've done if I hadn't had her there pushing me along. Me? Run my own garage? Sheri got me to do it. I was working for United Trucking then. Hated it. And she said, 'How much would you get if you logged off some of that timber down on your land?' And I said, 'Shit, I never thought of it.' And then she said, 'Al, you know what? You could probably get a bank loan against the farm.' And I'd never thought of that either. But there I was and I'd been in the army, and people seemed to think that made me responsible or some damned thing . . . and a wife and a baby . . ." He stopped talking suddenly; his face went hard. He gulped at the beer. "Well, shit, maybe I should have stayed on at United."

Evan pulled out a cigarette, offered one to Alex. "What the fuck's this you're smoking?" Alex said.

"It's my mother's brand. I don't know American cigarettes anymore."

"Too much filter. Like smoking air." Alex lit one of his own. "Hey, what's your girl like, Carlyle?"

"Well, she's young. Twenty-four. . . . It's a whole new generation, you know that? Just a few years and everything's different. Sex isn't a big deal the way it was with us, just something you do, eh? . . . Shit, I don't know what to say about her. She's fun. Bubbly. She likes clothes . . . not fashionable stuff . . . costume. Christ, the first time I paid any attention to her was at a party. Before that she'd just been my research assistant, you know . . . kid in blue jeans. But some people from the show had a party, and she came in a goddamned negligee with a leotard under it. And all of a sudden I was really paying attention to her." He laughed. "She says she's not in any hurry to settle down with anybody. She's got her own apartment, her own car. We spend, oh maybe two or three nights a week together. We get along fine."

"Yeah? And you don't need to get married? Sounds pretty good to me."

"Yeah, it is. . . . Except that I'm going to get transferred back east, and then . . . well, I guess I'll find somebody else."

"Is she good-looking?" Alex said.

"Good-looking?" *What does he want from me*, Evan thought, *a description of Dana laid out on the bed like a* Playboy *centerfold?* "Yeah," he said, "I suppose she's good-looking . . . if you like thin women. *I* like thin women. She's about five six, long brown hair. Got a good, strong face . . . not beautiful, but strong. . . . She makes the best of what she's got, knows how to dress, how to wear makeup. She's got fantastic legs. Likes to show them off. Yeah, she's a damned attractive woman."

"Sounds like you got a good thing going for you. Fuck, and you got money coming in, right?"

"Yeah."

"And you got a nice woman to screw. And she isn't going to tie you down, right? And you're doing pretty much what you want to. . . . Fuck, Carlyle, sounds to me like you got it dicked."

Evan laughed. "Yeah, I guess I do." *Why the hell doesn't it feel like it?*

"You know where I met Sheri? It was kind of funny . . . I'd just got out of the army and come back to town. Went straight back down to Wolchak's, right? Except it wasn't Wolchak's anymore . . . they'd all moved out of town. . . . Jerry Valacik had it, had a body shop in there. And I started in to working for him, and he had a kid working there, nice kid, Italian named Joe Tomerelli. And I got to loafing with him a bit, and he had a baby sister, see? And this was back when those miniskirts were big. Took the girls in Raysburg a long time to start wearing them, but Joe's little sister . . . shit, it didn't take her long. She wore her skirts . . . shit, if she tied a goddamned ribbon around her hips, it wouldn't have been much shorter than those skirts she wore. And that was Sharon. Haw! Senior in high school. Majorette." He laughed. "Jesus, Carlyle, going out with her was just like being back in high school."

"Sounds like Susie Galloway revisited."

"Yeah, she did remind me of Susie. That's right. . . . Fuck, I might of married Susie, except she went and married that ass-hole Eddie Gannister while I was away in the army. Well, it's a good thing. You should see her now. Big as a fucking barn. . . . But anyhow, there was Sheri, just a little kid, you know. Nice Italian girl. Shit, Carlyle, I just couldn't keep my hands off her. And the next fall she was pregnant with Al Junior."

"So you got married?"

"Yeah."

"Jesus, Warner," Evan said, laughing, "sounds like a story in a magazine. Hadn't you guys ever heard of birth control?"

"Good Catholic girl? Are you kidding? She'd never admit she was going to screw right up to the minute I was shoving my prick in her."

"So how come you haven't got fourteen kids by now?"

"She wised up. Doesn't believe all that crap anymore." Alex slammed his empty bottle down on the table, reached for the second one. "Reminds me, I better call her. . . . Shit, maybe we should get another case while we're here too."

"We've got a case in the car we haven't touched yet."

"Yeah, but nothing worse than starting to tie on a good one and then running out."

"Hey man, you're really hitting the fucking sauce, you know that?"

"Yeah," Alex said darkly.

"Some night, you get in one of your black moods and you've been hitting the bottle in the desk and the one in the glove compartment and the one in the closet—and for all I know the one taped inside the toilet bowl—" Alex allowed himself a faint smile. "And you get out there in your car, man, you're fucking well going to kill yourself. You scared the piss out of me tonight."

"I know. I scared myself." He shrugged. "I should call Sharon."

"What are you doing it for, Al?"

"Fuck, I don't know."

"You must have some idea."

"Oh, Jesus, Carlyle," he said angrily. "Because I should have kept on running and had a go at the world record? Because I should have been a coach? Because I should have been a racing driver? Who the fuck knows! I got to call Sharon." He pushed his chair back but then, instead of standing up, frowned and stared directly at Evan. "I'm not always drunk when I do it," he said.

"What?"

"You know that last fucking summer? Well, you was right. At the time I was pissed off at you, but you was right. You was always right, you bastard. Just look at you now and look at me. Shit!"

Evan couldn't say a word. Alex slapped his hand down on the table again. "And when I said it was the *last* run, I fucking well meant it. But just a few months ago . . . Shit, stone-cold sober. Didn't even have the excuse that I was hammered. . . . You know that horrible double curve on 88, out about ten miles? Blind both ways, you know the one I mean? I couldn't get that fucker out of my head. See, I'd never got around it at over a hundred. Back when Frank and me was stealing cars, there's more than one I left down at the bottom of that hill. It's a wonder I'm sitting here to tell you about it . . . but never got her over a hundred."

He smiled slightly. "Hundred and five and kept her on the road. And then driving back to town, I thought: 'Who the fuck would have taken care of your kids if you'd lost her out there?' I don't know what got into me. . . . Maybe I just never got it out of my system, I don't know. . . ." He looked at his watch, then back at Evan. "Goddamn Sheri, she's going to chew my ass up one side and down the other." He stood up. "Shit," he said, "maybe I got the wrong fucking wife," and walked away.

Evan sat like a stone and watched Alex elbow his way across the barroom to the wall phone: he was just a touch unsteady on his feet, not so much that a stranger would notice, but enough to see if you knew him and were looking for it. *Oh, God help me!* Evan thought. He drank the rest of his first bottle of beer without pausing for a breath, drank his second almost as fast. He drank what was left in Alex's second bottle and signaled the waitress for another round. *Yeah,* he thought, *maybe you can kill the fear that way. Sure you can, you simple fuck, drown it like a puppy.* He was getting drunk. He was going to get drunker.

Alex, his back toward Evan, was wedged into the corner on the far side of the barroom, gesturing with his left hand while he held the phone in his right, making short, choppy motions in the air as though driving nails, as though Sharon were right in front of him to see it and he was trying to bang his excuse into her head—whatever excuse he might have managed to scrape up to explain what the hell he was doing fifteen miles out of town on a weekday night, aimed south over roads covered with six inches of snow. And Sharon probably wasn't having any of it; the conversation didn't look like it was going to be a short one.

On all sides Evan was surrounded with West Virginia voices, that familiar tone and accent and inflection that he'd tried for years to erase from his own speech. "You-ins want anything else?" the waitress was saying; yeah, that's really what she was saying. He'd forgotten that particular grammatical monstrosity, not *you all*—have to cross the mountains into Virginia to hear that one—but the good old Appalachian *you-ins*. Shit, if he stayed here much longer, he'd sound just like any of them; he was already altering the way he talked to fit in with Alex, just the way he'd done back in high school.

The teen-age waitress bringing the next round of beer to their table was just like any of the girls he remembered from the old days; she'd rather be sexy than comfortable, working her six-hour shift in bright red platform heels. Oh, West Virginia girls with their trashy clothes, their slurring come-on voices, their middle-class ambitions! *Wrong wife, eh?* Evan thought. *Great parting line to leave me with, Alex Warner, you prick. You could have had any one of them you wanted, so why the hell* didn't *you marry Elaine? You would have been a damned sight better match for her than I ever was.*

But Alex hadn't married Elaine. And he hadn't married Susie Galloway, the princess of Raysburg High, Class of 1960. He'd married sweet Sharon, eighteen years old and right out of high school, a majorette just like Susie, bleach blond cutesy-pie and probably her father's little darling, just like Susie. But Sharon didn't have vacant blue eyes like Susie's; they were dark and brooding like Elaine's.

He'd drunk too many beers too fast. He burped. *Shit,* he thought, *if I'd stayed, I could have married a girl just like Sharon. Yeah, why not admit it?* That's what he wanted, not some witty, independent woman with her own car and apartment, cool and liberated, dynamite in bed and "see you in a couple days, kid," but a wife just like Sharon. He wanted a family; God knows why, but he did. He wanted a house with a mortgage, a couple of kids, and a wife to come home to with bleached hair, a peekaboo sweater, tight pants, and chipped nail polish. She could have his dinner cooked when he walked through the door, could do the dishes while he read the paper, and then he could take her to bed and screw the daylights out of her. It had been years since he'd been so turned on by a girl he'd just met. And Alex should have married Elaine, of course. He gulped more beer. He closed his eyes.

When Elaine's mother had gone crazy that hot afternoon in the restaurant, it hadn't been Evan who'd found a way to take care of it, but Alex. Naturally. Takes an old downstate farmboy to know how to handle a drunken downstate farmwoman when she's going nuts in the ninety-six-degree heat. Only three of them in the restaurant that day, he and Elaine and Alex, sitting back in their usual booth eating hamburgers and drinking Cokes. They'd heard Mrs. Isaac coming a long time before they'd seen her. Elaine had immediately shoved her cigarette at Evan, but he'd already been smoking one, so she'd handed it to Alex instead; he took it, cupped his hands around it to hide the red lipstick print on the end, and began to smoke it just like a cigar, drawing in and blowing out again without inhaling.

For some unknown reason Mrs. Isaac had gotten herself all dressed up at two o'clock in the afternoon. She'd tried to pin up her carrot-red hair, but it had fallen down in lank, unwashed strands. Her lipstick was on screwy and gave her mouth a lop-sided, clownish look. She'd painted most of her fingernails but had missed a couple on her right hand. She was wearing old-fashioned high heels with rounded toes and a print dress that she must have bought when she had more weight on her; now it hung slackly on her long, bony frame. She'd been talking away to herself before she'd even made it through the door from the kitchen: "Oh, he's so mean!" she was saying. "He's such a mean man. Good sweet Lord Jesus, a rattlesnake would care for his own more than that man does."

"Christ," Elaine said under her breath, "she's plastered like a wall."

Mrs. Isaac had given up on a glass and was drinking mint-flavored gin straight from the bottle. "He doesn't even take care of his own," she said, looking vaguely in the direction of her daughter. "Every cent he makes goes over to the hunky to pay for his drink. Oh, sweet Jesus, Elly, we never should have left Carreysburg."

Elaine didn't look at her mother at all but stared straight ahead at the wall. Mrs. Isaac teetered to a stop next to the booth, stood with her feet splayed on the floor, and droned on in that whining downstate voice: "He come out of the Moundsville Pen, he said he'd found Jesus and I thanked the Lord for it. He said Jesus was walking by his side. . . . Well, he's turned away from Jesus now and he's walking with Satan sure as I'm standing here. His people was always no-good trash. His uncle Warren Isaac was shot dead in the street, and that's a fact. And that's just the end coming for him, I can see it sure as day. He won't even buy me a new pair of stockings. Got to wear them two at a time 'cause they're all full of runs." And she hiked up her dress to show them two pairs of stockings hitched to her garter belt.

"Mother!" Elaine said. "Stop that now. You've had too much to drink."

"Oh, good Lord, Elly, it's a dog's life I've had with him." Fat, shiny tears were streaking the black mascara down her cheeks.

"Mother!"

"Oh, Lord, why'd we ever come up to this town? Why'd we ever leave Carreysburg? Oh, Lord, Lord, Lord, why'd we ever come up to this terrible place? Nothing but hunkies on all sides, and Sodom and Gomorrah was more godly than Raysburg, West Virginia, ever was. There's whores walking the streets and barrooms on every corner and every cent goes to the hunky for his drink. . . . Oh, Good Lord Jesus, girls grow up so fast in the city!"

Alex spoke for the first time, his voice gentle, slow, and just as downstate as you please: "Well, Mrs. Isaac . . . girls can grow up pretty fast down on the farm too."

Mrs. Isaac stopped talking a moment and appeared to be thinking about what he'd said. Tears continued to roll down her cheeks but she wasn't paying any attention to them. "May the Lord Jesus show his grace to you, Alex Warner," she said finally. "I knowed your people."

Elaine was not looking at her mother at all; she wasn't looking at Evan either. Her eyes were focused on the wall, and the blood was draining out of her face. "Oh, Lord, Elly, he done whipped you like a dog, swear to Jesus he did. Whipped you worse than any yellow dog."

"Shut up, mother." Elaine now was white as the plate in front of her; beads of sweat had broken out on her forehead.

Mrs. Isaac leaned down over the table to stare at Evan; despite the tears that were still running down her cheeks, her eyes were full of fury. "Evan Carlyle," she said, "if you've got a lick of common decency left in you, you'll marry her."

"Marry her?" Evan said before he could stop himself. "I'm not even out of high school!"

"Evan," Elaine said, *"get . . . her . . . out of here!"*

"Me!" Evan said.

Alex shrugged. He slid out of the booth and slipped his arm around the woman's shoulders. "Well, Mrs. Isaac," he said, "the Lord works in mysterious ways." He sent Evan the hint of a wink.

"Ain't that the truth now," the woman said.

"I think maybe you better go upstairs and have a little rest. All right? It's a hot day and all that gin goes right to your head."

"Oh, Lord, Lord," she said. She allowed Alex to guide her away from the booth and back toward the kitchen. "Oh, there's a bitter day a-coming," she said.

Evan and Elaine sat side by side in the booth and listened to the banging sounds of Alex guiding Mrs. Isaac up the stairs.

"Evan," Elaine said through gritted teeth, "will you . . . please get me . . . a glass of soda water? . . . Don't put . . . anything in it . . . all right?"

He walked around behind the counter, drew her a glass of plain carbonated water, and brought it to her. "Are you all right?"

"Yeah," she said. "Yeah . . . in a minute . . . Oh, shit, I'm going to barf . . ." She gritted her teeth. "No, I'm not." She drank from the glass. She clenched both fists and pressed them into her face just under the cheekbones; she clenched them so hard that her forearms knotted. Silent tears, just like her mother's, ran down her cheeks from closed eyes, but she wouldn't let herself cry. "Go away," she managed to say. "All right? . . . For a little while . . . but come back. Please come back." Out on the street, the afternoon sun struck at him as fiercely as a hammer blow.

Oh, my God, Evan thought, *I'll never come back to this terrible place again, never in my life.* He opened his eyes and saw that Alex had sat down at the table opposite him. "You crapping out on me, Carlyle?"

"Shit," Evan said and drank, "how'd Sharon take it?"

"Not too good, and that's putting it mildly." Alex wore his wolfish grin. "She's seeing red, white, and blue stripes. Well, shit, why don't we put it on the road?" Evan saw that Alex had bought another case of beer.

They slogged through the snow to the car. Alex came to a sudden stop and yelled: "Jesus!"

"What?" Evan said.

"Some son of a bitch hit me! Look!" The left rear quarter-panel of the car was crumpled; half the taillight was gone. Alex stepped back to look at the tire prints in the snow. "Some son of a bitch hit me pulling out of the lot. And then just fucking drove away. Jesus Christ!" He slammed the case of beer down on the hood of the car, walked around to inspect the damage, walked back, glared at Evan, pounded his fist into his hand. Then he stepped up to the back of his own car and kicked out the remainder of the taillight. "Jesus!" He laughed briefly. "Oh, fuck me, Carlyle! It's fucking ridiculous."

Alex started the engine and laughed again, a series of short, staccato barks. "You know, Carlyle, one of these days I'm going to get in this car and I'm going to drive away. I'm going to leave that fucking garage, and my fucking wife, and my fucking house, and my two fucking kids . . . and I'm going to drive away, and I'm not coming back!" He put the car in gear.

"Hey," Evan yelled, "the beer!" He jumped out of the car to retrieve it from the hood, set it in the backseat with the other case and a half.

"Fuck," Alex said, "open up one of those goddamned things, will you? Jesus, Carlyle, the way things are going, I'll be on the fucking assembly line by spring. If the fuckers is hiring. Can you see me on the assembly line? Jesus!" He pulled out onto the road. It had begun to snow hard again. "You know me," he said, his voice dark and menacing.

Three

Chapter One

The river road was straight and blank as a white ribbon, and Alex was burning down it as though it were high noon on a clear day and not late at night with snow coming down like confetti. The windshield wipers couldn't beat the snow back fast enough, and what Evan saw in front of him was a dim white swirl, like an effect in a science fiction movie; they were over-driving their lights by probably half a dozen car lengths; Alex had them up to sixty. "Hey," Evan said, "it's a little fast, isn't it?"

"Shit!" Alex said, the anger still clear in his voice. His shoulders were hunched and he was bent forward over the wheel. "Got to make our time down to Carreysburg, Carlyle. You should know that. The road back into Harrod's going to be a fucking nightmare. We're going to have to creep over it like a goddamned snail.... You want to still be on the road when the sun comes up?"

But Evan would have taken odds that Alex wasn't dreading the nightmare of the mountain roads. *Yeah, I do know him,* Evan thought: *bet he can hardly wait to get there.* And Evan had discovered that in spite of the idiotic slide down the hill earlier that night, his belief in the total infallibility of Alex's driving had mysteriously returned. And it was too bad that Dana wasn't here; she'd probably be scared half to death. The thought of her sitting in the middle of the seat, nervous, frightened, staring anxiously at the speedometer while Alex, stony-faced, rammed them down the road, was quite pleasant. Actually it was the thought that she'd ever be afraid of any man doing *anything* that was pleasant; she'd certainly never been afraid of Evan.

He'd never before Dana met a girl who could say casually about another man as she had: "He's a lousy fuck." So, of course, he'd had to ask her, "How about me?" When she was dressed up, she wore contact lenses; but to work, glasses with gigantic, perfectly circular plastic frames disguised as tortoiseshell; they gave her a wry and whimsical look, drained away her sexuality. When she had time, she put on false lashes to bring out her eyes through the thick lenses, but when she didn't, she looked as empty-eyed and dopey as Little Orphan Annie. Studio A had been a ridiculous place to be having that particular conversation, but that's where they'd been; she'd turned to him with that round, glassy glitter and said, "Well, you're pretty damn good . . . as long as the sex roles are clearly defined." He'd felt as though he'd just received a B minus with a handwritten note at the bottom: Evan shows promise but needs to be more attentive.

He glanced over at Alex and saw anger in every line of those hunched shoulders. Evan was angry too. If they were back in the fifties, he'd probably drink so much, he'd pass out like a stone and Alex would get in a fight or smash something; he didn't know what they were going to do with anger now in 1973. But Evan had reached the point of not giving much of a shit even if some farmer did pull out in front of them and Alex, at sixty miles an hour, sent them all smashing straight into their graves. They were drunk, they were on a bender where anything goes; he'd wanted to know since he'd met her, so why not ask him? "Hey Alex," he said, "how's your sex life?"

Alex didn't answer for so long that Evan began to think he hadn't heard the question or was simply going to ignore it. Then Alex said, "Shit, when she's not pissed at me and I'm not pissed at her, it's all right. . . ." He laughed. "Not too good lately."

Too bad you didn't bring the Sony with you, Evan thought to himself. *Got a perfect example of Middle America tooling down the road; you could run off a quick interview. Excuse me, Mr. Warner, just a few questions: How often do you screw? What are your favorite positions? Does your wife like it on top? Does she have orgasms? Have you found your interest in sex diminishing over the past few years? Did it change anything when you got married?* But neither he nor Alex were drunk enough yet for anything like that. Maybe he should interview himself. *Mr. Carlyle, how the hell's your sex life? Would you say there are any particular difficulties in screwing a girl eight years younger who calls herself a feminist?*

Stripped of her glasses, turned on, and juices flowing, Dana always looked like a cat. A Canadian lynx, maybe. She did have lynxy eyes, slanting and green and faintly threatening—maybe because without her glasses or contacts she had to be six inches away to see him at all. And when she wasn't coming on like a gymnast wired on speed, he did have a pretty good time with her in bed. *Oh, come on, Carlyle,* he said to himself, *more than pretty good; it's never been better with anyone.* But there were all those other times when she put him through nerve-grinding endurance sessions, and all he wanted to do was just hang on to his erection until she got her rocks off. The thing about her being on top was not so much that she was above him—that in itself would have been tolerable—but that she controlled the rhythm and the pace, and he had to respond to her. It made him see her with a kind of hard-edged clarity and he wasn't sure he wanted to watch her as those lynxy eyes focused in on his own from a few inches away and went soft and shining with approaching orgasm.

"All the goddamn whorehouses are gone," Alex said out of nowhere.

"Yeah, somebody told me that. . . . What the hell happened to Harriet Axford?"

"Oh shit, she's dead. Joe Patone's dead too. The rackets is all hidden away now. Got to know the right people and have good credit to even gamble in town anymore; shit, just like getting a bank loan. Not a whorehouse left, and Raysburg used to be wide open. Guys used to come from miles on Saturday night, you remember . . . all the way from Pittsburgh, fucking Columbus . . . just call-girl stuff now. Hotel rooms."

So that's it, Evan thought. "What are they charging these days?" he said, keeping his voice as expressionless as possible.

"Fuck, you wouldn't believe it, Carlyle. Fifty bucks and up."

The speedometer sat there, pegged on sixty. The view through the windshield was as useless as if somebody had sprayed it with white paint. *Maybe I should be scared,* Evan thought; he still wasn't. Would Dana be, or would she just lie back against the seat and chat away brightly in that faintly British voice she'd mysteriously acquired at Kitsilano Senior Secondary and drink beer out of the can right along with them? Evan had always wanted to be with a woman who was a little scared of him, just a titillating flash of fear every now and then. But all he'd ever seemed to bring out in women was a desire to dress him up for a part in their own personal fantasies. Starting with his mother, who'd put him in short pants and knee socks in Raysburg, at a time when little boys could practically get stoned on the street for looking like that. And then Elaine, who'd told him a million times how great he looked in a suit, and who had actually got him into a tuxedo for the senior prom. And good old California girl Beth, who'd thought he looked best with a beard, even though it had been wispy and unconvincing; she'd made him half a dozen shirts out of unbleached cotton and had decorated them with her own embroidered daisies. And now Dana; she wasn't simple, that was the problem with her. If she'd been nothing more than one of those aggressively liberated ladies in jean coveralls and peeling, thousand-year-old Adidas runners, they never would have made it to bed in the first place. But she was as theatrical as any of the other women who'd drifted in and out of his life, and he'd been cast—as what?— God knows. Mick Jagger? His birthday present had been a perfect example. Dana had put on her highest heels, and then, without explaining a thing, had driven away with him in her orange Datsun. Their destination was a little shop in the East End where they specialized in handmade boots. The sour Italian man had a face that surely couldn't have smiled in fifty years, but Dana had actually got a laugh out of him. She'd told Evan to stand back-to-back with her and then had said to the boot-maker: "All right . . . he's got to be taller than I am." And here he was wearing the result, heels fit for a flamenco dancer, a hundred and twenty bucks' worth. He'd ended up paying for half, because she couldn't afford to give him presents like that, for Christ's sake.

Evan sneaked a glance over at his friend: Alex Warner, still a good-looking man in his own hard-faced way, still attractive to women, even though he was huge and thick now, no longer that bony lean kid he'd been as a runner. What would Dana think of Alex? Would she find him amusing, interesting, and—what was the word she used from her free-lancing days to mean a good-talking, colorful character? A *natural*, yeah, that was it. Or would she think Alex was just an American redneck, just another male chauvinist pig? Would she want to go to bed with him? Evan remembered watching TV with her one night when some folksinger had been on doing a song called "Ladies Love Outlaws." Dana had said, "Christ, what a sexist song!"

"You mean they don't?" Evan had said.

"Maybe ladies love outlaws, but women don't." And then she'd added after a moment, "And I'm no lady, eh? . . . I find that song positively offensive."

"What do you mean, 'no lady'? You're just a modern version, that's all. I've met your mother." And there they'd been, starting another therapy session that had lasted for hours. But no matter what she'd said or how firmly she'd said it, he still didn't believe her. Maybe it was true, maybe it was just his own fucked-up fifties West Virginia head, but he still felt it in his guts: No matter what they might say about how they really want men who are concerned, gentle, soft, sensitive, and all the other modern etceteras, what they really want, in bed at least, is some fucking outlaw, some Alex Warner. Evan had never been able to shake that old conviction that there was no woman in the whole goddamned world who could possibly prefer him to Alex Warner.

Chapter Two

Alex held the car steady on the white road, but what he wanted to do was ram the accelerator to the floor and push that fancy Detroit junk right to the edge of doomsday. *Shit. The son of a bitch comes back here dressed in his goddamned three-hundred-dollar suit and asks me how my sex life is. After everything that happened, Carlyle still comes up smelling like a rose, has a real talent for it and always did. Got him a good job, free as a bird, screwing some little honey who ain't going to tie him down, and he comes back and asks me how my sex life is. Jesus, what's he think? Fucking going broke, mortgage around my neck, turning into a goddamned drunk, got a fuck-up son and a wife pushing me up the ass like a billy goat. McClain Hotel call girls all know how to go through the motions. Off come the shorts and the blouse quick as a wink, no underwear, because that'd slow them*

*down, leave their high heels on because you're supposed to
think it's sexy, and yell and scream like your prick was the best
thing that ever happened to them. All the time wondering if
they'll be able to get in another john or two that night. How's
my sex life? Jesus, Carlyle, you don't understand a thing and
never did.*

Alex remembered sitting in the P.A.C., listening to Carlyle
say, "Jesus, Elaine's got a wonderful imagination, doesn't she?
She ought to write stories. All that stuff about the snake people
was really great." *And when you finally figured out what he was
thinking, you just had to say to him, "Carlyle, you're a goddamned fool."*

Alex tried to imagine what Carlyle's woman must look like.
The best he could come up with was long legs and a smile. *A
young girl who don't want him to marry her. Free pussy, a free
life, free as a goddamned bird. He got out just the way he
always said he would. Well, he always told everybody exactly
what he was going to do, so nobody should be surprised that he
went and did it, least of all you or Elly. Maybe it would have
been different if he'd known about everything, but he didn't. So
don't hold it against him. Have a few more beers, and what the
hell. When he leaves this time, he'll probably never come back.*

Alex couldn't stop the sour feeling in his throat.

He started thinking about the time that Elly's father walked
into the garage with his right hand all covered with blood. So
drunk he could hardly stand up, of course. "Excuse me, Alex
Warner, do you mind if I set down here?" His deep voice as
sorry as if he was already talking to the judge.

"Hell no, John. Help yourself."

John lowers his big fat ass right down onto the concrete,
shoves his back up against the wall of the garage. Then he holds
up his right hand like it belongs to somebody else. "Goddamn
my soul," he says, "I just left my wife laying up on Short
Market Street."

"Oh, yeah?"

"Yeah. She just wouldn't stop talking. She just went on talking and talking. I asked her to stop and she wouldn't stop. Well, I suppose the police will be by for me directly. The police or the sheriff, one. I suppose all I have to do is set here and they'll be coming for me." He sighs. Tears are running down his face. He wipes them away and leaves a blood smear around his eyes. " 'Knock and it shall be opened unto ya.' . . . What do you think of that, Alex Warner? Well, I done knocked and knocked. Maybe I committed the sin you can't get forgiven for, I don't know. Well, the sheriff will be down, or the police."

"What did you do, John, hit her?"

John tilts his head to one side. His forehead knots up. "You know, Alex, I don't rightly remember. Ain't that something? Shit, I just don't remember. You know, I left her laying up there on Short Market Street. Flat on her back. One of her shoes come off. What do you think of that? Do you suppose Jesus has got enough blood to wash me clean? A man like me? Goddamn, Alex. I just don't know. I left her laying up there on Short Market Street bigger than shit, and she's still talking to me. Now how can that be?"

"Beats the hell out of me, John."

"Satan's walking in the world as sure as I live," John says and stares at his feet.

Then the cops come. They don't even turn on their sirens. A couple of young guys. They get out of the car and walk over to John slow and careful. "Okay, John, you want to come along with us now?"

"Is she all right?"

"She's over at the R.G.H. Got a concussion. But she ain't hurt all that bad. So you just come along with us now."

"Yeah, I'll do that. I ain't goina give you no trouble." He pushes himself to his feet. It's like he's moving a thousand pounds. "Could you give me a hand, son? I ain't walking so good." The cops put the handcuffs on him, and then they each take him by an elbow. "Suppose one of you fellows could call my boy?"

"We already called him, John. Don't worry about a thing."

But old lady Isaac wouldn't press charges, and all he got was sixty days. He came home and sat around the restaurant playing his old Stella guitar and singing Hank Williams songs, sometimes hymns. Alex would come in and hear John back in the kitchen. One time he was even yodeling. His voice was wheezy and thick, a fat man's voice, too many cigarettes and not enough breath, but it was true as a bell. "He's kind of quiet now," Alex said to Elly.

"Yeah, but it's the quiet before the storm. He's been like this before. He's building up to something."

Elly's brother was still living at home then, one of the sorriest fuckers Alex had ever seen in his life. Since they'd come up from Carreysburg, the Reverend Earl Bob had been working on the line at Consolidated and preaching at a little church down back of Scottsbog, The First Tabernacle of Jesus Christ, Savior of the World, Incorporated. Alex would see him coming back late Sunday driving the old man's beat-to-shit Dodge, dressed all in black like an undertaker. Earl Bob seemed to get thinner every time you looked at him, and his face whiter. His mouth was pinched shut, and he looked like a crow. "They're both crazy as loons," Elly said. "I'm afraid the old man's going to kill him."

When Big John finally blew up, it was fall. Alex remembered that because it was football season, and he didn't know about it until afterward because he was at practice. It was their first year at Raysburg High; Elly came home from school, and the minute she walked in the restaurant, she knew that something was up, because John wasn't playing his guitar. He was pacing up and down in the back talking to himself, or maybe to Jesus, she wasn't sure. The first thing he said to her was, "You take that paint off your face, you whore."

If she'd had any sense, she told Alex, she would have walked right back out and on up to the library, but she didn't know how bad he was. She went to her room instead. He followed her, walked right in. "Will you please knock?" she yelled at him, and then she saw that he had his shotgun.

"Get down on your knees, you whore," he said.

She tried to humor him out of it, but he wasn't going to be humored, so there wasn't a damned thing for her to do but get down on her knees. He shoved the shotgun right up in her face and said, "Now, I want you to pray to Jesus to forgive you for your sins."

"Jesus, please forgive me for my sins. Can I get up now?"

"No, you just stay right there, girl. You ain't done yet. You tell Jesus how you been fornicating and committing abominations with all them men."

"But Daddy, I haven't been committing anything."

"The hell you ain't. I know. I seen it all. Jesus told me all about it. 'As is the mother, so is her daughter,' and you're your mother's daughter sure as God made little green apples. Now you start telling Jesus about all the things you done, and don't leave nothing out."

"I haven't done anything," she yelled at him.

"You start talking to Jesus, girl, or I'm goina blow your head off right here and now."

She was pretty sure he wasn't going to shoot her, but his eyes looked as crazy as she'd ever seen them, and she figured the only thing for her to do was start talking to Jesus, but she didn't know what to say. "Give me a hint," she said.

"Don't you be laughing at me, you whore."

"What am I supposed to say to Jesus?"

"Tell him about your fornicating."

"Jesus, I've been fornicating right and left. Please forgive me."

"Go on, tell him all about how you done it."

Then she got really scared because she couldn't think what he wanted her to say, and he had that shotgun pushed right up against her face, and she knew that even if he wasn't intending to shoot her, it'd be easy for his finger to slip and then she'd get both barrels right in the teeth. She knew he kept the damned thing loaded with deer shot, and as close as it was, it'd blow her head clean off. She felt herself start to cry, but she was damned if she'd give him the satisfaction. "That was really dumb, wasn't it?" she said to Alex. "I'd rather have my head blown off than let him see me cry." But she couldn't find much to say. "Well, I've been fornicating, you know."

"Tell him about them big cocks you had shoved in you both front and back."

"Jesus, I had big cocks shoved in me both front and back."

"And in your mouth too."

"Yeah, Jesus, in my mouth too."

"Go on, tell him what it felt like having them cocks shoved in you."

Elly had never had a cock shoved in her in her life, but she closed her eyes and tried to imagine what it must be like because that seemed what her father wanted to hear. "Well, Jesus, the first time it hurt like hell because the cock was so big, you know, but after a while I got to like it."

"That's right," John yelled. "You tell him."

About this time her mother came in. "John Isaac, just what the hell do you think you're doing to that poor girl?"

"You shut your mouth, woman."

"You just take that gun away from her head and let her up, John. She ain't done nothing."

"You shut your mouth, you fornicator. Look at them eyes she's got. Them ain't Isaac eyes. Just who the hell was her daddy, will you tell me that? It was when I was in the pen you was fornicating with any man that'd have you. So you just shut your mouth, you adulterous woman. You bitch. You fornicator."

Her mother turned white as a sheet. "I swear to Jesus it ain't true. Why John, you know she was born long before you ever went to the pen."

"Well, you was sneaking behind my back then," John yelled at her. " 'As is the mother, so is her daughter.' " Elly gave her mother a look, trying to tell her to shut up so maybe he'd calm down. John went on yelling. By then you probably could have heard him six blocks away. "Look at them eyes she's got. Them black eyes. Snake eyes. Her daddy was a big black buck nigger sure as I'm standing here."

And then her mother said one of the dumbest things Elly'd ever heard in her life: "John, you know there ain't any niggers in Wetzel County."

"Shut up, Mama," Elly said from down on her knees. Her mother shut up and never said another word.

But the niggers had set John off on a new track. "Go on, girl," he said, "tell Jesus about all them niggers you been committing abominations with."

So Elly started making it up by the yard. "You know the damnedest thing," she told Alex, "was that once I got started, it was kind of fun. I just made up the worst things I could think of, and the worse they were, the better he seemed to like it. He stood there with the sweat pouring down his face, saying, 'Go on. Don't leave out nothing.'"

Well, about the time that Elly had got around to telling Jesus about how she'd gone from door to door in Nigger Town and screwed every man who'd wanted her right there on the sidewalk with the neighbors all watching and cheering her on, Earl Bob came home from work. She'd been down on her knees with that shotgun pointed at her head making up stories for damned near an hour. Earl Bob walked in and said in his preacher's voice: "John Isaac, you put down that gun."

"John Isaac? I ain't John Isaac to you, you snake. I'm your father."

"Jesus said, 'For I am come to set a man at variance against his father, and a man's foes shall be they of his own household.' The Holy Spirit is with me, John Isaac, and he's telling you to put down that gun and repent."

So finally John took the gun away from Elly's head and pointed it at Earl Bob instead. She'd been so tense the whole time that she fell right over on the floor. She was shaking in every muscle. Her mother was still standing there, white as a sheet and not saying a word, and Elly looked up at her brother and her father and she couldn't tell which one of them was crazier. Earl Bob was still wearing his overalls from work, but he had his preacher's face on, and he didn't seem to be the least bit afraid of that shotgun. "I should kill you where you stand," John said to him. "You snake worshiper."

"Hear the word of the Lord," Earl Bob said, "Matthew Seven. 'Judge not, that ye be not judged. For what judgement ye judge, ye shall be judged.' "

"Snake worshiper. Snake worshiper. Snake worshiper," John yelled back at him.

But Earl Bob went right on just like he was in church: " 'Not every one that saith unto me, Lord, Lord, shall enter into the kingdom of heaven. But he that doeth the will of my Father which is in heaven.' Now put down that gun, John Isaac, and repent of your sins."

"My sins? My sins? Before Jesus I'm white as the new driven snow compared to them bitches there . . . compared to you. False prophet. Snake worshiper. You're no son of mine, you minion of Satan. Look at that bitch there on the floor who calls herself my daughter with them black nigger eyes she's got. Them ain't no Isaac eyes. Them's snake eyes."

Earl Bob stepped forward and grabbed the shotgun by the barrel. It was a miracle, Elly said, that the damned thing didn't go off right then and there. But maybe John didn't have his finger on the trigger. Earl Bob twisted it around so it was pointing at the wall, and the two of them stood there and hung onto it.

"You goina raise your hand to your father?" John yelled out. "I'm goina beat you with my fists. I'm goina beat you down to a yellow dog."

"With me and Jesus on the one side," Earl Bob said, "and with you and Satan on the other, let's see who's the stronger," and they started wrestling back and forth.

"It was a good day for Jesus," Elly told Alex. "Earl Bob wrestled that shotgun away and took the shells out of it and threw them out in the hall. And the old man came after him, but skinny Earl Bob just grabbed him and squeezed him and pushed him right down on the floor. I don't know how he did it."

John was all out of breath. He lay there red in the face and yelled, "Get out of my house, you snake. Get out and never come back."

Earl Bob said to Elly, "I don't know where I'm going, but I'll let you know. And no matter where I am, there's always a place for you. May Jesus protect you and guide you both by day and by night," and he walked out and never came back. He drew all his money out of the bank and took the Greyhound bus to Detroit.

It was only a matter of days until John came over to the garage, drunk again, and flopped down a few feet from where Alex was working under somebody's Packard. "I done drove my own son out of my door," he said, and started crying. He cried hard, his whole fat body shaking. It sounded like a band saw tearing through sheet metal. "Jesus done turned away from me," he yelled out. "I done drove my own son away, my own flesh and blood, that godly boy who never done nothing but try to do good wherever he could do it. What's goina happen to me now? Oh, Jesus God, what's goina happen to me now?"

Chapter Three

Alex liked to make time between Scottsbog and Carreysburg; that was county jurisdiction, the sheriff's problem, and the sheriff had better things to worry about than who might be speeding on his road. Alex pushed the gas pedal to the floor and wound out the pickup truck. There was a lot to wind out; he'd dropped a '58 Corvette engine under that battered gray hood. The road was straight and Alex shot them down it at a hundred and twenty. The sign, too quick to read, whisked by, but they both knew what it had said: Mason-Dixon line. "South," Alex said, laughing.

"Save your Confederate money, boys," Evan said.

"Love to push this fucker, hardly get the chance. . . . Goddamn, Carlyle, feels good to be moving again. Open me another beer." Evan popped the cap, handed the bottle over; Alex tilted back the bottle and drank down half the beer without stopping. "Goddamn," he said, "Frank should be here."

The thought of Frank seemed to have punctured Alex's moment of elation; his face went hard. The speedometer was edging gradually up to a hundred and thirty. "Don't see him in months and then I come around to ask him to do me a favor," Alex said. "So he does me the favor. Then I can't very well tell him I don't want to loaf with him anymore. Shit, Carlyle, I feel bad about it.

"Same damn thing keeps happening," Alex went on after a moment. "I get to loafing with Frank. . . . It's not that I don't like it, right? But it just ruins me. And then I say: Come on, Warner, got to straighten yourself out. And the only way I can do that is if I don't loaf with him. And his feelings gets hurt. Shit, it's just like last summer when him and me run McCarthy off the road. You remember that?"

"Yeah, I knew you did it, but—"

"Didn't I ever tell you about it?"

"You didn't tell me the whole story."

"Well, you know McCarthy, right? That cop in Hallies Rise? You know the kind of reputation he's got? Running a real tourist trap out there. Making a fortune every year knocking off the poor fuckers coming through from Pittsburgh or New York. You know how you're just burning down the road from Little Washington, and all of a sudden there's this little tiny sign that says Slow to Fifteen and McCarthy's sitting right there next to it waiting for you? Shit, in the summer he must knock them off one an hour." Evan leaned back in the seat, prepared to drink his beer, watch the road roll by, and collect another story.

As Alex told it, Hospidarski had been the one who'd cooked up the plan. Frank was going to park in Hallies Rise facing into town, and then Alex was going to come from the other direction, speeding. McCarthy was going to go after him, of course, and Alex was supposed to open up a wide lead. As soon as Alex went by, Frank was going to pull out and head straight for McCarthy, taking up both lanes so the bastard would either have to hit him head-on or leave the road. Frank was betting that McCarthy would leave the road because, as he said, "Who the hell wants a head-on collision at a high rate of speed?" But if he didn't, if his reactions weren't fast enough, or if he "got paralyzed with fear," then Frank was going to cut over just in time and push him off the road. So they picked the spot to do it, a pretty good drop over the side of a hill but not a big enough one to kill him.

Frank was pissed off at McCarthy for a couple of reasons, the first that the fat fucker had given him at least a dozen tickets, the second that McCarthy had bought a new police car with all his fine money, a big blown Chevy, and it annoyed Frank that a cop should have a car that hot. But thinking about the top end of that Chevy, they knew they'd have to find something really fast for Alex to be driving, and thinking about the pushing that Frank might have to do, something really substantial for him. It took them a week of looking to be able to steal exactly the right two cars on the same night. Frank found an old Packard and Alex a new model Corvette. Pilsudski went out with them in his car, parked over a couple hills to pick them up after it was finished because they figured there'd be nothing left on the road but scrap.

But they hadn't planned on the rain. Frank got situated, and Alex came through Hallies Rise at damn near a hundred. He even saw McCarthy in his new car—a big, fat, old man just sitting there sound asleep. Alex went and told Frank. It was raining so hard by then that Alex was beginning to get a bad feeling about it, but Frank said, "Fuck it, Warner, run through again." This time Alex made sure McCarthy knew he was coming: squealed the tires, blew the horn, did everything but send the bastard a telegram.

McCarthy woke up, got it in gear, and away they went. Alex pushed the Corvette to the floor, but that cop's Chevy was hot and in no time McCarthy was half a car length behind. Alex knew he'd never be able to open up the kind of lead they were planning on and he just hoped Frank would let them go on by. McCarthy had his siren going, the red light on. Alex couldn't get anything more out of the Corvette, and McCarthy was damned near pushing him down the road. Could see him in the rearview, a big fat man madder than hell.

There were a few good curves before the straight stretch where Frank was waiting. Alex thought: *It's now or never. Can't outpower him, got to get him on guts.* So he accelerated into those curves at way over a hundred. It was raining hard, and the Corvette was all over the road. "It's the only time," Alex told Evan, "that I remember being scared while I was doing something instead of later." He almost lost it, but power-slid into the straightaway and pulled it out. He'd picked up maybe fifty yards on McCarthy, but as soon as the bastard came out of the curves, he started closing fast.

And there was Frank in the Packard pulling out onto the road. Alex even got a quick look at the big fucking grin on his face. *You goddamn fool,* he thought, and held the Corvette full out, the speedometer buried at a hundred and thirty, and nothing to do but hold on. Nowhere near enough room for Frank to get in, but nothing was going to stop old Hospidarski. He sideswiped McCarthy. Alex watched it in the rearview mirror. And the next thing he knew, there was a tractor trailer from Little Washington coming down the road straight at him.

Raining like hell, slick road, run out of straightaway, going way too fast for the curves, out of control, and there was a tractor trailer coming straight at him. Alex stopped thinking about Frank or McCarthy; if he hit that truck head-on, they'd have to scrape him off the road with a putty knife. He hauled her over hard to the right, but he was afraid to break because of the wet road, and the trucker was cutting to the left just as hard as he could, and there was almost enough room. Then, *wham*, Alex was nailed in his left rear quarter panel and went into a spin.

He didn't know how many times he went around, but each time he was amazed that he was still on the road. Finally he saw his chance, tramped her down and ran that Corvette right into the mud and then into a rock face. Scrap iron. It took him a minute to make himself let go of the wheel; he'd been hanging on to it so tight his forearms were sore for days afterward. He climbed out, shaking like a leaf, started walking down the road in the rain, not even sure where he was going, and there was Hospidarski coming along at a jog trot. Big gash on the side of his head, blood all over his arm, but grinning like a son of a bitch. "We did it, kid!" he said, and slapped Alex on the back.

Frank had pushed McCarthy off the road all right and then had lost control of the Packard. Of course the next thing he saw was the semi coming down on him, so he'd just run off the road to get out of the way. He hadn't been going anywhere near as fast as Alex had, so he got off all right. Totaled the Packard. "And that poor fucking trucker," Alex said. "Jesus, he must have had himself one hell of a night."

McCarthy got a broken leg and a mild concussion out of it, but his car was a total wreck. "Which is what we'd wanted," Alex said, "but the whole thing left a bad taste in my mouth. It had been great to plan, and even the run had its good points, but shit, four people could have been killed deader than mackerels over it. And you know who I felt worst about? That poor old trucker. I mean Frank and me had planned it, so anything we got we deserved, right? And McCarthy, well . . . shit, that's his job. But that poor trucker was just out there trying to make a living and almost got himself killed by these two fucking maniacs. And I even had to give it to that fucking fat-ass McCarthy for the way he'd stuck to me in the rain. I mean, shit, that took a lot of guts for an old man like him."

Alex fell silent. To encourage him, Evan said, "So you decided you'd better straighten yourself out, huh?"

"That's exactly right. I even told Frank what I was thinking, but he couldn't understand it. 'What the fuck's bothering you, Warner?' he said. 'Shit, nobody's going to get us. Nobody can fucking touch us.'

"But the football team had already gone into training, and there I was running around with Frank. It was fucking killing me. And I was also thinking about how it wasn't right to be out there risking other people's necks . . . like that poor old trucker.

"I thought: Shit, you either run cars or you run track. If you keep loafing with Frank, you're going to wind up dead or in jail. It was my goddamned senior year, and I really wanted to do something, so I quit loafing with him. I *tried* to tell him, but he just didn't understand it.

"Well, you know all the records I broke. Shit, you was there. And that one I done at the Invitational is going to stand on the books a long time. . . . There's a crazy kid from the Island going to come along and bust it, but it's going to stand till he gets there." Alex let up on the gas and the speed began to fall off. They were only a couple miles outside of Carreysburg. "We're making good time," he said. "You know, Carlyle, I think I'm going to make one last run . . . with cars I mean . . . and then quit it for good. I owe it to Frank, for one thing. Everything I know about racing cars, I learned it from him. We must of stole fifty cars when we was really doing it. I don't know why we didn't get killed. We'd steal them and run them down to scrap, and then we'd sit over at the P.A.C. and talk about it. He'd tell me where I fucked up, you know, braked too soon, or didn't brake soon enough . . . or whatever it was. And I'd sit there and listen to him, and it would all get real clear in my mind. . . . So I owe it to him. Yeah, one last good fucking run, and then cash her in."

Why doesn't he ever take me on one of those things? Evan thought. But what Alex always said was: "I'm not going to take risks with somebody else's neck." But what would it be like to see him *really* pushing a car?

Alex flicked a glance down at the clock on the dashboard, then over at Evan. "Carreysburg," he said, "right on time." He seemed to be wearing a hint of a smile, but before Evan could be sure, had turned his face back to the road. "I told you it'd take two hours," Alex said.

Chapter Four

At Carreysburg they'd turned southeast, away from the river, and were rattling back up into the hills in the hot summer night, getting higher all the time. Soon they'd be drifting along a narrow strip chopped out of the side of a mountain, so high that if the truck slid over, it'd be just like Alex always said: "Hardly find enough of us to bury." It was almost dark now, but a splash of blue light in the west left Evan just enough to catch sight of vistas that took his breath away; he seemed to be peering a million miles down into dark, mysterious valleys with faintly glittering creeks running at the bottom like tiny lines drawn by a silver pencil. It was already cooler out here in the hills. Evan was pretty drunk, and he was happy—glad to be getting out of Raysburg and away from Elaine for a while. He didn't think he'd ever understand girls; they seemed as strange to him as a whole separate race of people. Like Susie. Whoever would have thought that she would have gone out with Alex? "Hey, Warner," he said, "are you serious about Susie Galloway?"

Alex didn't answer immediately. Then he said, "Depends on what you mean by serious."

"You know, *serious*."

"Hey, fire me up one of them stogies, will you?"

"Sure." The only admission that Alex ever made that he was working hard at the driving was if he asked Evan to light his cigars for him. Evan picked one out of the box on the floor, peeled away the cellophane, bit off the end and licked it just the way he'd seen Alex do it a thousand times, lit it and passed it over.

There was nothing left of Alex's face in the growing darkness but a black silhouette, cigar jutting upward, red glowing ember at the end. "Well," he said, "you serious about Elaine?"

"Depends on what you mean by serious," Evan said, laughing.

"You know, *serious*," Alex said, and they both laughed.

"I don't know," Evan said. "I really like her, but . . ." He didn't have the right words for what he wanted to say. Yeah, he liked her an awful lot, but he didn't know what that had to do with anything. He was leaving in the fall.

"Yeah, I like Susie all right too. But she's such a . . . *cream-puff*. She's out of high school and her daddy still wants her in by one. 'That's the magic hour,' she says. 'After one, he knows we're up to no good.' Fuck me, man, I never thought I'd be dating a girl like that."

"Get in her pants yet?"

"Are you kidding me?"

"Jesus, Warner, what ever happened to all that crap you used to tell me all the time. 'Come on, Carlyle,' you used to say, 'who the hell wants to date one of those piss-ass girls? They just get you going and then leave you with your prick sticking up in your pants like a hammer.'"

"Yeah," Alex said, "but then you don't marry one of Harriet Axford's girls either."

"Shit, you thinking about getting married?"

"Well, not right now. But some time."

"You!"

"Why the hell not me? I ain't got two heads."

"But you're only fucking eighteen."

"I said not right now, didn't I?"

"You thinking of marrying Susie?"

"I don't know . . . maybe." Alex began to laugh. "Frank and me stole cars from her old man's lot for years back in the old days. He had to hire a guard around that place, did you know that? That's how many cars we stole. And here I am dating his daughter. Shit, I wonder if he suspects? . . . But goddamn, it's funny."

It's not just funny, Evan thought, *it's fucking weird.* Everybody in their class had been surprised when Alex had asked out Susie Galloway and even more surprised when she'd said yes. She'd not only been head majorette that year, but the football team had elected her Homecoming Queen, first time anybody could remember that a girl had been *both* head majorette and Homecoming Queen. And she was a real doll, no doubt about that, had a perfect majorette's figure: forty-inch tits and long showgirl legs. But she was also a good girl. Shit, he couldn't think of anybody who was more of a good girl than Susie Galloway. She dressed for school every day just like she was going out to dinner, not sexy or trashy, but just nice, in skirts and nylons and ballerinas. She was a genuine strawberry-blonde, and if anyone should dare to suggest that she got any help from a bottle of peroxide, she'd fly into a small ladylike rage, would thrust her gleaming, set curls into their face and demand: "Do you see anything but blond? Anywhere?"

Alex had been the number one athlete that year, All-Valley, and undefeated in wrestling, and breaking all those mile records. But Susie Galloway go out with him? With his reputation? Everybody knew about the stolen cars, the drinking, the street fights; in fact the legend had grown totally out of proportion to anything he'd really done. If he'd raised as much hell as everybody said he did, he wouldn't have been able to finish a mile, let alone break records in it. Yeah, it was true that he'd had the clap. But it hadn't been a big deal. The doctor had cured it with a dose of penicillin.

Alex had invited Evan and Elaine to double-date with him and Susie half a dozen times, but until the senior prom, Evan had always found an excuse not to. He liked Susie well enough, and could have talked Elaine into putting up with her for a night, but the problem was that Evan and Susie knew each other too well. The Carlyles and the Galloways were both old valley families; his mother and Susie's mother had been friends for thirty years, and he was sure that Susie knew just as much about him and his family as he did about her and hers—which was everything. And worst of all was that Evan and Susie had taken tap lessons together at the Mateski School of Dance, had been in the same goddamned class for years until Evan had turned ten or eleven and had finally managed to say no loudly and convincingly enough for his mother to hear him. So what if he did know all the embarrassing things there were to know about Susie? He still couldn't trust her not to say, right there in front of Alex Warner, something like: "You should have seen Evan in the dance recital when we were nine. He was the *cutest* little thing." Nothing he knew about her could top that.

"How the fuck do you get along with her old man?" Evan asked.

"He puts up with me. I don't know. . . . I'm always nice as pie when I go over there." Alex chuckled. " 'What is it exactly your folks do?' he says to me. 'Well, my father runs the farm and my mother teaches school.' . . . Shit, that's a joke! My old lady goes on over to Harrod when one of the regular teachers calls in sick, and my old man draws welfare and lays around and drinks. Haw!"

By the time the senior prom had rolled around, Evan hadn't been able to contain his curiosity any longer, had told Alex that, sure, they could all go together. He'd been dying to see just how the hell Alex acted when he was around Susie.

Elaine had turned out to be more of a problem than he'd expected. "You want *me* to go out on a double date with *her*?"

"Well, sure. Why not? It could be a real joke."

Elaine sat in the booth and stared off into space. "All right," she said. "We'll go with Alex and that little bitch. But you rent a tuxedo, and I'll go as Marilyn Monroe."

"What?"

"A joke? Isn't that what you said? And wouldn't that be something wonderful? Everybody would think we were serious, but we'd be laughing at them the whole time."

"A tuxedo!" But he wouldn't have to rent one; he already

owned one. It had been his father's from some earlier day when the old man had been thinner, and it fit Evan perfectly. "Marilyn Monroe?" he said. "You'll bleach your hair?"

"No, but I'll do everything else. You won't be able to believe it."

Susie's father lent Alex the best car in the lot for the night, a dark blue, four-door Cadillac. ("Some joke, huh?" Alex said.) And Susie was a knockout, of course. She'd bought her silver-gray formal in Pittsburgh, wore matching heels and white elbow-length gloves with it. The skirt was so full that Alex said, laughing, "Is there going to be room enough for me to drive?" Evan had studied himself and his tuxedo for damned near an hour in front of his mother's full-length mirror; he thought he looked like a Coca-Cola ad.

Elaine must have been waiting for him. She made the grand entrance, using the entire length of the restaurant as a runway. Her dress was black crepe with a neckline that was plunging, to put it mildly; her breasts were pushed up into dazzling white curves; her cleavage was so deep, he could have dropped a quarter down it. (How the hell had she managed that?) And she had Marilyn's walk down to perfection, that honey-smooth, hip-swinging, fantastically sexy glide. Her sheath skirt fit skin-tight all the way to her knees, then flared out to the floor just wide enough so she could manage to walk in it at all. She'd got herself a black bag, black shoulder-length gloves, and black sling-back heels. Her hair wasn't blond, that was true, but she'd set it just like Marilyn's, and her makeup job was incredible: Marilyn's pale, creamy skin, spiky eyelashes, flaming lips, even that black beauty mark on one cheek. She'd been right; he was stunned. "Jesus Christ, Elaine," he said, "you're gorgeous."

"Yeah, I am," she said, and that voice wasn't her own; it was Marilyn's to a T, that high, breathy whisper. "And I keep my undies in the icebox too."

He was already beginning to think about what the other kids were going to say. *Oh, my God!* "Even my old man was impressed," she said in her own voice, under her breath. "First nice thing he's said to me in weeks: 'Good Lord, Elly, you're pretty as a picture!' Come on, Evan, take my arm." He took her arm. She was wearing a rhinestone bracelet over her black glove. Too short, he followed her through the door.

Alex watched them walk over to the car, his pale eyes absolutely expressionless. "Elly," he said, "you're crazy as a bedbug." She said nothing. Evan opened the door for her.

He walked around to the other side of the car and got in. From the front seat, Susie was staring back at Elaine. Evan didn't know why it should be happening, but Susie was blushing all the way up to the roots of her naturally blond hair. "Why, Elaine," she said, "you look . . . lovely." Elaine smiled and smiled and didn't say a word. Evan reached for his cigarettes.

"About halfway," Alex said. They were skimming around yet another backtracking loop, beautifully high up into the hills now; the last of the daylight had faded away entirely, and there was nothing left to see but the road ahead unwinding toward them in the yellow headlights, the dark, hairy shapes of treetops sticking up above the brim on the one side, the ominous, blank cut of a rock face on the other, everything rolling by like a dream. "High as we're going to get," Alex said. "It's all downhill from here . . . right on into Harrod." He sounded pleased with himself. The stiff truck-suspension pounded and rattled them through the night. "Goddamn, Carlyle, I love this road."

"What did you think the night of the prom when you saw Elaine walk out to the car all dressed up like that?" Evan said.

"Oh, fuck me, man, I didn't know whether to shit or go blind. I didn't know she was going to pull a stunt like that . . . at the prom, for Christ's sake. She sure is good when she does something like that. Remember our junior year when she played that little old lady in the school play?"

"Yeah."

"Well, she just had to come over to the garage and try it out on us. It was incredible."

"I didn't know she did that."

"Yeah, well she did. It was about quitting time and there was me and Tony Wolchak . . . don't know where the hell you was that night, but Pilsudski was there, I think, and I don't remember who-all. About five of us back there. And all of a sudden here comes this little old lady with a black dress on, walking on a cane, you know, all bent over, comes hobbling on into the back. She says, 'Hey, boys, you got any hot cars back here? Heard you boys keep some good hot cars back here.' And shit, we all thought she was just some crazy old lady. I didn't know anything about the play, right? And she completely had me fooled. She stayed back out of the light so we couldn't get a good look at her. 'Land a Goshen,' she says, 'you know, boys, got to get me a good hot car, drive down that river road, and the Lord help me!' We figured out that something was up pretty quick. I mean, shit, she had us rolling on the ground laughing. 'Goddamn,' she says, 'got to get my creaky old ass down that river in a good hot car, boys. Think you can fix me up?' Had us going for about ten minutes before I figured out who she was. 'Christ,' I said, 'Elly!' And she straightened up and started laughing. 'You should have seen your faces when I walked in here,' she says, 'it was something wonderful.' "

"Yeah, she's great," Evan said. "She really ought to do something with it."

She sure as hell had done something with it at the prom. He'd been expecting to spend most of the night watching Alex and Susie, but he hadn't been able to take his eyes off Elaine. Nobody could. *Oh, it was a wonderful night*, Evan thought, *a night to remember*. They'd damn well let him graduate and he was out; he couldn't believe it. And Elaine was the sexiest thing he'd seen short of a movie screen. The Sunset Room was hung with balloons and streamers, the syrupy old band that always played for formal dances was winding out fox-trots through all their smooth saxophones, and he and Elaine floated around the floor pressed tight into each other. Everywhere they went, the other kids were staring at them. There were only two or three other guys in tuxedos, but there wasn't a single girl who looked remotely like Elaine. After two or three slow dances, Evan began to feel like he was carrying around a crotch full of rocks and gravel. Sometimes out on the dance floor his erection got so stiff he could feel it poking right into her leg; so could she, and she smiled at him wickedly from behind her makeup. "I'm not bringing up a painful subject for you, am I, Mister Carlyle?" she said in Marilyn's voice.

Evan took Alex aside and said, "Hey, lend me the car."

Alex winked. "Don't leave us stuck here till two in the morning, you crazy fucker."

And Evan was off with Elaine, speeding along the dark park roads under those huge drooping trees. "Christ, where the hell can we go they'll never possibly find us?"

"Go out toward Route Eighty-eight," she said. "Just before the turnoff there's a private road on the left. You wouldn't even see it if you didn't already know it was there."

"How do you know about it?"

"Been exploring," she said mysteriously. "I see a road and I just have to know where it goes. That one goes all the way out to Revington Crescent, cuts back around behind the golf course. Nothing there but some fields where those rich bastards ride their horses. I bet they hardly ever use that road. I bet they always go out the other way."

"Yeah, and I'll bet there'll be a thousand cars parked back in there."

"It's too early yet. Not a thousand . . . maybe a couple." Only one, it turned out; Eddie Watinka's Thunderbird was parked just inside the high hedge. It was still only ten o'clock and they'd beat the crowd by an hour. *Just us horny bastards,* he thought; *give her hell, Watinka! Shit, you couldn't even wait to get her down the road, could you?*

Evan drove slowly on back over the narrow ruts and parked by an overgrown field. They were sheltered on all sides by woods. He turned off the lights, killed the ignition, and grabbed her. "Evan," she said, "you get it on my dress, and I'll kill you."

"Take it off."

"Christ, I can't take it off! What if somebody comes by?"

"You said yourself nobody's coming by."

She wasn't even wearing a slip. All of her cleavage had been created by an astonishing contraption: a bra—well padded but cut low—that pushed her breasts up and forward and barely covered her nipples, kept on going down to squeeze her waist into a Hollywood hourglass, and ended in garters trimmed with lace. A "merry widow" she called it; the damned thing had more bones in it than a catfish. He thought it was the sexiest thing he'd ever seen. She had more room on the backseat of the Cadillac than she usually did in cars. She had on tiny black lacy panties. "You knew you'd have that dress off before the night was over," he said, "didn't you?" The thought that she'd planned ahead for it was giving him a hard-on that just wouldn't quit.

"Well, I figured there was a good chance of it." She arched back and stretched; her small pointed nipples popped out easily, free for his fingers. "Hey, don't be so rough, Evan!"

"Jesus Christ, Elaine!" He was burning up; he couldn't even give her time to take her gloves off.

"Well, that was fast," she said in a wry voice. "There's a hankie in my purse."

"That's all right. I've got one in my pants." He wiped it all up from her smooth thighs, pulled on his shorts and pants. "Goddamn this cummerbund," he said. She helped him with it.

Then she stepped out of the car, slipped her dress over her head. "Here, zip me up." They sat in the front seat and smoked cigarettes.

"Goddamn, Elaine," he said, "I just think you're fantastic. I just think you're wonderful."

"I don't know what Marilyn would say. . . . I know what I'd say: Oh, I love you, Evan. You're a real sweetheart." She leaned against him, her head in the hollow of his shoulder. "You want to go back?"

"No, let's sit here a minute. . . . Christ, Elaine, we're out of Raysburg High. Do you realize that? It's incredible. Can you believe it? Don't you feel great?"

She didn't answer. After a moment she said, "You know, you embarrass me sometimes."

"I do?"

"Yeah. Like just now. My God, Evan, you attacked me like an animal."

"Well, Christ, you were driving me nuts."

"I like to get into the mood for it, you know, but you just grabbed me. I like to feel all relaxed and at ease, but I sure as hell didn't. . . . If I knew how you felt toward me, it would help. . . . If you don't mind doing it, I wish you'd tell me." Her voice sounded stiff, almost formal.

"I love you, Elaine," he said automatically.

"Do you?"

"Yes. You know I do." *Oh, Christ,* he thought.

She seemed to be satisfied with that. At least she didn't say anything more, just dragged on her cigarette, French-inhaled it, blowing smoke out her nostrils. The only light out on this lovely back road was from a brilliant half moon, and in that pale, white shimmer she really did look like Marilyn. It was almost scary; it gave him a bit of a shiver when he looked at her face. Her eyes were half closed and her painted mouth gleamed like an oil slick. "You've got to get out of Raysburg," he said. "You've really got it, you know that?"

"Yeah, I know . . . but I don't know what to do with it. I'm scared, Evan. I've saved some money. I could go to New York. I could try to get into the Actors Studio. . . . Wouldn't that be something, Evan? Marilyn went there. Jimmy went there. . . . Wouldn't that be something?" She sighed.

"You ought to do it."

"I'm scared. What if I screwed it up? What if they didn't like me? I'm just a dumb kid from Carreysburg. I keep thinking about that. Just a dumb kid who grew up back of Carreysburg. Who the hell am I to think I'm going to be an actress? . . . But wouldn't it be incredible if I turned out to be rich and famous?" She giggled. "Just think what I could buy for everybody. I'd get the old man a lifetime's supply of Jack Daniel's . . . get Alex a racing car. You know what I'd get for you?"

"No. What?"

"A harem." He laughed. She laughed too. "I'd put Susie Galloway in it," she said.

"Oh, would you?"

"Yeah, I see how you look at her."

"I'm not looking at anybody but you tonight."

"Yeah, I'd put her in there in one of those little harem costumes—you know, silk pants and gold bracelets—and you could screw her as much as you wanted . . . and she'd have to do it every time whether she wanted to or not."

He was surprised at the anger in her voice. What the hell was she thinking about now? But she was already gone, off on another track: "It's a real tragedy that Jimmy's dead. He could have helped people like us, you know? He had so much to give. If he were alive, I could write to him and ask what to do. I know he'd answer me. . . .

"I remember when I heard about it. I was just thirteen. I came in the restaurant and my mother said, 'I just heard on the radio that some actor died. Got killed in an auto wreck. James Dean, I think his name was.' And I just walked on by her and went upstairs. I didn't want her to see how I felt, you know. And I went in my room and shut the door. I felt just like something had been ripped apart inside me. I couldn't even cry for hours. I was just numb, you know. It felt like I was bleeding inside. I turned on the radio and waited for the news, and there it was. He really was dead. I couldn't even cry. And then I woke up in the middle of the night and I was crying in my sleep. And I just cried and cried all the rest of the night."

He'd heard all of these stories about Jimmy before, of course; she told them over and over. She kept a scrapbook about him full of clippings from screen magazines. She'd bought every paperback book they'd ever put out about him. She'd seen all of his movies dozens of times. "You know, he set a pole vault record when he was in high school," she said. "They didn't even know he was practicing for it. He practiced all alone at home without telling anybody and then he went out and broke the record. Everybody thought it was incredible, you know, because they didn't even know he could do it. And he never pole-vaulted again after he broke that record. People keep saying how strange it was, but I don't think it was strange. I know exactly what he was thinking. He just did it to prove to himself that he could . . . you know, to prove that you can do what you already know you can do. I really understand that, Evan. . . . I'd like to drive in a race just like that. I'd like to practice all alone without anybody knowing and then come out and drive in a race. Just once. And win it. Just to prove I could do it. And then never do it again."

He didn't know what to say to her when she got going like that. It didn't make any sense to him. You did things to show people, to get ahead, to make your mark in the world. You didn't practice all alone and then do it just once. "You're crazy," he said, "you know that, don't you?"

"Yeah," she said, "I suppose I am. . . . You have everything planned out. *You* know exactly what you're going to do, don't you?"

What was that supposed to mean? "No, I don't have everything planned out," he said, "but I know one thing. I'm getting out of Raysburg and I'm never coming back."

"Yeah," she said, "that's what I've got to do too." She sighed again. "I think about you when I'm going to sleep at night. Did I ever tell you that? Sometimes when I've got a migraine and I can't sleep, I think of you and then I go to sleep. It's amazing, isn't it? . . . Oh, Evan, I don't want to lose you!"

"You're not going to lose me. I'm just going to Columbus, for Christ's sake. We'll keep in touch."

"Will we?"

"Yeah, of course we will."

"Do you promise?"

"Sure."

"I know your mother hates my guts—"

"What's that got to do with anything?"

"Yeah, that's right," she said. "It doesn't matter if your mother hates me . . . or my old man hates you, does it?"

"No, of course it doesn't. . . . Hey, we should go back. People are going to start wondering where we are."

But she lit another cigarette. "In a minute," she said. "They all *know* where we are. . . . Jesus, Evan, you look good in a tuxedo. You look just great. You always look so good when you're dressed up."

"Well, Christ, Elaine, you look just great too. You look fantastic. If your hair was blond, you'd look just like her."

"I did it for you."

"Did you?"

"Yeah, of course I did."

Her voice had that smoky, sullen sound that meant sex to him. He was beginning to feel like making out again. Jesus, he'd just come a few minutes ago, and he was already feeling like it again. "Elaine," he said, "why don't we make love sometime? I mean for real?"

"No."

"Why not? What difference would it make? We've done everything else."

She turned and looked directly at him; with all that makeup, her black eyes seemed enormous, like something you'd see at night in the woods from a long way away. You'd see it there a few yards back from the road, and you wouldn't know what it was. "It may not make any sense to you," she said, "but it really matters to me. I know what people think of me, what they say about me—girls like Susie Galloway—that spoiled little bitch. *Trash*, that's what I am to her . . . to people like that. I know I'm not, no matter what they say. . . . And it may be really dumb to you, Evan, but if I let you do it, then I really would be trash."

Chapter Five

Since turning away from the river at Carreysburg, they'd been climbing the mountain road to Harrod at speeds from five to fifteen miles an hour; Alex held the car in tight to the rock faces, coaxed it up the steep grades somehow or other, the tires slipping. They'd spun out three times in nerve-jangling slow motion, and each time Alex had managed to do the right thing to keep them on the road. Once they'd actually begun to slide backward down the way they'd come, aimed right for the edge of the road hidden under the snow, no fence to stop them from dribbling over a forty-foot dropoff down into an invisible valley. But Alex had spun the tires, let up, spun the tires again, and gradually goosed the car back up the hill. *Well,* Evan thought, *at least it's stopped snowing, or we'd probably both be dead by now.*

"You know, Carlyle," Alex said, "this is crazy. They should fucking well lock me up for being out here on a night like this."

Right, Evan thought. He was sick of Alex; the ride was taking too long and neither of them had found much to say since they'd turned off at Carreysburg. "Hey, light me a smoke, will you?" Alex said.

"Sure." The match flame went up with the sharp biting smell of sulfur, and Evan saw that Alex was looking over at him: the face in the quick flare of harsh yellow light seemed old and lined, tired; the mouth was set into a bitter, downward curve; the remote eyes looked out from baggy pouches etched deeply into the skin. Then the flame went out and Alex fell back into inexpressive silhouette. *Do I look that old?* Evan thought. *I can't possibly look that old, can I? Fuck, we're only thirty-two. That's not supposed to be old. That's supposed to be the prime of your life.* He handed Alex the cigarette.

"Thanks. . . . Hey, Carlyle, what's your work like? I know you work on the radio . . . but what do you do every day?" It didn't sound to Evan as though Alex really wanted to know what he did, more that he was asking for talk about anything at all that would fill up the endless time it seemed to be taking them to get nowhere on this weird mountain road.

"What it feels like is being a ringmaster in a circus . . . a three-ring circus." Evan laughed without humor.

"I get up at four or four thirty in the morning . . . usually four thirty. The alarm goes off at four and I usually just lie there and think about what the hell I've got to do that day. It's always black as pitch. Nearly two fucking years I've been doing it, and I never get used to it. Never. I jump up at the last minute, don't usually take the time to eat. Just shave and throw some clothes on, run down and jump in the car. . . ."

"What kind of car you got?"

"Volkswagen."

"I hate those fuckers."

"Why?"

"I don't know. I just do."

"Yeah. . . . So I get in around five. The studios are in the Hotel Vancouver. Really a crazy place for them. For months I kept getting lost in that damned hotel; it's like a goddamned maze in there. All right, so I come in. I've got a couple doughnuts and a double coffee. I'm not awake yet. The technician's already there. About a minute or two later the announcer comes in. There's a stack of tapes on my desk halfway up to the ceiling. The first thing I do is grab the sports editorial out of the box. It's on cassette and it's got to be dubbed onto seven-and-a-half-inch tape. I pick up the folders with stories from yesterday afternoon. I open up the newspaper to see if there's anything we should be covering. I drink my coffee, smoke a cigarette. Nobody's awake, and everybody's in a fucking awful mood. Dana's always late. She's late every goddamned day."

"That's your girl friend, right?"

"Yeah. . . . All right, so we sign on at a quarter of six. . . . Marine weather forecast. There's a couple guys in the newsroom. I'm sitting there watching them, you know, from the other side of the glass. Then at six fifteen we start the taped items. Item, news, music, item, news . . . it goes on like that. I've got to keep an ear out for what's going over the air, and I've got to do a quick run through the *Province*, and I've got to look at all the stories piled up from yesterday . . . all at the same time. When we start having live items—that's about a quarter of seven—it gets pretty hectic. If the interviewer's off the wall, I've got to feed him questions. And the phone's going to start ringing. Most of the calls I've got to take myself because I'm the fucking producer, eh? They can be anything at all, some idiot pressure-group. Completely out in left field, saying: 'Why the hell don't you give us more space?' Or it can be a lawyer threatening to sue the balls off me and the CBC for some item I did yesterday. We're on the air for three hours, and by the time it's over, I'm shot. Dana calls it 'Dixie-cup radio.' . . . Shit, sometimes it's a wonder to me we make it on the air at all. Every day it's another fucking crisis, like we've got this unbelievable prima donna announcer, and everytime I get a freelancer in to do an interview—you know, to cohost the interview with him—the announcer goes slightly bananas because the freelancer has some brains and knows about the subject—that's why I got him in the first place—and all the announcer has is a voice, so I've got to make sure he remembers how much we appreciate him. Or maybe there'll be a call from Toronto, and I've got to take that. . . .

"So we go off to lunch at nine, usually just go downstairs to the Spanish Grill. Then we have a staff meeting, do a postmortem on that morning's show, plan what we're going to do for the next day. And I've got to keep an eye on everything that happens because I'm the fucking producer. It's me, baby, and if something screws up, it all ends up in my lap. Amazing how people can pass it all back to me. I'm supposed to be out of there by one in the afternoon, but I never am."

"You like it?"

"Sometimes. I like running things."

"Well," Alex said, "at least you work inside." And when Evan turned and looked at him, Alex laughed: "Haw!" A *joke*, Evan thought. *Some joke.*

The morning show had a reputation for burning out producers. It usually burned them out in six months, but he'd hung on well into his second year. He'd been offered the show, he knew perfectly well, because no one on staff had been able to face it. He'd thrown himself into it full of fire and drive and had completely revamped the structure. He'd originated the snappy and aggressive format they were using now, and he'd had to step on a few toes to do it, but it was paying off: Toronto had noticed. Toronto was like Big Brother; he was constantly aware of that gray, specterlike presence peering over his shoulder from three thousand miles back in the mysterious East. And Toronto was pleased with him. He wouldn't be doing the morning show out of Vancouver much longer. Then some other poor asshole could get burnt-out nerves, insomnia, raging headaches, the shakes, and an incipient ulcer producing the fucking thing. He was going on staff, by God; he was going east.

Right now it didn't feel like much of a victory. Wherever they sent him, he'd have to start all over again: proving he could get a show out every day and not only get it out but find new, exciting, zippy, and dynamic ways to do it. Having to prove once again that he could get along with everybody, not only with the other nice guys but with the burnt-out idiots. He'd have a whole new set of politics to figure out. He'd have to be right there, Johnny-on-the-spot, but he couldn't come on too pushy. He'd never become a Canadian citizen, and he never knew when he'd run into another one of those raging nationalists who wouldn't mind chopping up all the Americans in Canada into small, bloody pieces and shipping them back across the border in a green plastic garbage bag.

Wherever he went, he'd have to find another understanding doctor with an automatic right hand, quick on the draw with the prescription pad, who wouldn't bat an eyelash at the fact that he was eating Dalmane like candy, that he occasionally needed a hit of Valium to keep his nerves from blowing apart like electric cables hit with a vicious power surge. At least he wouldn't need a doctor to get the 222's he ate the way some people ate Rolaids, or the two packs of Craven A's he smoked a day, or the bottle of Scotch to help out the Dalmane on those nights when nothing he was doing made the least bit of sense and the Canadian Broadcasting Corporation had begun to look like some disgusting monster with an open mouth, a four-million-pound baby robin who had to be fed a thousand miles of brown recording tape every day just to keep it satisfied.

The hell with Dana, let her stay in goddamned sleepy Vancouver and mildew in the rain if she doesn't have the guts to try it in the east, where it counted. "Evan," she'd said with that damnable icy wit of hers, "you've got ass kissing down to a fine art. You understand perfectly how you've got to do it just right so they don't even feel your tongue." But how the hell else were you supposed to get ahead in this fucking world? He'd always had rotten luck with women, always been stuck with some woman who made him feel like an asshole. Why couldn't he find just one who'd appreciate him? Beth with her dozen hippie lovers. Elaine, who'd fucked his best friend. How the hell could she have done it?

The ride was interminable. And his old best friend was boring the shit out of him. He should never have come along on this lunatic jaunt. Alex had turned into some goddamned suicidal drunken redneck, and here he was, like a fool, stuck with him at one in the morning out in the middle of nowhere in the goddamned snow. *Oh, fuck it all!* Evan unsnapped his seat belt, bent over into the back, and hauled out another can of beer. "Yeah," Alex said, "I'll have one of those."

Evan handed the beer over without a word. "What I told you earlier was just bullshit," Alex said.

"What's that?"

"All that shit about blaming it on the valley . . . blaming it on this fucking oil crisis . . . yeah, blaming it on *anything*. . . . It's just me, right? I'm just a fuckoff, that's all. There's a lot of guys in the valley in the garage business making money hand over fist. Even now they're making money, oil crisis or no fucking oil crisis. I could have done it too if I'd played it by the book, right? I just fucked it, that's all."

"Sounds like you're being a little hard on yourself." Evan's anger had suddenly walked away like a bad actor abandoning an unconvincing speech in midsentence, and he felt a wave of maudlin sentimentality gurgling up from inside him, assisted by the case of beer he'd just drunk. *Why the hell should you feel guilty?* he asked himself. *You don't owe him a thing.*

"I ain't any harder on myself than the world is," Alex said. It sounded like something Alex's mother would have said. "In business, Carlyle, you either make it or you don't. It's just like running, right? You either beat the son of a bitch or you didn't. That's all there is to it."

Evan said nothing. Alex was working the car slowly around yet another of those rising, blind curves. *Maybe that's all there is*, Evan thought. *You just keep grinding on and on, and every curve looks like every other curve, and you never get anywhere, and eventually you just get tired and lose it, the car slips off the road, and that's the end.*

"Hey Alex," Evan said, "you should come to British Columbia."

"What the fuck's in British Columbia?"

"For a good mechanic like you, there's plenty . . . towns all over the province where you could walk right in and pick up a job. Lumber towns. Fishing towns. Jesus, man, it's beautiful up the coast, you should see it. Beautiful mists and fogs, huge stands of trees, all these little islands . . ." Evan listened to his own voice; he felt as detached from it as if it were a radio broadcast he'd prerecorded. He was talking about his first years in Vancouver when he'd been a free-lancer. He'd driven all over the province with his Sony, talked to Indians in Alert Bay,

Finns in Sointula, crazy old characters in the interior, trappers and loggers. He hadn't made much money, but now, remembering it, he realized that it had been one of the few times in his life when he'd been happy. "If you ever saw B.C.," he said to Alex, "you'd never leave."

"You make it sound great. If I was single . . . But shit, I could never get Sheri out of Raysburg." At the top of a rise Alex pulled over to the side of the road. "I'm just glad one of us got the fuck out," he said. There was nothing to see anywhere for miles but more snow, trees and hills, and road and snow. He turned off the engine, rolled down his window.

"What the hell you doing?" Evan said.

"Just look, man. Just look at it a minute."

Evan looked. The road was a bright, unmarked white mat under a dazzling moon, risen into a fiercely glittering country sky. In the valley below all the trees were glowing with white frosting. They were far enough out of Raysburg by now that the air was clear; the wind blowing in the window was bitter and sharp as a knife. "That's why I come down here," Alex said. "Sometimes I just got to get out and come down here. . . . But when there's one of those goddamned inversions, the air stinks even out here. The whole state probably stinks. . . . You don't know how lucky you are, Carlyle." He lit a cigarette, dragged on it, and stared out the car window. "Can you imagine what Raysburg must have been like a hundred years ago, what a nice little place it probably was? And then the bastards went and fucked it up." He snapped the cigarette out the window and rolled it up, started the engine, and drifted the car over the rise and down the next hill.

Lucky, he calls me, Evan thought. *Jesus Christ! Why? Because I got out of Raysburg? Out of the country? And if I like British Columbia so much, why am I so eager to get out of there?* "Hey," he heard himself saying, "you know the only goddamned thing in my life I'm proud of?"

"No. What's that?"

"Telling the United States Government to kiss my ass."

Alex laughed.

"Christ, you just can't let them screw you forever," Evan heard himself saying desperately. "You've got to tell them where to get off sometime. I mean that fucking war, that fucking ridiculous, obscene war. I was damned if they were going to screw me with their war. . . ."

"Yeah, Carlyle, that's right."

"I mean, you've got to do *something*. Shit!"

"Yeah."

"So I bloody well told them to shove it and left the country."

Evan was horrified at himself. What the hell had he been saying? No, it wasn't the only thing in his life he was proud of; there was nothing in his life he was proud of. He might have been proud of it if he *had* been telling the United States Government to kiss his ass, but he'd just been looking out for number one, the same as he always did. "A suckhole," Elaine had called him back in Raysburg High School; well shit, he'd been a suckhole then and he was still a suckhole. Liberation be damned, there's something the matter with you if your wife screws twenty other guys, if your very first girl screws your best friend. What the hell was wrong with him anyway? Dana was perfectly right. "Let's play it by ear," she'd said. "All right? You're not the kind of guy to get serious about. Oh, I understand perfectly why you want to hang on to your American citizenship. If you get a good job offer in Los Angeles or New York, you want to be able to flip right back across the border like it didn't exist." *Oh, Jesus*, he thought, *you don't need women to make you feel like an asshole. You are an asshole.*

"Proud?" Alex said. "I don't know what I could say I was proud of . . . the way I kept a car on the road sometimes. Or playing sports . . . the last time I broke the Valley mile record, I guess I was proud of that." He laughed. "That's all years ago . . . I guess I'm proud of my kids . . . Lori, anyway."

They'd finally come to the end of the road, were rolling down that last hill into Harrod. The little town, shut up for the night and covered with snow, looked to Evan just like some silly

Christmas card. Alex drove down the short main street and turned onto Rural Route 1 that led back to the farm. "Shit," he said, "now that we're down out of there, I'll tell you something, Carlyle. . . . You know how close we come to getting killed?"

"No . . . I guess I don't."

"I was hoping you didn't. There was four different times that we come *that* close." Alex held up his right hand, showed Evan a half inch of space between his thumb and index finger. "*That* close," he said again. "See if there's another beer back there, will you? We're going to have a fuck of a time getting down the hill."

"What hill?"

"You know. That big hill down to the house. Don't you remember? It just goes straight down. And there's going to be snow piled in there by the goddamned ton."

Evan had an idiotic cartoon vision of the car transformed into a toboggan, the two of them sailing off in it like Santa Claus. "Sure," he said. "Yeah."

Alex made the turn at the top of the hill, very slowly, and they started down at five miles an hour. "Shit," he said, "can't see a thing."

For no reason at all, Evan was suddenly wildly happy. He heard himself giggling. Alex opened the door, stuck his head out, steered with his right hand. "Here we go," he said, "nice and easy." The house began to appear in the distance: a flat, gray shadow. Evan watched in fascination. They were rolling down, not, as he'd imagined, in a great *Dr. Zhivago* sweep, but bumpily in slow motion. The house swam up on them ridiculously slowly, like a mirage, but they were picking up speed. Alex braked. Nothing happened. "Useless," he said, and gave Evan an odd smile.

The house was coming up faster now; it was turning into something three-dimensional, a ghostly cube. Alex started to laugh. "Nothing I can do," he said. "We'll just have to slide until we stop." Evan began to laugh right along with him. *We sound like a couple idiots,* he thought. Alex raised his right hand in a gesture of helplessness, looked at Evan with a mime of surprise. A fence on the right moved in out of the swirling snow. Evan stared as it approached. Very slowly, discreetly and gently, the car hit the fence. There was the sound of breaking glass. The right headlight went out. The car stopped. Evan was laughing so hard that he was doubled up in the seat.

"Well, fuck me," Alex said dryly, "if I ever get this thing back to Raysburg, I guess I can sell it for scrap. Haw!" He looked over at Evan, who had collapsed in a heap, laughing until tears ran down his face. "Well, what's the matter with you, fuckhead? Didn't you ever see anybody screw up their car before?"

"It's just so . . . so fucking . . . ridiculous!" Evan went off again into another painful spasm of laughter.

"Fuck me, Carlyle. This just ain't been my day. Come on, grab some of that beer. Let's get in the house and get a fire going."

"Christ," Evan managed to get out, "you know what I thought . . . earlier tonight . . . when we left your house and you slid the car down the hill? I thought: 'Oh, dear God, don't let me die in West Virginia!'"

Chapter Six

Inside the farmhouse, Evan was stumbling dizzily around in the dark. He hadn't known, until he'd climbed out of the car and tried to walk, just how drunk he'd managed to get, and now he felt like a bat without its radar, as though he could easily take off and fly straight into a wall. "Jesus," he called out to Alex, who had disappeared, "it's cold in here." The big room had a slight echo.

"Got to get a fire going." Alex's voice came back from off to the left. "Whole shitload of firewood back here in the pantry." Evan walked carefully in the direction of the voice, one hand stuck out in front of him so he wouldn't bump into anything. "I stacked it up in the fall," Alex was saying. "Knew I'd be down here before the winter was out."

Turning the corner, Evan saw huge black shadows projected high onto the walls. Alex had lit a couple of kerosene lanterns. "Christ," Evan said, laughing. "Feels like we're in a horror movie." Now that they'd actually arrived, the exhaustion and gritty gloom that had been pressing on him all the way down had lifted, and he felt giddy and elated. Alex must have been feeling something of the same thing; his voice was positively cheery: "Nothing's hooked up. Don't use the crapper, huh? The cistern ain't hooked up."

Evan couldn't remember from the last time whether they'd had indoor plumbing or not. He picked up a lantern and went exploring, found the bathroom. *Yeah, they must have had it last time*; he surely would have remembered if he'd had to stumble out into the night in search of an outhouse. He set the lantern down on the floor and began to wipe snow off his boots with toilet paper. *Goddamned kid leather,* he thought. *Not meant to stand up to this kind of treatment.*

"Hey," Alex yelled, his voice echoing through the bare rooms, "don't use the crapper, huh?"

"Yeah," Evan yelled back, "I heard you."

"Hey, fuckhead, why don't you give me a hand with some of this wood?"

"Sure. Coming right up." Evan grabbed the lantern and lurched back toward the pantry; he set the light down, bent over, scooped up wood. He couldn't see what he was doing, felt as though he were diving right into the woodpile. He got a sizable stack of it in his arms, bent his knees, stood up, and heard a loud rip. He began to giggle crazily. "So much for English tailoring," he said.

"What?"

"I just ripped my goddamn jacket in half. . . . Where the hell am I going with this fucking wood?"

"Just follow me. Jesus, if I didn't know better, I'd think you'd been drinking. Here. Just throw it down here." Alex was crouched in front of the fireplace, building, with absurd speed, a small scaffolding of kindling. "Ripped your jacket, huh?"

"Yeah, ripped my fucking jacket. Jesus, Alex, you look like a demented Boy Scout."

Alex winked at him, stood up, and poured a great splash of kerosene over the entire construction. When he threw the match in, the blaze went up with a loud slam like a gigantic handclap, but the flames were easily contained inside the fireplace. "That's the ticket," Alex said, rubbing his hands together. He set the screen back in front of the fire. "Let's have another beer."

"I'm not sure there is any more."

"Oh, fuck, man, got to keep track of the beer." Alex grabbed a lantern and lurched off. Evan shoved one of the old stuffed armchairs up in front of the fire; it was getting quite warm in the room already. He shed Alex's overcoat, then his own jacket. He examined the rip. "Fuck. Goddamn these Englishmen," he said. "They make clothes so all you can do in them is sit around and look fatuous." He looked up and saw that Alex wasn't around to hear him. He fell into the chair; it smelled of old dust and mildew.

Evan sat and stared into the fire; he found, surprised at himself, that he was fondling his ripped jacket. His hand had located that familiar rectangular lump in it: his notebook. He fished it out, flipped it open, and looked at his own scrawled writing, something about MacMillan Bloedel. He didn't try to read it. He turned the pages until the writing stopped and nothing was left but blank lined paper.

An idea for a feature story seemed to be prickling away in the back of his drunken head. That Atwood business again, victims and failures; there had to be some way he could use it, tie it all into West Virginia, the oil crisis. Shit, it could be really interesting. He'd use Dana's line about the American Empire starting to crumble with the Tet offensive. Yeah, the United States sliding into second-rate status among world powers, the oil running out, the age of the automobile over. That's what Alex had been saying all along, anyway. Christ, he had it! He laughed out loud, wrote across the blank page: IF YOU CAN'T COME TO CANADA, MAYBE CANADA WILL COME TO YOU.

Evan drew a series of curlicues across the page. *Shit, Carlyle,* he thought, *you're drunk. It's not a marketable item, it's just sheer craziness.* He sat for a moment with his pen suspended in the air and looked down at what he had written. "Jesus," he said out loud. He tore the page out of the notebook, crumpled up the paper, and threw it into the fire. It burst into a small puff of flame and was gone. And a huge explosion of sound came racketing out of the kitchen: breaking dishes, falling silverware.

"Holy shit!" Alex sang out. He sounded pleased with himself. "Damn near killed myself that time." Evan laughed.

Why the hell had he never thought of it before? It was incredible that he'd never thought of it before. "Jesus Christ, Carlyle," he said to himself out loud, "you can tell Toronto to kiss your ass," and threw his pen and notebook into the fireplace.

He stood, carefully folded his suit jacket, stepped up to the fire, and flipped the jacket into the flames. The fire was momentarily smothered. Then it began to lick the edges of the material. Evan grabbed the can of kerosene, doused the jacket with it: an enormous whoosh, a roar of flame. The entire room rose for a moment up with a surge of blinding white light. "What the fuck you doing, Carlyle?" Alex yelled. "You're going to burn the fucking house down!"

Evan stepped back sheepishly, caught with the kerosene can still clutched in his hands. He could easily have ignited the can, set himself on fire. "Just fucking off," he said.

"Jesus, man, you're crazier than I am." Alex was proudly swinging a dusty demijohn over his head. "Look, Carlyle, I found it. The old lady used to make wine years ago and then hide it from the old man. Only problem was she'd forget where she put it. I knew there was still a jug of this shit stashed away out there someplace." He'd uncorked it already. He lowered the jug, offered it to Evan. "It's really beautiful wine, man. Plum. Must be the last batch she made."

Evan took the jug, laid it into the crook of his arm, index finger through the loop at the neck hillbilly style, tilted it up and drank. "Ain't that some fine shit?" Alex asked, smiling.

"Yeah, sure is. . . . Sweet, but not too sweet."

"She really could make wine. Jesus. Her daddy made it and her grandaddy too. . . . Shit, those old boys made more than wine back here in the old days." He drank again, sank down into the other chair. "Well, here we are, you dumb fuck . . . after all these years. Up yours," and passed the jug back to Evan. "If it wasn't for the kids, I'd put the whole works into bankruptcy in a minute. I'd be up there in Canada scratching on your fucking door like an old dog: 'Hey, Carlyle, let me in!' " He laughed. "But shit. Kids. I don't know."

"Not working out with Sharon, eh?"

"Did for a while. First couple years I was just like a cat in the cream dish. Didn't even mind her pushing me . . . wanted her to, as a matter of fact. Thought, 'Christ, Warner, without some woman on your ass, you'd never amount to a tinker's damn.' And by God, she pushed me too."

"Yeah," Evan said, "when I got together with my first wife—" He stopped, hearing what he'd just said. *Jesus,* he thought, *if Dana were here to hear that, she'd hit me with something.* "With my *ex*-wife," he said, correcting himself, "when we first got together, it was like living in a wet dream. Jesus, I don't remember us doing anything but screwing for six months. I know we had to do something else, I mean we had to eat. I was working. But I don't remember anything at all except just us in bed. And then a couple years later I was looking at her across the room and thinking, 'Who the hell is this? She hasn't got a brain in her head. She bores me silly.' "

"Sheri's never *boring,*" Alex said. "Might be better if she was. She just chews at me, that's what she does. She just fucking chews at me all the time."

"Yeah," Evan said. The drive was over and his nerves were relaxing. Beer, warm fire, plum wine; he was mellowing out. For the first time since he'd come back to Raysburg, he felt like he'd come home. It really was good to see Alex again, seemed ridiculous now that he'd avoided him for thirteen years, that all the times before when he'd been in town, he'd stayed hidden away in his parents' apartment, that he hadn't even gone out to a bar for fear of running into him. *He remembers the last time all right,* Evan thought, *but it doesn't matter. Either he's forgiven me for it years ago, or it just never mattered as much to him as I thought it did. And I don't even care now if he did screw Elaine. Why the hell shouldn't he have? He stayed and I didn't.* "Yeah," he said again.

The fire had burned the last chill out of the room; Evan was comfortable in his shirt-sleeves. There was something about being out here at the farm, drunk, in the snowy night that felt good to him. He wouldn't even mind talking about Elaine now; he wanted to talk about her. "You said Elaine's dad was dead, didn't you?" he said, approaching sideways.

"Big John? Yeah, been dead for years."

"What did he die of?"

Alex stared into the fire a long time before answering. Then he said, "I figured you'd heard about it."

"Heard about it? Where would I have heard about it?"

"It was in the papers. Thought maybe your folks would have sent you a clipping or something."

"Oh, hell, no. You know how my mother felt about Elaine. She hasn't even mentioned the Isaacs in years."

Alex turned back to the fire; he drank from the wine jug, wiped the back of his mouth, frowned. But then, surprisingly, he looked directly at Evan, grinned, and said in his best storyteller's voice: "Heart attack . . . Must have been eight or nine years now because it was just after Sheri and me was married. He was coming down Chicken Neck Hill and some damn fool teen-ager clipped the back of his car. And you remember how fat old John was?"

"Oh, yeah. He was enormous."

"Well, he got even bigger, right? I mean he had to kind of fight to get in and out from behind the steering wheel. And he come down off the hill and this kid clipped him, and you remember what a temper he had? Well, he was yelling like a fucking madman and struggling to get his belly out from behind the steering wheel and he just fell out on the road. And when they got to him, he was dead as a post."

"How about her mother?"

"Moved back downstate. Some little town down there. Her people was from down there."

"Yeah? . . . And what about Elaine? What's she doing?"

"Oh, still working over at the R.G.H."

"You see her?"

"Yeah, have a beer with her every now and then."

"Is she happy?"

"Hell, I don't know, Carlyle. What do you say to something like that? . . . She looks damn fine, I know that. Hasn't let herself go to pot like some of the other girls in our class. Jesus, Carlyle, you really ought to see Susie . . . Shit, I almost said Susie Galloway, but she's Susie Gannister now. She must weigh two hundred pounds."

"But Elaine still looks good?"

"Shit, she can't be a pound heavier than when we graduated. She's probably lighter. Really kept her figure, she don't show her age at all. She could be twenty-five. Wears her hair real long now, halfway down her back. Still black . . . black as coal."

Evan felt an unpleasant twinge in his chest. "She seeing anyone?"

"Yeah, there's a fellow she sees. Works at the bank down on the corner of Twelfth and Main. Looks a little like her husband used to . . . another one of these suit-and-tie assholes. Nice enough guy, I guess, but I never took to him . . . too much like Jamieson. Seems to be good for her, though. He's really young. He's even younger than Sheri. I think he's twenty-four, twenty-five, something like that."

"She going to marry him?"

"If she is, she hasn't told me about it."

"Shit, I always thought she should get out and try to do something with her acting. I never really thought she'd do it, but I always wanted her to."

Alex wasn't looking at Evan at all now, was staring again into the fire. "Of course she should have. I guess she took some classes in it out at Raysburg College, but then . . . Well, that fucking Bill Jamieson come along, and she married him. I come back to Raysburg on leave and there she was married. 'What the hell'd you do that for, Elly?' I said. 'I don't know, Al,' she said, 'just seemed like the thing to do at the time.' Jesus, was he worthless! Bill Jamieson. What a goddamned piece of shit he turned out to be. When she got sick of keeping him, he just took off, left his goddamned kid behind. She don't even know where he is to this day."

"When was that? When'd he leave?"

"Oh fuck, I don't remember. A few years ago. So I said to her, 'What are you going to do?' and she said, 'Well, Al, it's not a big deal. I'm glad the son of a bitch left, don't think I could of stood much more of him. Well, I've got a profession.' And she's been working at the hospital ever since." He glanced at Evan, then away. "I keep her car running," he said. "Never charge her for labor, just for parts, but I always write the bill up so she don't notice, right? They don't pay them nurses for shit."

"What the hell was her husband like anyway?"

"Oh, shit, Carlyle, he was an asshole. A real smoothie, con man, good talker, life-of-the-party type, right? Always out for the fucking good time. Hard not to like the son of a bitch, had more jokes than some fucker on television. Could have been a damn fine salesman if he stuck with it. Well, I tried to like him when I first met him, but after a while I got to really hate his guts. Came really close to punching him out once."

"Christ, how'd you come to do that?"

"I don't really want to go into it, all right? It was just stupid. I'd had way too much to drink and I was feeling mean." Alex took a long drink from the wine jug.

"I didn't mean to stop the conversation," Evan said.

"Yeah, I know. But there's some things you'd just as leave forget. Shit, I'm just glad Pilsudski come in that bar that night and was there to talk some sense into me because I think I would of killed that son of a bitch."

"Christ, man, you've got to tell me now!" Evan said, laughing.

Alex didn't laugh. "No, I don't. I said too fucking much already." He turned and passed the jug to Evan. "Have a drink," he said. "I've been nursing this goddamned thing like a baby." Evan took the jug. "There is something I will tell you though." Alex smiled slightly. "Something I bet you don't know. Shit, after all this time, it can't hurt to tell you."

Oh yeah! Evan thought, his skin prickling. *Are we that drunk?* "What's that?" he said.

"Elaine run me from Harrod to Carreysburg once."

Evan stopped with the jug halfway to his mouth. He wouldn't have been any more surprised if Alex had just told him that all during the war he'd been a secret agent for Ho Chi Minh. "In cars?"

Alex was grinning now. "She told me: 'Don't say a word to Evan, or he'll shit a brick.' So I never did. But fuck, it couldn't matter that much anymore whether I tell you or not, right? Jesus, Carlyle, did we have a run! It was incredible."

"Christ, man, when the hell was that?"

"The summer right after we graduated from high school. She come in the garage in her old man's clunker Dodge and said, 'Hey, Al, I want to run you.' I thought she was kidding, right? I said, 'Sure, Elly, where?' And she said, 'Harrod to Carreysburg,' and the minute she said that, I knew she meant it."

"Jesus Christ!"

"I told her, 'Fuck, in that old Dodge, you'd be killing yourself. Tires bald as Eisenhower. The transmission's shot. Nothing left to the brakes. You're out of your fucking mind.' She said, 'The car doesn't matter. It's *me* that matters.' I said, 'Elly, you've got that wrong. You're talking about something that I know about, so I'm going to tell you. You get the car right. You get it as right as you can possibly get it. And *then* you're what matters.' She looked at me, and I saw that she was really disappointed. So I said—shit, don't know to this day why I did it—I said, 'You leave that car in here a week and I'll have it running like a clock, and then we'll talk about racing somewhere.'

"That fucker hadn't had that much work done on it since it left the factory. I put a whole new set of tires on her, new brake linings, tuned the son of a bitch up ... set her up for racing, not for the street, right? I mean I worked on that old Dodge like it was going to Daytona.

"So I went across the restaurant and said, 'It's ready, now where do you want to do it?' And she said again, 'Harrod to Carreysburg,' and I said, 'All right.' "

"Jesus, Alex! I *never* would have thought you would have raced a girl."

"Oh, it wasn't that. Shit, she could drive, couldn't she? It was just that fucking stretch of road she wanted to do it over. Well, you just seen it again. Suicide Road. I knew I could stay on that road, but I didn't know whether or not she could. But she said to me: 'Al, I grew up in Carreysburg same as you grew up back of Harrod. We both know that road,' and I believed her.

"Well, fuck, man, we took off just after noon and drifted on down to Harrod just as slow and easy as you please. Got there about three, had lunch at Froelich's. And I said, 'Look, we'll start just outside of town, and the first one into that parking lot at the Baptist Church outside of Carreysburg, that's the winner.' ... You know that big lot they've got there, right? Could turn a tank around in it, and I figured we might need us some room to stop. .... So my Chevy was a fuck of a lot hotter than that old Dodge, that's for damned sure. Had a blower in it, you remember, so I got out a fuck of a lot quicker than she did, and started up into the hills doing way over a hundred. But on the curves it don't matter much how hot your car is, the main thing is if you got good tires and good brakes and can keep her on the road, right? So I come into them curves about a mile ahead of her, but damn if she wasn't on my ass by the time we come off

Round Bottom Hill. God, she must of been scrambling! I'd expected her to catch me, but I figured it'd take her damn near to Carreysburg to do it. Then I'd just burn her to death on the straightaway and get enough lead so she'd never catch me until we was almost out the other side, and then on that last straightaway I'd burn her to death again. That's the way I'd figured it, but it didn't work like that.

"We was scrambling over them fucking roads like you wouldn't believe it, Carlyle. I'd power-slide her on a blind curve just hoping that if some poor farmer was on the other side, he'd hear me, right? And get out of the way if he could. And I'd look back in my mirror, and damned if she wasn't doing the same thing I'd just done. She was smart, fantastic how smart she was. I was a better driver, but she had me going ahead of her, and everything I did, she done the same damn thing right behind me. I don't know how the fuck she could think that fast. Some of the damn finest driving I'd ever done in my life, and swear to God she was right with me the whole way. And we come down onto that last straightaway, and I thought: 'Okay, Elly, we've had our run and it's just been incredible, but here's where auto mechanics is going to enter the picture. As soon as I kick her down with that blower under the hood, it's going to be bye-bye, kid.' But damned if she doesn't pull out into the left lane just like she's going to *pass* me. I couldn't believe it. She's right on my fucking ass, and that poor old Dodge was screaming like a yellow bitch. So I was just going to stomp it down and leave her. Except that there was this goddamned blue Nash sitting right smack in the middle of the road. Some poor fool had taken it in his head to make a U-turn right that minute, and he was taking his time with it. Like maybe in about fifteen years he'd get the car turned around and head back up the way we was coming.

"Well, the fucker's blocking the whole road, right? But most of him is in my lane. And damn, Elly's not going to give me any room to get out left. I mean, if I'd tried it, I would of had to hit her, that's all. And she's still got that Dodge to the floor. I mean she just didn't let up a fucking inch. . . . Jesus, Carlyle, it was happening so fucking fast, but somehow it felt like we had all the time in the world. Nothing for me to do but start braking her down and hang on. And Elly goes by me on the left, and shit . . . we even had time to look at each other. She's fucking laughing at me. And that poor fucker in the Nash don't know whether to shit or go blind because here come these two damn fools in both lanes straight at him, so naturally what he does is nothing. He just comes to a dead stop. And it's a damned good thing he did too, because Elly goes right in front of his nose, swear to God she missed him by inches, and she's gone.

"And I'm still going too fucking fast to stop. I'm braking, easy, you know, so I don't spin her out, but I'm still way over eighty. And . . . shit, it's amazing how fast you've got to decide. See, if he sits there, I can go right by him on the left, just in front of his nose the way Elly did. But if all of a sudden he takes it into his head that it's time to move and I'm trying to go around, then it's all she wrote, Al Warner home in a garbage pail. But if he *doesn't* move, if he just sits there like he's been doing and I try for the right, I'm either going to take him out like a bowling ball or I'm going off the road.

"Well, I figured he was going to jump. Shit, it was like I could read his mind or something. I could almost hear him thinking: 'Christ, I've got to get out of here!' So I made for the right. And to this day I don't know how I knew he was going to do it, but he did it. He jumped like a rabbit, and I shot right behind his ass. It was some of that miracle driving you hear about, you know? And as soon as I got by him, I stomped her down, got her up to a hundred and thirty, but I'd lost too much time and Elaine was long gone.

"I almost caught her. I was in that parking lot less than a car length behind her, swear to God. And I jumped out and yelled at her, 'Elly, that fucking Nash hadn't been on the road, I would of whipped your ass.' And she just sits there and laughs at me. Shit, I didn't think she was ever going to stop laughing." Alex was grinning ear to ear. " 'But it *was* on the road, Al,' she says."

Evan was so stunned, he couldn't find a single word. All he

could think about was the absolute certainty in his mind that the next thing that must have happened was that Alex and Elaine would have searched out the nearest dirt road up some cornfield, parked their cars out in the middle of nowhere, and worked off all that high-power fever pitch they'd just cranked up on the highway with a good quick fuck in the backseat of Alex's Chevy. "Christ," he said finally, "that's some story."

"It was the only time," Alex said. "She never wanted to do it again. She said, 'I just had to do it once, Al . . . just to prove I could.' Shit, but that was an amazing run. She was good. I mean she was damned fucking good."

"How good?"

"Damned near as good as Frank."

"As good as you?"

"Shit, Carlyle," Alex said, laughing, "nobody was as good as me."

Evan stared miserably at the fire. "Hey, Al . . . you know that last run?"

"Forget it, man," Alex said, shrugging and turning away. "I never held it against you."

Four

Chapter One

Evan woke and didn't know where he was. Then the size and heat and sound of the day moved in on him, and he knew. He turned onto his back and kicked off the single sheet; he was sweating. He lay with his eyes closed and listened to the drone of the locusts, that old melancholy hum. A hundred times he'd driven south with Alex on the river road, sometimes all the way to Harrod, but this was the first time he'd been this far south. If he'd conned and cheated his way out of Raysburg High, if he felt like a phony to himself, well at least Alex didn't know it. Alex obviously liked him. He'd asked him down to the farm.

He opened his eyes to the dazzle of sunlight. He reached out, pulled his watch from one of his loafers where he'd put it for safekeeping, and found that it was nine thirty in the morning.

He sat up. The windows were open but the curtains were drawn. The wind blowing through the screens was hot; it made the translucent white curtains swing gently in the bright sunlight. He couldn't remember the last time he'd slept as soundly. He looked over at the other twin bed. It was empty; Alex must already be up. Then he realized that he had been hearing the voices from the kitchen and the bangs and rattles of cooking. He smelled the food: meat, hot grease. He found himself strangely reluctant to go out and face the day, lit a cigarette instead, and looked around the room that Alex had shared with his brother, Bob, years before.

Faded wallpaper was flaking off the walls, a pattern of dogs and shotguns. Two small bookcases were stacked with magazines and old schoolbooks. Ribbons were pinned on the wall by the door, as was a large framed photograph. He climbed out of bed and wandered around to look. The magazines were old *Strength & Healths* with pictures of enormous muscular men. Standing in the corner was an Enfield rifle. The ribbons on the wall were athletic awards. On the dresser were a bowie knife, a World War II bayonet, a wrecked model airplane, and cups and trophies won in football, wrestling, and track. The largest trophy—it must have been a foot high—a runner caught in midstride atop something that looked like an ornate funeral urn, was engraved:

CANDEN INVITATIONAL TRACK MEET—1960

ALEX WARNER

First Place Mile Run, Meet and Regional Record
4:29.5

The framed glossy photograph was of Alex, as lean as Evan remembered him having ever been. Alex was walking, or rather lurching toward the camera; he appeared ready to fall. But another boy—Evan recognized Johnny Pilsudski, the sprinter— had stepped forward to catch him. Alex was sliding one arm around Pilsudski's shoulders; Pilsudski was grinning wildly. If the picture had been extended to the right about ten feet, Evan would have been there too in his manager's sweat shirt screaming right along with everybody else, with the other runners, the ones from other schools as well as their own, with the people in the bleachers who'd risen to their feet. And Alex was looking up, high to the right of the camera; his lips were drawn back like a snarling dog's (Evan could see the teeth quite clearly); his face was twisted with what could have either been intense pain or rapture; and his eyes—the flashbulb must have done it—gleamed strangely, like polished stones. Someone, probably the photographer from the *Times* who'd taken the picture, had written in ink at the bottom: BEST OF LUCK WITH YOUR RUNNING, SEE YOU IN THE OLYMPICS.

Evan butted his cigarette in the saucer on the floor, pulled on his socks, shorts, and pants. He had to piss, but he was still hesitant to walk out into the kitchen. He sat on the edge of the bed, worked his feet into his loafers. He wanted to taste the day, savor it slowly, to soak it up so he could remember it. He might never be down on the farm again with Alex; once he left next month for Columbus, he might never be in West Virginia again. Well, of course he'd come back to visit, but he knew he'd never live in West Virginia again.

He lit another cigarette and looked across the bedroom at the shining gold trophy and the photograph of Alex. *A fine way to end high school*, he thought, *with a trophy, a record, and even a picture of the event.* Some other hot-shot kid would come along and break that mile record, but it would always be on the books; it'd be there forever, nothing could erase it, and Alex would have it in his memory forever. But what the hell did *he* have? His picture in the year book with an entry that read: "Keep smiling, Evan!" A letter in track with an M for manager marked on it. Grades that weren't quite high enough for a B and not quite low enough for a C, just barely enough to get him into Ohio State. It was all just empty crap. He'd barely got his ass out, and nobody was going to give him a trophy for that.

He was going to make love to Elaine, that's what he was going to do. He'd be damned if he was going to leave West Virginia in September still a virgin. They'd come so close so many times, all it would take would be one final push, and they'd be over the edge. Christ, if you've played with a girl's breasts, if you'd had your finger in her pussy, if you've come all over her legs, if you've come in her hand, why draw the line?

But Elaine did draw the line, no doubt about it. It didn't make any sense. Her parents thought they were screwing, his parents thought they were screwing, Alex thought they were screwing, everybody in their whole class thought they were screwing, so why the hell shouldn't they be screwing? *It'd probably even be good for her,* he thought. She couldn't very well go off to be an actress in Hollywood or New York and still be just as much of a virgin as Susie Galloway, and he didn't want to go on pretending to every guy he ever met that he'd been laid when he damn well hadn't been.

He stood up, yawned, and stretched. He felt great. If he stayed down here over a week, he was sure that Elaine would really be missing him. Yeah, she'd be really glad to see him. It wouldn't be exactly easy, but he was sure he could talk her into it. He stretched all the way up until he touched the ceiling, heard his elbows pop; he wandered out of the bedroom and down the hall to the bathroom. It felt wonderful to stand in the country heat letting the piss flow out of him, feeling the big day all around him and the ease of his body after a good night's sleep. The smell of food had made him hungry as a hound.

In the kitchen Alex was working on a plate of fried eggs, fried potatoes, and pork chops. Mrs. Warner, a great round column of a woman whose breasts seemed a single swelling ledge under her dress, greeted him with: "Well, hello there, son. I'm Alex's mother as you probably could have guessed for yourself. Yes. Well, sit yourself down and we'll see what we can do for you. This restaurant ain't much for service, but the food's always good. Well, sit down, sit down now. I hope you like to eat, son. Yes. Well, now, what did you say your name was?"

"Evan Carlyle."

"Well, Evan Carlyle, how do you like your eggs?"

"Anyway's fine. Scrambled?"

"Scrambled it is. Did you sleep well? Yes, I suppose you did. Everybody does down here. It's the air. I've been telling Allie for years that he ought to come back down here and stay with us for a while. It would do him a world of good. Yes. But Allie, he was always one for pottering around with cars. I suppose you know that. He always loved taking things apart. Yes. And putting them back together too. Now Bob, he just took them apart. Haw, haw. And left them that way, you know? Have you been down this way before?"

"No, I haven't."

"Well, I hope you'll come back and see us again. And what do you do with yourself?"

Evan looked up. Her eyes, pale as her son's but sharp and inquisitive, peered out at him from a great round, fleshy face. "I'm going to school in the fall," he said. "Ohio State."

"Well, good for you. That's what it takes to get ahead in the world these days. That's what I've always told Allie. I've always told him that he shouldn't spend all of his time pottering around with cars. School, yes. That's what it takes. Well, maybe he's going too. Wouldn't surprise me a bit if he did it, went on down there to the university. That'd just be the thing for you, Allie, I'm sure it would. School's what you need. Times are changing, the Lord preserve us. My other boy's in the marines, you probably know that. I never thought he'd amount to a tinker's damn anyway, haw haw. No, he was a good boy. But it just goes to show you. Two chops or three?"

"Two's enough."

"Are you sure now?"

"Yes. Two's enough."

"Maw," Alex said, "the cows have been in the onions again."

Mrs. Warner sighed and continued more slowly. "I know, son. They do that. They just go right through the fence where it's broke down. I've told your father about it a hundred times. I might as well have saved my breath for all the good it's done me. But that's another story. Well, son," she said, dropping one of her large red hands onto Alex's shoulder, "it's a great life if you don't weaken."

Chapter Two

Alex squatted on his heels at the top of the hill and squinted against the sun. Evan had never felt comfortable hunkered down like a garage mechanic; whenever he tried it, his legs cramped, but Alex seemed to be able to rest that way indefinitely. Evan had fallen right down on the grass on his butt and had drawn his knees up. But Alex remained balanced there, squatting. "You can see the property line," he said, pointing to the left. "That's the Froelich place on the other side of the fence. Then our property goes all the way around here"—he swept his arm in an arc—"and over to there. . . . See that road? That's the run that goes back up the hollow."

Evan couldn't see the property line at all, except where it was obvious, along the edge of the fence. The Warner farm rose and fell over these hills like a staircase; from up here it looked like a crazy quilt. The house was directly below them. Evan could see Alex's father sitting on the rocker on the porch. "Hey," Evan said, "your old man didn't have much to say."

"Oh," Alex said, smiling slightly, "he's got his moments."

After breakfast Evan had met Mr. Warner, six feet of gnarled veins and dark-colored lumps like an old twisted tree. The old man—he was much older than Evan had expected—had stood up politely, taken Evan's hand, avoided his eyes, and spat a thin stream of tobacco accurately over the porch rail. "Howdy," was all he'd said.

"Shit, from the way you talked about him," Evan said, "I expected . . . I don't know what. A fucking madman, I guess."

"Like I said, he's got his moments. Right after school was

out, Frank come down here looking for me. See, I'd told everybody I was coming down to the farm for a few days, but where I was"—he grinned—"was over in Harrod visiting a young lady." Evan was surprised. That was the first he'd heard of any young lady over at Harrod. "Well, so Frank come down, right," Alex said. "He'd been drinking and it just seemed like a good idea. Give him a chance to wind out his Chevy. And so he got in around eleven at night, walked up on the porch, and banged on the door. And the next thing he knows he's looking down the barrel of a Colt Thirty-eight Police Positive Special . . . jammed right up in his face, he said it was. And then my old man looks out and sees who it is and says, 'Oh . . . sorry, son. I thought you was Alex.'" He rocked back on his heels and laughed.

Evan laughed uneasily. "Shit," he said, "what was he going to do?"

"What do you think? Goddamn, he done his best to kill me for years. Shit, he probably still thinks about it. . . . And of course if you're going to get here at eleven at night, he's going to be pretty well plastered. . . . But he's calmed down considerable in the last few years. Now he just drinks at home, but back then . . . Well, Christ, Carlyle, you've got no idea what it was like growing up here. Some mornings I'd get up, and he'd be laid out right there on the road," he pointed, "because he hadn't been able to make it up to the house. The dogs loved it when he done that. They'd go down and sleep with him. You'd look out and there he'd be sleeping it off with five dogs." Alex's lips drew back a moment into that toothy grimace. He worked a cigar out of his jeans. It was broken in the middle. He frowned at it, tore off the broken end, and lit the remainder.

"See the run there?" Alex said. "Shit, we could drive up there right this afternoon, and if we went slow and careful, we might even get back out alive. And if we went up to the right place, we could buy ourselves a gallon of moon that would fucking well knock the back of your head right off. . . . But if we went up there at night, shit, we'd be committing suicide. Fuck man, tonight, I'll tell you what we'll do. We'll go down to the foot of the run and fire off a shot with my old Enfield. Just one shot, right? And then we'll just sit down there at the bottom for the next two hours and watch the fireworks. Them crazy fucking fools will be shooting at each other for hours. . . ."

"Come on, Alex, you're bullshitting me."

"No, man, I'm not. I'm dead serious. See, the folks that live up the hollow, what they do at night is they take *sound shots*. . . . Now you know what a sound shot is? Well, I'll tell you. You're sitting out on your porch and you hear a sound, so you shoot at it. Now why do you suppose they're doing that? Well, I'll tell you. If it's an animal moving around out there, you want to kill it. That only stands to reason, right? And if it's some *person* coming up the road, you want to shoot him because you know he's up to no good. If he was a friend of yours, he'd be singing out the whole way, 'Hey, Jake, it's me . . . Hey, it's me, coming to see you.' Now, if it's one of your neighbor's dogs, then he's got no business on your property. And if it's one of your *own* dogs and he hasn't got the common sense to hang right around the house after dark, then you better get him now before he gets any older and gets into trouble." Alex nodded to Evan and laughed.

"Christ, man, it sounds like a movie."

"Well, it ain't no movie down here, and that's for damned sure."

Evan wanted Alex to go on talking, but he couldn't think of anything to say to encourage him. The heat was terrific; Evan was already sweating in torrents, and it wasn't even noon yet. His breakfast lay heavy as cement in his stomach; he didn't want to move, didn't want to do anything. He could lie down in the grass and go to sleep. Alex rolled his cigar around in his mouth and stared off into the distance. "See him up there," he said.

"What?"

"Right *there*, fuckhead."

Evan saw a black speck in the distant sky, small as a gnat. "Yeah," he said.

"Hawk," Alex said.

Evan followed the bird until the glare of the sky made his eyes water. He couldn't fight it any longer. He let his eyes fall shut.

Chapter Three

"Started running down here," Alex said, but then he saw that Carlyle was sound asleep. Alex laughed. *Not used to a country breakfast*, he thought.

From up on the hill Alex could see the whole three-mile path he used to run over to the Froelich place. He'd been really proud of himself the first time he'd made it the whole way without stopping; he must have been ten or eleven then. And later on when he got bigger, he'd taken to running into Harrod, not the whole way, but running and hitchhiking. A few times when there hadn't been a car on the road, he had covered it all on foot, and he'd been pissed off at himself for having to stop and walk so much, for letting it get him so tired that he couldn't do a thing for days afterward but crawl around the farm like a cripple. *Didn't know a damned thing about track then*, he thought. *Didn't know what I was asking myself to do. Shit. Twenty miles.*

But talk about a bottom, he sure had one built by the time he went up to Raysburg High, and he didn't even know it. First day out at practice, nobody in shape yet, and Rurak called for a tryout for the mile. Alex thought he'd do all right, but he didn't expect what happened: he beat everybody on the field. The first time in his life anybody'd had a watch on him, and he did a 5:06. Rurak took him aside and said, "If you really train hard,

kid, you'll break the Valley record by the time you're a senior."
But Alex broke it his junior year, and broke it again this past
year, and he still had it. He'd never understood why he'd
worked at it so hard; being a runner was something he'd never
really planned on.

He turned on his heels and looked up the run toward where
his grandfather's place used to be. He wished the old man had
been alive to see him break that first record. He remembered the
sick feeling it'd given him when his mother had come back from
visiting with him and said, "Your granddaddy wants to see you.
And if I was you, Allie, I'd be going right up because he don't
look to me like he'll last out the week." So Alex had slogged on
up in the spring mud.

The old man had got real sick that winter, but he wouldn't
hear any talk about going to the hospital; shit, he wouldn't even
move down to the house. He just sat it out up there all by
himself, and by the time Alex went up to see him, he was pretty
much wasted away, must have lost forty or fifty pounds. Alex
found him on the front porch wrapped up in a couple of quilts,
and the first thing he thought was: *Well, he won't be toting no
more bags of sugar.* He'd always been old as long as Alex could
remember, but before it'd never been a kind of old to be afraid
of. Now he really looked old. Alex was sorry he hadn't been to
see him sooner. "Set down here, Alex Warner, I want to talk to
you."

Alex couldn't figure out what it was the old man wanted to
say to him. He was talking about some war. He'd been around
for so many of them, and they'd got so mixed up in his mind,
that Alex couldn't tell which one they were fighting at the moment, whether it was the one with Spain or maybe the first one
with the Germans, but he kept hearing the name of Billy Morgan so he figured out that his grandfather must be all the way
back to the War Between the States. "Listen to me now. Uncle
Jake Warner, he held with the Union, so he went up there to
Blantons Ferry and enlisted in the Ohio National Guard, but
Uncle Fred Warner, he held with the Confederacy, so he rode

with Billy Morgan. But my pappy, that's your great-grandpappy —boy, are you listening?"

"Yeah, I'm listening."

"Well, my pappy said it was none of our business, so he stayed home. . . . All right? So Uncle Fred, he got hisself shot dead by a Yankee, and Uncle Jake, he lost a leg and was never right after that and died a couple years later. But my pappy, he lived to be ninety-seven years old and was just as spry as you please right up to the day he died. He was setting out on the porch one day and he said to me, 'Well, I think I'm goina die now,' and I said, 'Oh no, you're not,' and he said, 'When your time's up, your time's up, and I done run mine out.' And he said to me, 'Son, you hang on to the land because the Warners done lived here forever,' and he went in the shack and laid down with his face to the wall and he died right then and there. Do you understand what I'm telling you, boy?"

"I don't know. Tell me more."

"All right then, listen. When I was a little bitty boy, we had a big picnic and all our people come. They come from miles around. And I remember my great-grandmaw. Sweetest little lady you could ever imagine, had snow-white hair hung all the way to her waist and she wore it all wrapped up on the back of her head. And they put her out in the sun, you know, in her rocking chair, and she set there and smoked her pipe. And I couldn't of been older than five or six I reckon, and I come up the way little kids will, asking questions, always wanting to know the whys and the wherefores, and I asked her, 'How long you been here, Grandmaw Warner?' and she kind of laughed and said, 'Oh, I been here close to a hundred years now.' And I said, 'But how long have *we* been here?' and she said to me, 'Listen, boy. When I was a little bitty girl, I remember my great-grandmaw, and she'd lived here all her life. And she didn't come from nowhere. And her people didn't come from no-where. So I reckon we been here forever.' . . . Are you getting what I'm trying to tell you, boy?"

"Yeah, I think I'm getting it."

"Well now, I've been watching you grow, and I've got you figured for one of the straight Warners, so don't you go proving me wrong now. You see, what I done is, back last fall I went up there to Carreysburg and had it put in writing. And I done passed over your father and your brother, Bob, and all what I own around here is going to you. And when your old folks die, more than likely there's goina be another chunk of it coming to you, and boy, I want you to keep it. What do you say to that?"

"I don't know, Grandpaw. . . . Sure, I'll keep it, but what about Bob? He ain't goina be—"

"Don't you pay no attention to Bob. He's not goina live long. Now you go in the shack there and fetch me a drink. And you've got to listen to me real careful because I'm fixing to die later on today."

Alex brings the old man a Mason jar of his own white corn liquor, and a cup, and pours it for him. The old man sips a bit and then lays back in the chair. The skin on his face is hanging down in big folds, like on a dog's neck, from the way he lost so much weight over the winter, but his eyes are still clear, that pale yellow-brown just like all the Warners. "Listen to me. This here's ours, and we got to keep it. That's number one. You know they call it God's country out here and that's because you can do what you damned well please, and only God's goina care."

He takes a sip. He's looking out into the trees. "Some people hold to the notion that his name's Jesus Christ, but I ain't so sure." Then he turns his eyes back to Alex. "But that ain't neither here nor there. Number two is this, boy, and you listen just as hard as you can. I know you're only fourteen years old, but I want you to remember what I tell you to your own dying day. Now if somebody does wrong to you or your people, you remember, and you get 'em, even if it takes you years. Even if you got to wait fifteen, twenty—shit, boy, fifty years—you get 'em in the end, right? But on the other hand, if somebody does good to you or your people, you remember that too. Be they man, woman, or child, if they done good to you, you never forget, and when they come to you in need, you give to them, right down to takin' the shirt off your back and handing it over. ... Now I want you to go on back down to the house and don't say nothing to nobody, but you fetch your daddy back up here around suppertime and then you can tote me down. Get that preacher at the Baptist church, not the new fellow but the old one—you know the one I mean. Get him to say a few words. Don't matter much what they are. And then there's about fifty gallons of corn liquor up the hollow. You know where it is, don't you, boy?"

"Yeah, I know."

"Well, I'd appreciate it if that liquor was brung down so when our people come, they could all have a drink of it and say, 'Yeah, the old man sure made good whiskey.'"

"And he never paid no whiskey tax," Alex says, smiling.

"Yeah. Haw! That's right, boy."

Alex doesn't know how to say good-bye. He stands up. It seems like there's something he should do, but he doesn't know what. Finally he holds out his hand. The old man takes it, and they shake. "I ain't never goina forget you," Alex says. The old man just looks away at the sunlight, and Alex walks back down the hill.

And it was just like his grandfather had said; when they came back up, he was dead as a post. "Don't that beat all?" Alex's father said, and they tied him to the cooling board and toted him down the hill. "It runs in your family," Alex's mother told him. "All the Warners seem to know when their time's run out," and Doctor Steinrod said it was a mercy because with all that cancer through his belly like that the old man must have been in terrible pain, and if he'd hung on for another few months, he would have had to go up to the hospital at Raysburg, and everybody knew how the old man said he'd never die in a hospital. Alex never told anybody about the empty bottle of rat poison he found in the back of the shack.

The sun was beating down like a forty-pound sledge, and

Carlyle was sound asleep, lying on his back with his arm over his eyes, snoring. Alex looked down the lumpy hills, then back up the hollow. *What the hell does it mean to own something anyway? How could you own something like this?* And the thing he remembered the clearest about the funeral was all the cars and trucks winding along the mountain road to the cemetery. There were Fords and Chevys and Packards and every damned kind of car, there were pickup trucks, there were cars so old, they could have had antique plates on them, and they came for miles, one after another along that twisty road. Alex looked back and saw them like that, moving slow, at fifteen miles an hour, taking the old man to bury him with the Warners. And all their people came, not just the Warners but the Scotts and the Oreys and the Shins and the McAlisters. And all the neighbors, the Froelichs and the Yohos and the Calendenes and the Smiths. Seemed like hundreds of cars with their headlights on in the middle of the day, spring sunshine falling down on them, easing along that narrow road, all in a row like that.

Back at the house, they drank and told stories about him. They asked Uncle Gladney to tell about the time the old man had to go to court, and Gladney, who was a shy man, looked at the wall and drank, and told it in a voice so quiet they had to strain to hear him. "Yeah, it was back in the thirties and them banks were foreclosing right and left, so the old man, he went up to Raysburg and borrowed some money from one of them loan shark fellows that was tied up with Joe Patone, you know, and he come back down and paid off the bank and kept his land, but he never paid back that debt. So Joe Patone, he said, 'Now, we can't have them hillbillies thinking they can get away with shit like that. We got to make an example of him,' so he sent up to New York City for a couple hired killers. And they come down to Harrod and started in to asking around where they might find old man Warner, so of course he heard of it. Well, one night they come up to the shack and knocked on the door. His wife opened it and stepped back out of the way, and he shot them both dead before they could bat an eyelash, so they arrested him and took him to court up to Carreysburg.

"Well, the prosecuting attorney, he argued it for two days. He said it was cold-blooded murder. And then the defense attorney, that was old T. R. Johnson from Harrod, he got up and called the police to the stand and had them testify about the records them dead men had, about how they'd committed this crime here and that crime there and done time for it. And then he called the old man to the stand and had him tell just what he done. He said, 'I heard them killers was coming for me, and when they come, I just took my gun and cleaned that trash from outen my doorway.' And then old Johnson he leaned up against the jury box and he said, 'Now don't we have the right to protect our own?' Whole thing took no more than an hour, and the jury was out deliberating no more than ten minutes, and they done found the old man innocent by reason of self-defense."

People laughing at that story and other stories and drinking the old man's liquor. Alex walks out onto the porch. It's a cold, clear night, must have been March or early in April, and his father follows him out and says, drunk, "Boy, what the hell you think you're goina do with all that land?"

"Keep it."

"Do you think that's fair and proper with your brother Robert not owning a pot to piss in?"

"Paw, I don't give a shit."

"Jesus, boy, do you know who you're talking to?"

They stand and look at each other with the light from the house on the sides of their faces. Alex knows that his father hasn't got it anymore, that he could take him right then and there. He knows the bastard knows it too. His father spits a stream of tobacco over the railing and says, "I should of pinched your head off the day you was born."

Chapter Four

It was the same spring Alex finished up the eighth grade at Carreysburg when the old man died, and his dying changed everything. Even when he'd stopped coming down the run so nobody had to see him unless they wanted to walk up there, he'd still been old man Warner, and what he'd had to say always counted for something. Now Alex's father should have been the one to have the say, but nobody paid the least bit of attention to him, and it made him drink more than ever. And the fact that the old man had left the land to Alex didn't help.

Alex was beginning to get his full growth, and while he wasn't quite ready to take on his brother in a straight-out fight, he was big enough to discourage him most of the time, and when that didn't work, he could always outrun him. But that summer he mostly stayed away from home, spent a lot of time in Harrod seeing one particular young lady from his class at school. And then in July, the best he remembered it, on a hot Saturday his father had butchered a hog, and his mother had said to him, "Now you be home for dinner, Allie, and I mean it." When she said, "I mean it," she meant it, so he started running and hitchhiking back to the farm about two in the afternoon. He got there in one ride because Stacey Yoho picked him up and brought him right to the end of the road.

The minute Alex got out of the truck, he could hear Bob and his old man yelling at each other. *There they are*, he thought, *both of them drunk as skunks again, and the sun not even down*. He felt like turning right around and starting back to Harrod, but he couldn't do it because the old lady had planned something special. And Alex thought, *shit, really going to be special with Bob and the old man going at it like that.* About the best he could hope for was that they'd both pass out by suppertime. All of the Warners were coming over, and a lot of the Scotts and the Oreys too, and he thought how ashamed the old lady was going to be for everybody to see them like that with the sun not even down. She was hiding out in the kitchen because the old man had knocked her down more than once and she knew enough to stay out of his way when he was tying on a good one.

So Alex was walking up the road to the house, and he was just tired of it. They didn't even give him half a chance to get there before they started in on him, his brother singing out: "Well, Jesus Christ, look who's here. It's the landowner." Alex didn't say a thing, just walked up onto the porch, and then he saw that they weren't just drunk, they were blind, crazy drunk from hitting the white moon since morning. More than likely they were going to get into it again, and then Bob might kill the old man this time, and Alex didn't give a shit if he did. Or maybe the old man would get his gun and blow Bob right off the porch. He'd threatened to do it a hundred times.

And back in the spring on one of the first good days they'd had, the old man had started in to mend the railings on the porch. Naturally he got about one rail done and then crapped out for the rest of the day, but he left the nails in a big paint can, and he left the hammer too. And seeing as the old man had started it, he should have finished it, so nobody around there was going to pick up the hammer and nails and carry them back into the house, least of all Alex, so they'd just stayed there and got rained on. Two inches of standing water in the paint can, and the nails was rusting away. The hammer was just laying there next to the can. It was a big ball peen. Alex had used it around the farm a million times, and he knew it'd been on the porch for weeks, but he'd just stopped seeing it. He didn't have any idea of hitting anybody with that hammer.

Alex walked up onto the porch. He was just going to go on

by them and into the kitchen to talk to the old lady, but somehow or other he didn't do that. No matter how much he thought about it later, he'd never be able to understand just why he did what he did. Alex's father was standing up, taking swigs from the Mason jar, waving his arms in the air and yelling. It was all about what fucking trash his sons were and what had he ever done to deserve sons like that. He should get his gun and shoot them both down like dogs on the road. And all Alex could remember thinking about was how he wished he could have some peace and quiet around there for a change. Then he turned around and hit his father. He hit him in the solar plexus. He didn't know the name for it then, wouldn't be till he was in high school that he'd hear somebody call it the "solar plexus," but he knew it was a good place to hit somebody.

The old man stopped yelling, and his face went funny, and he bent over. Alex blocked him low just like he was playing football and lifted him up and dumped him off the porch and down the stairs. He lit at the bottom and he just lay there. He didn't move a muscle.

Bob froze up for a minute, all red in the face with his mouth hanging open. Then he ran at Alex like a bull. He must have figured he was going to beat the crap out of Alex again because he'd been beating the crap out of him for years. Alex stepped back and let him come. He wasn't even thinking about the hammer. Later on he thought and thought about it, but he could never remember picking it up. But Alex hit his brother in the head with that hammer.

Bob dropped in his tracks. It was amazing how he dropped. Alex had seen plenty of fights, so he expected Bob to stagger or something like that, but Bob dropped like a stone. Alex was sure he'd killed him. He pitched the hammer out into the yard, and all of a sudden it was as quiet as a tomb. And Alex thought: *Now that's the way it ought to be around here.*

His mother stuck her head out the door because she must have heard all that quiet. "Oh, my God, Allie," she said, "what have you done?" and all he could think about was how he'd really ruined her dinner.

He said, "I think I killed them," and she started in crying. She raised her apron up over her face saying, "Oh, Lord, Lord, what are we going to do now?" and he couldn't stand to see her like that so he took off running.

She took off after him, but she was so fat, she couldn't go very far, and she stopped at the end of the road and yelled after him, telling him to come back, yelling, "Allie, Allie, come back," but he knew he couldn't come back, so he kept right on going. He caught a ride that took him on into Harrod, and he kept on going, got another ride into Carreysburg and started hitching up the river road. He wasn't thinking about going to Raysburg. It was just the direction he was aimed. North. And the funny thing was that all the time he kept thinking about how he'd spoiled her dinner.

He'd never forget that day, and he hoped to God he'd never feel that low again. Walking and hitchhiking north with a feeling in his chest like a stone because he'd done something so terrible he couldn't stay, because he was leaving, and he'd let his mother down who'd always been good to him, and let his grandfather down too, old man Warner who'd left him everything. And when he was riding along with some salesman who'd picked him up, he finally figured out that if his grandfather had still been alive, he probably wouldn't have done it.

He got dropped off in Millwood, and that was the first time he thought maybe he should go see his uncle Gladney who lived up there. Before that he'd been planning to just keep going north forever. And Gladney was expecting him, of course, because they'd called him. He met him at the door and said in that quiet voice of his, "They're both all right, no thanks to you."

But he couldn't go back, and that stone in his chest wouldn't go away. Gladney got him a job with old man Wolchak, and he started in at Raysburg High where he didn't know a soul. He went out for football, and he was surprised how easy it was to scare the city kids. He kept to himself. And he'd never understood before what lonely could mean, but he understood it now. It was with him all the time until he thought he'd die of it, Jesus, really crazy the way you could miss a place that's only two or three hours' drive away. All twisted up inside himself, not talking to anybody, just thinking: *Well, I'll play football and wrestle and run track and I'm goina be good, so fucking good that they'll know my name. "That's Alex Warner," they'll say*. But that stone in his chest never went away.

And then one day he and Tony Wolchak went over to the restaurant across the street for lunch and there was a girl in there waitressing, a tall skinny kid with black hair and long legs. He'd seen her before in school, and he was hoping she'd wait on them but she didn't, the fat man did, but she came around later and said, "You-ins all right over here?" and that voice just cut right through him. It was like music that voice, because she talked just the way they did down home.

"Where you from?" he asked her.

"Back of Carreysburg," she said. She had eyes like what people used to call sloe eyes, big and black.

"I'm Alex Warner," he said. "I'm from back of Harrod," and it was the first time he ever felt good about being in the city.

Chapter Five

"Hey, Carlyle."

Evan woke with a jerk in his muscles; he slapped his hands flat onto the ground and felt the grass. He sat up. He didn't remember falling asleep. They were still sitting on top of the hill, but now the sun was directly overhead. Sweat was pouring down his sides; it burned like acid. He stripped his shirt off, found his cigarettes in his shirt pocket. "Did you say something?" he said.

"Fell asleep, huh?"

"Yeah, I guess I did."

Alex had about an inch and a half of cigar left. He was relighting it. "I was just thinking," he said. "What are you going to do about Elly?"

It was the same question Evan had been asking himself, but he was surprised to hear it from Alex. "I don't know," he said.

Alex had got the cigar going; his eyes were squinted down to slits against the bright light. "You going to marry her?" he said.

"Marry her?" Evan was astonished. "Did I ever say I was going to marry her?"

"No." Alex dragged on the cigar. "So you're just going off to school, huh?" he said. "That's what you're going to do?"

"That's what I'm going to do."

"What you going to take up in school?"

"I don't know."

"Shit. I wouldn't know either . . . if I went."

"Aren't you going?"

"I don't know whether I am or not."

"Oh, for Christ's sake, man, you've got to."

"Why?"

"Jesus, man. How the hell else are you going to get out of Raysburg?"

Alex shrugged. "Maybe I shouldn't get out of Raysburg. Maybe I should just keep on working for old man Wolchak."

Evan was fully awake now. It seemed absolutely ridiculous to him that Alex could think of doing anything but accepting the athletic scholarship he'd been offered at WVU. "Christ, you're registered and everything."

"Carlyle, I hate school. I just fucking hate it. Fucking amazing to me I even got through Raysburg High."

Evan stared at Alex's impassive profile. He knew he was good at talking people into doing things, and he also knew that for some crazy reason he didn't understand, he had to talk Alex into going to school. "You liked playing sports, didn't you?"

"Yeah."

"Well, you'd have four more years. Just think how fast you'd be doing a mile in four more years."

"Do you have any idea how hard it is to run a mile under four thirty? Any fucking idea at all?"

"No, I guess I don't."

"It's like killing yourself. You've just got to be ready to go out and kill yourself. Jesus, that last quarter just feels like goddamned death."

Evan was at a loss for a moment; then he decided to open up his attack in a new direction. "What the hell you thinking about, Warner? Why the hell are you thinking you're not going to go?"

"I'm not very smart," Alex said.

"That's bullshit too. Look at the way you work on cars. You can't be dumb and do that."

"I'm not smart in books."

"Listen, Alex," Evan was practically yelling, "you can take my word for it. You don't have to be smart in books to get through fucking college, all right?"

"Maybe *you* don't."

"Oh, Jesus . . . you've got to get out of Raysburg! Listen, man, you've got to get out. All right."

Alex shrugged. "I'd like to."

"All right then. They've offered you a goddamned scholarship, for Christ's sake!"

"Go down to Morgantown and bust my ass. I'll get fucking killed trying to play college ball at my weight."

"Look, I can't believe you didn't like playing football."

"No, I didn't exactly like it," Alex said slowly. "I *did* it." He frowned. "I guess I did like football. I mean wrestling was hard for me. I really had to work at it. And I busted my ass at track. But football was more fun, you know? I just didn't take it all that serious, so it was fun. But Jesus, in college, it'd be pretty fucking *serious*." Alex rolled his cigar around between his teeth; then, suddenly, he looked over at Evan and grinned. "I'd be a fucking good quarterback," he said. "You don't have to weigh a million pounds to be a quarterback."

Evan laughed. "Shit, man, are you going to go or not?"

"Yeah, I guess I am. Give her a try. Why the hell not?"

"Great!" Evan slapped Alex on the shoulder; he felt as though *he'd* just won some kind of sports contest.

"It's the same fucking thing all over again," Alex said. "It's why I come down here. I've either got to play sports or drive cars . . . just can't seem to do both."

"All right, then. Now does it make sense? You've got to get out."

"Yeah, it makes sense. *You* always make sense, you know that? Shit, you've got it figured all the way down the pike. If you don't amount to something, I'm going to be surprised."

Evan was surprised; he was pleased too.

Alex stood up. "Let's get out of this sun. It's getting impossible out here." He began walking down the hill. Evan jumped up and followed. "Have to give her one more run," Alex said, "and then cash her in."

"That's what you've been saying all summer."

"Yeah, and this time I mean it. Just one last time. Really do it. I mean fucking do it, really run her one last time so I can say: 'By God, I ran her!' "

"Why?" Evan said. "Why's it so fucking important?"

Alex jerked around; his face, before he could catch himself, seemed totally surprised. "You know why."

Evan shrugged. He thought he did know why, but he wanted to hear Alex try to put it into words.

"There's Frank for one thing," Alex said. "I'll tell you, Carlyle, he was like a brother to me. And I just want to do something with him again one last time." Alex rubbed the back of his neck and began walking again. "And I want to do it for *me* too, that's all. . . . Fuck, I don't know why." He stopped suddenly. "Carlyle, you've been giving me all this goddamned advice, now I'm going to give you some," he said. "Hang on to Elly."

Evan stopped dead; he felt like Alex had punched him in the stomach. "Yeah?" he said uncertainly.

"You're never going to find another woman worth a quarter

of her." Alex said, "That's the fucking truth, man," and walked away.

Evan was left standing in an open field with the sun beating down on him and the locusts humming for miles around. Alex just kept on walking through the field and back toward the barn. Eventually Evan took off and trotted after him. "Hey," he yelled, "Al!"

"What?"

"When you make that last run, you know? . . . Take me with you."

Alex smiled slowly. "Don't say it if you don't mean it, Carlyle."

Fear struck at Evan like a snake. "You mean . . . you would?"

In the strong light, Alex's eyes were washed out to nearly nothing; they were looking straight at him. "Sure," he said.

"What's all this shit you used to tell me about how you don't take risks with other people's necks?" Evan said desperately.

"Man, if you decide to come, *you're* risking *your* neck, that's all."

Evan said nothing.

"All right?" Alex said.

Evan swallowed. He found his voice. "I want to come," he said.

"That's it then," Alex said. "You're coming."

Chapter Six

Alex couldn't understand why he'd lied to Carlyle about the way John Isaac died. That was the only thing he'd lied to him about, unless you could count what he hadn't told him. *Shit, after all these years maybe he should have told him, maybe he's* got a right to know, but how do you decide about something like that? The snow seemed to be turning to rain or sleet; Alex could hear it pounding on the windows. Something from a song. "Cold wind a-blowing and freezing to rain." Something his granddaddy used to sing. Alex threw back the blankets, got up, and pulled on his pants.

Drunk as ten skunks and still can't sleep. He walked back into the living room, where there were still coals left in the fireplace, threw another log on. It caught; flames licked out from under the sides. He waited until it was going and then laid on another one crosswise, then another one on top of that. Only light in the room was from the fire and he liked that; wind and rain pounding outside, shaking the whole house, rattling the windows in their frames, and he liked that too. Evan Carlyle sleeping in the next room, that crazy fucker brought it all back with him. "Al Warner," Alex said out loud to himself, "you're a goddamned fool." A few cans of beer left. He opened one.

If he didn't watch it, he'd turn out as crazy as John Isaac, pacing up and down in the middle of the night going over it all in his mind until it knotted up permanently. *Shit, he grew up in this house, could remember his mother plain as anything sitting on that couch, could remember when they hadn't got electricity put in yet and there'd be kerosene lanterns burning at night. Gives a nice light, makes everything soft, makes nice shadows in the corners. Shit, you either get out like Carlyle did or else you go all the way back to the beginning, and how the fuck do you do that?*

He walked through the house sipping at the beer. The sound of the wind outside had a howl in it like a dog and he could feel how drunk he was by a shiver on the back of his neck. He stopped by the closed door, could hear Carlyle snoring in there: shit, dead to the world. Almost knocked, almost yelled, but went back instead to the fire to warm his hands. *Sometimes you get fooled into believing you got it all under control, like a fine-running machine, got it tuned and purring, know where you're going and you'll get there right on time. But it's all false, every bit of it, and you don't know the road or the car or yourself and you could be driving over the side of a cliff for all the control you got over it.*

He came back from Morgantown with nowhere to go but back to Wolchak's; of course he could always go back to working for Wolchak, no problem there. Think about joining the army. Why not? Let somebody else run his life for a while. And it takes all these years looking back to make him understand that he came back because of Elly.

"He's really going crazy this time, Al. He's going crazy as a coot."

"Does he know?"

"I don't know if he knows, but he sure as hell suspects."

"Why don't you get out?"

"Where am I going to go?"

"Go stay with your brother in Detroit."

"Yeah, but he's still the *Reverend* Earl Bob, and what's he going to think?"

"He's family, ain't he?"

But she doesn't want to go to Detroit, and Evan Carlyle, that son of a bitch, is off at Ohio State, and this is the worst John Isaac's ever been.

John can't sleep at night anymore. He walks up and down talking to himself. "If thine eye offend thee, pluck it out," he says. He sits down in the kitchen in the back of the restaurant with only the one overhead light on reading the Bible out loud. "And they have healed the hurt of the daughter of my people slightly, saying, Peace, peace, when there is no peace. Were they ashamed when they had committed abomination? Nay, they were not at all ashamed, neither could they blush." Elly can hear him muttering away down there for hours, the rise and fall of his downstate voice.

Alex comes over in the afternoon for coffee. John serves it to him and just like he might say, "Do you think it's going to rain today?" asks him, "Is there no balm in Gilead?"

"What's that, John?"

He repeats it in that same ordinary everyday voice: "Is there no balm in Gilead?" and when Alex doesn't answer, he turns back to the grill, lays on a patty of meat. John stands there, must weigh two hundred and eighty pounds if he weighs an ounce, and the meat hisses, and he leans up against the wall with his arms folded in front of him looking away like there's a television set hanging up in the corner of the ceiling and he's watching a program that nobody else can see. Talking away to himself, and doesn't care if anybody hears or not. "The harvest is past, the summer is ended, and we are not saved."

He finishes cooking a cheeseburger and sets it down on the counter. Alex hasn't ordered any cheeseburger. "Thanks, John. Kind of chilly for this time of year?"

"Oh, that my head was water . . . my head was water," John says, "and my eyes was a fountain of tears." John puts on another patty of meat. Alex is the only customer in the restaurant.

"What do you think?" Elly asks Alex later in the day.

"I'd get the hell out of there if I was you." But damn her, she's still waiting around for something that's never going to happen.

At the end of the day Elly and her mother have to throw away all the food that John's cooked for nobody. John sits upstairs reading his Bible. There doesn't seem to be any time now when his voice isn't going like a radio you can't turn off. Elly wakes up in the middle of the night, can be one or two or even five in the morning, and always somewhere in the house there's her father's voice. He's beginning to have conversations. One night she hears him yell: "No, you don't tell me that, goddamn it. I don't want to hear that. Shit, don't be saying that. Goddamn it, didn't I tell you? Shut up now and don't be saying that."

Elly's mother is no help at all. "You just stay out of his way. He'll come around in a week or two. He's taken these spells before, long as I've known him." Mrs. Isaac's drunk constantly, sips mint-flavored gin from the time she gets up in the morning until she passes out in front of the television set after supper. "Just let him alone," she says.

When it finally happens, the first thing Alex knows of it is the scream in the street. Before he's even awake, he's jumped straight out of bed and is pulling on his pants and boots as fast as he can. It won't be until later that he'll hear how it started.

Elly'd been in bed only half asleep. For a minute she thinks it's part of her dream, that she's made it up herself because she's been so afraid for so long. But then she's wide awake and knows she didn't make it up: her father has quietly pushed her door open. He's standing there with the light behind him and his shotgun pointed at her. He doesn't yell. That quiet slow voice is worse than if he'd been screaming his head off. "Get up, you harlot," he says, "you serpent. You mother of abominations."

"Go on back to bed, Papa, for heaven's sake. It's three o'clock in the morning."

"Now you listen to me, girl. You get your ass out of there or I'll blow you to pieces where you lay."

Very slowly she slides out of bed. She's got on nothing but a pair of old shorty pajamas. "What do you want, Papa?"

"You just come down in the kitchen so your yelling won't wake your maw."

"Let me put some clothes on."

"You won't need no clothes."

"At least let me put something on my feet. It's really cold."

"You won't need nothing on your feet. Come on, girl, get moving. Don't get too close now, or I'll blow you to pieces." He stands back, aims with his gun the way he wants her to go. She walks ahead of him down to the kitchen. "Harlot," he says in that quiet voice. "You got serpent's eyes."

He lights all the lights in the kitchen so it's blazing like high noon.

"Papa, what the hell do you think you're going to do?"

"I knowed you was not my own. You ain't got no Isaac eyes. I been studying it day and night, and Jesus just come to me and made it plain. The woman said, 'The serpent beguiled me and I did eat.' And the Lord God said unto the serpent, 'Because thou hast done this, cursed art thou. Upon thy belly shalt thou go, and dust shalt thou eat all the days of thy life.' . . . Oh, it all come plain to me, how I've been nursing a viper in my bosom all these years, in my very house. You harlot. You scarlet woman. You mother of abominations."

"Papa, you're talking crazy." She's scared to death now, ice inside her, and she knows she's got to do something. She reaches for the gun. He jumps back and points it right into her face.

"You stop right there. I ain't goina kill you unless I have to. But if you make me, then I'll blow you to pieces. Hear the word of the Lord, harlot. You ain't none of mine. You come out of your harlot mother's fornications and abominations. You got serpent eyes, and you been fornicating with Satan to bring forth new abominations. Behold, harlot, I will gather all thy lovers with whom thou hast taken pleasure. I'm goina start with that goddamned Evan Carlyle. And I'm goina kill them all every one. But first I'm goina fix you so you can't do no more evil in this land."

It's so horrible she can't move. She can't even scream. "Now you just set down there on that chair," he says. She sits down on the chair. "You look at that light over there on that ceiling because it's the last look you're ever goina get." He picks up a soup spoon.

"What are you going to do?"

"I'm goina dig out them serpent's eyes of yours."

All of a sudden she can scream. He shoves the gun right up in her face again. "Goddamn it, would you rather die? You set still and let me dig them eyes out now, and then I'll let you alone."

She pushes the gun away. She doesn't care if he does kill her. She runs for the front door. Behind her, she hears the hammers fall, first one and then the other: *click, click.* The gun doesn't go off.

She's out in the street. The cold pavement burns her bare feet like fire.

Alex is already running down the stairs by the time Elly gets to the front door of the garage. He unlocks it and she runs through, her legs flashing in the streetlight. "He's got his gun."

"Get back of the counter." Alex sees John Isaac stop under the streetlight to shove the shells in. Then he snaps the barrel back up into place and runs straight for the door, big and slow as a cement truck. Alex locks the door, turns and sprints back away from all that plate glass. He's flat on his belly next to Elaine behind the counter. The twelve-gauge goes off, both barrels, and the front window's gone, glass blown everywhere, and the air ringing like thunder.

"It didn't go off before. Jesus, Al, it didn't go off before."

"Yeah, I took the powder out of the shells damn near two years ago."

"You come out, you harlot," John yells, "or I'm coming in to kill you."

"What the hell we going to do, Al?"

"Be quiet." He pushes her down flat on the floor. "Stay down and be quiet. We've just got to stall him till the cops come." On his belly, Alex peers around the end of the counter. John's standing just outside the broken window, a huge black shadow. Alex hears him reloading. "I've got you covered, John," he yells.

"Who the hell's that?"

"You know damn well who it is. It's Alex Warner. And I've got a fucking Enfield rifle aimed right at your big belly."

John stands there not moving. Alex can almost hear him thinking. "You ain't got no gun," he says.

"You want to bet your life on it, fat man?" *Shit*, Alex thinks, *and me laying here with nothing in my hands but air.*

"You're bluffing me, Alex Warner. You ain't got no gun."

"Not goina argue with you, John. But if you're still standing in that window with the light behind you like that making such a pretty target . . . if you're standing there about a minute from now, you're goina be dead."

John doesn't move. "John Isaac," Alex yells, "you know who's talking to you, don't you? It's me, Alex Warner."

Very slowly John walks away from the window. "You send my daughter out, and I'll let you alone. I ain't got no quarrel with you."

"He's going to come around back," Elly says, whispering. "He's just stalling you."

"Yeah, I know. Come on, Elly. Move fast and stay down." He grabs her hand, and, bent low to the ground, runs through the back to where the truck's parked. Opens the door to the cab. "Quick," he says, "get in there. Stay flat down on the floor. Here's the key." He finds her hand in the dark and presses the key into it. She's shaking. "Now listen. When you hear another engine start, you start the truck. But stay down on the floor. Keep your hand on the accelerator so it don't stall."

Wished he could make it clearer, but it's all the time he's got. Back inside the garage, feeling in the dark along the row of nails where the keys are hanging. Third one from the end is for Bud Clark's Ford. He's got it, then crawling on the ground, in the shadows, moving fast as he can. John's just coming around the corner. "Hold it right there, John."

"You ain't got no gun."

Jesus, where are the fucking cops? Alex slips into Bud Clark's Ford, rolls himself up into a ball with his head below the window line.

"Don't try to drive out of here, Alex Warner," John says not more than ten feet away. "I've come for my daughter. Harlot. Mother of abominations." Alex starts the Ford. He hears Elly on the other side of the lot start the truck. John's yelling: "Upon her forehead a name was written. Mystery. Babylon the great. Mother of harlots and of the abominations of the earth." Walking straight toward the Ford with his shotgun aimed at the windshield.

Alex puts the Ford in gear, takes off the emergency brake, leaves it in idle, and slips out the passenger's side. Running fast as a dashman for the truck. In the cab, Elly's pressing on the accelerator. "Stay down," he says.

Black as a coal bin back here on the lot, and he knows John

can't see a thing, but that Ford with its high idle is drifting toward the street. John, that shadow, is watching it come. Will he think there's somebody in it? "I told you, Alex Warner."

Blam. Shattering glass. *That's right,* Alex thinks, *and now the other barrel, you damned fool. I want to hear that other barrel.* The Ford's still rolling toward the street. John jumps back, points and shoots. *Blam.* That poor old Ford is scrap, but Alex has got the truck in gear and is screaming out, burning rubber the whole way. He sees John jerking the spent shells out of his shotgun, but it's too late, Alex is on the street, accelerating. He's laughing. "Suckered him, the son of a bitch."

"Oh, Jesus," Elly says from the floor.

Alex drank the last of the beer and looked at where the fire was dying down again. *Goddamn,* he thought, *even then she felt something for her old man.* They'd parked all the way up on Chapline Street, listening to the sirens. Elly was shaking like a leaf. He held her. "Goddamn it," she said, "don't shoot at them, Daddy. Don't shoot at them." They heard the twelve-gauge go off, then the cops' pistols, like the barking of dogs. *Well, he was a hell of a good target, that fat man.*

Chapter Seven

Evan woke and didn't know where he was. Then he felt the cold all around him and he knew; he had to find someplace quick to throw up. Dressed only in his T-shirt, he jumped out of bed, fumbled the door open, and ran down the hall to the bathroom. He bent over the toilet, and purple liquid squirted out of him. He unrolled a strip of old toilet paper and wiped his mouth with it. But he wasn't finished; the next spasm bent him double. He was getting solid stuff now, partially digested food turned shit-brown by his stomach acids. He needed water. He twisted the tap. Nothing happened. Of course: the cistern wasn't hooked up. He hung on the sink, his forehead pressed against the edge. He felt as though his skull were being cracked by sledgehammers. He ran back into the bedroom and buried himself under the two mildewed quilts.

He was so cold that he couldn't remember what it was like to be warm. The snow light from the windows filled the room with a harsh unyielding glare, and his mind felt as definite and harsh as that icy light. He looked around the room. The old wallpaper of dogs and shotguns was peeling off the walls in disintegrating strips. The same old magazines that had been there thirteen years before were still there, and so were the athletic awards, even the trophy, even the picture hanging on the wall. He could see Alex's strange eyes. *Nineteen sixty,* he thought. He was too far away to read the lettering, but he remembered what it said: BEST OF LUCK WITH YOUR RUNNING, SEE YOU IN THE OLYMPICS. *Shit,* he thought, *he must have gained sixty pounds since then.*

Somewhere—it seemed very far away—a great animal was snarling to itself: *Rurr, rurr, rurr.* An engine. And the window frames rattled and banged. The torn drapes were billowing as though a wind were blowing right through the walls. He heard a sound like a sandblaster fired in short bursts at the window-panes, but he couldn't see what it might be because the glass was totally frosted over. *Sleet,* he thought. *Hail?* And some-where off in a white vicious world, that engine kept going: *Rurr, rurr, rurr.*

Finally the snarling stopped; Evan heard someone walk into the house and stamp his feet. Then Alex pushed through the bedroom door. His coat was covered with snow, his short hair was covered with snow, even his eyebrows were lined with it. "Awake, huh? How you doing?"

"Awful."

"Well, I got a fire going if you want to come out."

Evan pulled on his clothes as fast as he could and ran into

the living room. Alex was hunched over the fire, warming his hands. "You look like death," he said.

Evan touched his head, meaning the gesture to say everything there was to say. He leaned over the fire.

"Yeah. Haw! Horrible, ain't it?"

"Well, I finally figured a few things out," Evan said. "It's not the booze, it's the cigarettes. Only took me fifteen years to figure that out."

Alex laughed. "That's right. I never got hangovers that bad when I wasn't smoking."

"And we just can't bounce back the way we did at eighteen. Jesus, is there anything to drink?"

"No."

"What the fuck you mean, no? Isn't there at least a beer left."

"We drank every fucking one of them, Carlyle. The wine too. . . . Go eat some snow. Stick your head in it. Fix you right up. That's what I did."

Reluctantly Evan left the fire. "Hey," Alex called after him, "take a jacket."

"What the hell's it doing out there?"

"Don't know. Was sleeting a while back."

Evan grabbed Alex's overcoat, wrapped himself up in it, and stepped outside onto the porch. A blast of icy rain struck him on the side of the face; he winced. The view from the porch was awesome: everything was buried in snow as far as he could see. The sky overhead was a uniform gray; on the horizon it was a swirling black like liquid shoe polish poured into milk. Wind was driving nearly horizontal bursts of rain. The snow was pelted with it, but the water wasn't biting in; it was skittering along on the top and freezing. The surface of everything was slicked with a glassy sheen of murderous ice. Alex had cut a trail out to the white lump that must have been the car.

Evan felt his stomach kick. He grabbed the railing; it burned like fire under his hands. A thin squirt of something came out of his mouth and was blown away. He knew he couldn't get down the steps without falling. At the side of the porch where the snow had piled up against the wall, he broke through the surface crust, scooped out white powder from underneath, and ate it by the handful. It seared his tongue and throat. Then he ran to the railing and threw up. The snow came up stained green. Alex had followed him out onto the porch. "You're in a bad way," he said.

Evan's head was beating him nearly blind. He stumbled into the house, shed the overcoat, and threw himself down on the couch in front of the fire. "Too cold to go right in your stomach that way," Alex said. He set a cast-iron Dutch oven full of snow to melt in front of the fire.

"Sick as a dog," Evan said.

"No shit. Well, you just lay there and get yourself together. We still got a good bit of wood left."

Wood? Evan thought. *Wood?* "What happens when we burn it all up?" he said.

"I guess we start burning the furniture."

The rain beat on the windows. After a while, Alex said, "Some of it's melted now. Sit up and drink it." Evan sat up. Alex handed him a cup of faintly dirty water. "Sip it. Don't just gulp it down. Got to get some fluids in you."

Evan took the cup and drank a mouthful. It tasted wonderful. "No food, I suppose?" he said.

"Nope. Just some shit the old woman canned years ago. I wouldn't want to trust any of it."

Evan wanted to get Alex to talk. He didn't care what about; anything to distract himself from the pain in his head. "It's amazing," he said, "how much your room looks the same."

"Yeah, the old woman kept it that way . . . even after we'd both been gone for years."

"So what's your brother doing now?"

"Bob? Fucker got himself killed in Vietnam." Evan opened his eyes. Alex's face was unreadable. "That's what you get for being a lifer," he said.

"When? When did it happen?"

"Sixty-seven I think it was. Or sixty-eight. Shit, I never cared much for the son of a bitch, but he sure didn't deserve *that*. Well, fuck . . ." He spat into the fire. Then he gave Evan an odd smile. "You know, we can't even call Sheri. The phone's not hooked up. . . . You feeling any better?"

"Yeah, a little." Although he wasn't.

"I wanted to wait to spring it on you until you was feeling halfway human. That car ain't going nowhere."

"Guessed that from the look of it." Evan forced himself to sit upright. He had to try to function. "Is it bad?"

"Fucking buried. The rear wheels is sunk in to the axle, and then they're frozen in there. For a while I didn't think the fucker was even going to start. And then I got it started and I had it in my mind I was just going to drive out of there. Shit, still trusting to blind luck, right? But I put her in gear and nothing happened. Out to lunch."

"So what are we going to do?"

"Number of things we could do," Alex said meditatively, his odd smile widening. "We might dig it out. But that would take us years. And even then we wouldn't have any guarantee we'd get up the hill. And once we got it up the hill, I don't know how we'd go anywhere over the road the way it is now. . . . Or we could walk into Harrod and find somebody to stay with . . ." He was looking directly at Evan. "Or we could sit here and wait for spring."

"Some joke," Evan said. "Why don't we walk over to the Froelich's place and call in to Harrod and get a tow truck to come out here and pull us out?"

"Well," Alex said dryly, "now that's a good suggestion, but there's a few things wrong with it. The first thing is that the Froelichs don't live there anymore. They had to give it up because they couldn't pay the taxes on it, so the phone sure as hell ain't hooked up. . . . We could keep on going to what used to be the Medley place. Bunch of young kids got it now. You know, the ones that come down from New York and buy up our land . . . but I think they're only there in the summer, and I kind of doubt if their phone's working. . . . And suppose we did get to a phone and I called the wrecker in at Harrod? You think he's going to drive out here over these back roads all covered with ice and snow and pull me out? Shit, he's going to hang up on me."

Evan laughed weakly. "Sounds like you've got it all figured out. So what do you want us to do, walk into Harrod? How far is that?"

"If we take the road, it's about twenty miles. But if we go over the hills, I figure we can cut a couple miles off it."

Evan looked closely at Alex. *What the hell was he doing with that smile on his face?* He must be nearly as hung over as Evan, so how could he be so goddamned cheery? And Evan was suddenly angry. "I'm not going anywhere," he said.

"Well, we're going to burn up the rest of this wood. And then maybe we *could* start burning the furniture—"

"Shit, Sharon knows where we are."

"Sure she does. What's she going to do about it?"

"Send somebody down."

"How they going to get here?"

Evan didn't answer.

"Nobody's driving out here, Carlyle. Nothing's going to move out here until it melts."

Evan couldn't believe it. "There's got to be some way."

"Name it."

"Snowmobile."

"God, you're funny, Carlyle. You've been living in Canada too long."

Evan lay back on the couch and closed his eyes. "You go off to Harrod if you want. I'm staying here."

"That's a good one. If you think I'm going off and leave you, you're out of your fucking mind." Alex was beginning to sound angry. "You'd freeze to death before I got back."

"I'm not leaving here, that's all. You know the weather in this valley," Evan said. "Hold off a day and it's going to melt."

"You ain't in the valley anymore. You're in the fucking hills. This snow could lay out here for weeks."

"It's raining."

"The rain's freezing."

"And you want to go out in it?"

"Carlyle, there's no fucking way I can come back in and get you, can you get that through your head?"

"We could die out there, man! How many miles you talking about? Seventeen? Eighteen? You're out of your goddamned mind!"

"We're not going to die out there."

"All right, asshole, you go and do it then. I'm sick as a fucking dog. I couldn't walk around the block."

"Show me a block to walk around."

Evan sat straight up and stared at Alex. *Jesus*, he thought, *I'd like to kill the bastard.* "Go on," he said, "get the fuck out."

Alex grinned and shrugged. "I'll just sit here until it dawns on you where the fuck you are, that's all."

"Listen to me," Evan said. "I can't do it, all right? I just can't walk eighteen miles with fucking snow up to my asshole and a goddamn ice storm coming down on my head."

"Carlyle, that's no ice storm. You should see a real one."

"I did an item once on assholes just like us dying of exposure."

"Yeah? Did they know where they was going? Was they right in the same place where they grew up so they knew every hill and valley in it? Did they have lots of warm clothes? . . . Shit, man, you should see what we've got in the closet. We've got coats coming out our ass. We've got sweaters. We've got old fucking rubber galoshes. We've got hats with ear flaps—"

"No."

"It ain't going to be no picnic, that's true. But we're going to make it . . . if we don't piss around here so long that it gets dark. Shit, we'll get on into Harrod, have a good appetite worked up. Have a steak, a few beers—"

"Alex, you bastard, stop trying to humor me."

"I'm not trying to humor you, just trying to put some spirit back into you, you dumb fuck. . . . You're just feeling sorry for yourself. Once we get moving, it'll be all right."

Evan stared at the cobwebs on the cracked ceiling. *How had he ever got himself into this?*

"You can't walk away from this one," Alex said in the same easy voice. Then he laughed. "Well, I guess you can. I guess that's exactly what you've got to do."

"Alex," Evan said from flat on his back, "you may be the toughest son of a bitch I ever met in my life, but you're not a fucking superman."

My gut feeling was absolutely right, Evan thought. *I never should have come back to West Virginia, or at least I should have stayed off the street so I wouldn't run into him. I never should have let myself get talked into that insane drive down here.* "More damn fools dying of exposure just because they've got to prove something," he heard himself saying. "Jesus, Warner, you've always gone around creating disasters just to prove you could get out of them. Well, it doesn't matter to me."

But Evan knew that it did matter. The past should have been erased like an old show that would never be aired again, but it was too late for that now. He hated Alex Warner—and he loved him too. He'd hated and loved him for years.

Evan knew he'd come too far this time to back out. He had to know. "Al," he said, "did you screw Elaine?"

He sat up. Alex was staring at him with his head cocked slightly to one side; the expression on his face looked genuinely puzzled. "You're bullshitting me, ain't you, Carlyle?" he said. "You're not asking me that straight."

"Yeah, I am asking you that straight."

"I never would of believed it."

"Come on, did you or didn't you?"

"Christ, Carlyle, did you forget who you're talking to? It's me. Al Warner."

"Yeah, I know who I'm talking to. Did you or didn't you?"

"Jesus, she was your girl!"

"I know she was my girl. Did you screw her?"

"I still can't believe you're asking me that."

"Well, I am asking you that."

Alex threw his cigarette pack down at his feet, hard. "No," he said, lips drawn back, teeth showing. "No. I never screwed her."

"Come on, be straight with me, Warner. It doesn't matter after all these years. Just tell me straight, okay?"

"Carlyle, I *am* telling you straight. I never screwed her."

Evan stared at his friend. It was unbelievable, but he almost believed it. "Not even after I left?"

"Jesus! . . . I was down at Morgantown a fucking month and a half and then I was in the army."

"Not any time after I left?"

"I told you I was in the army. . . . Don't you listen, asshole? I was back on leave a couple times and I seen her, but we sure as hell didn't screw. And when I got out, she was already married to that prick, Jamieson."

"Oh, fuck."

"Look, Carlyle, do you believe me or not?"

"Yeah, I guess I believe you. . . . Sure, I believe you . . . but Jesus, Alex, didn't you ever want to?"

Alex shook his head. "You never let up, do you?" he said, his voice hard. "Goddamn right, I wanted to."

"Why the hell didn't you?"

"She was your girl, goddamn it! You don't screw your friend's girl. That's all. Did you think I would? Did you think I was that kind of guy?"

"Shit . . . But after I left, she wasn't my girl."

"Oh, Carlyle, you dumb fuck, lay off, will you?"

"No, I'm not going to lay off. . . . Look, that time you raced up from Harrod to Carreysburg. You mean to tell me that when you got up to Carreysburg, after all that tension and excitement . . . that you didn't drive up the road somewhere and pull off a quick one?"

"You're fucking nuts, you know that?"

"Didn't you?" Evan was yelling.

"Stop pushing me, Carlyle. This is something you don't push me on, all right?" The color had drained out of Alex's face; it was the old murderous look he used to get just before he beat somebody up.

"Didn't you?" Evan yelled. *Let him beat me up,* he thought. *That'd just be perfect. Let him kill me. To hell with him.*

"Stop pushing me."

"Didn't you?"

"Fuck no, I didn't, you prick. She was your girl. I told you that once. I don't have to tell you again. I'm not going to tell you again." Alex picked his pack of cigarettes off the floor, pounded one out. His hands were shaking.

"But you were in love with her," Evan said. The minute he said it, he knew it had to be true. "You *were,* weren't you?"

"Yeah," Alex said flatly.

"Why didn't you screw her then?"

"Carlyle," Alex said slowly, "I told you not to push me on this, didn't I?"

"I've got to know."

"All right. So you've got to know. Well, I'll tell you. Where did she go that first year you went off to school?"

"To Detroit."

"That's right. What did she go there for?"

Evan began to panic. "To get out of Raysburg. She always wanted to get the fuck out of Raysburg. She went and stayed with her brother. She got some kind of job. She sent me letters from Detroit. She went to Detroit to get out of fucking Raysburg."

"Carlyle, you dumb shit. She went to Detroit to have your baby."

"Bullshit, man! Bullshit!"

"Count it out. End of August to the end of May."

"Oh, Jesus!" Evan felt tears rising to burn his nose and throat; it was too late for them. "What was it? . . . Do you know?"

"It was a girl."

"What happened to her?"

"Who the fuck knows, man? She gave her up for adoption."

The enormity of it seemed as wide and impossible as the landscape outside the farmhouse. His daughter would be thirteen. "But why didn't she tell me?"

"Did you ever know why she did anything she ever did?" Alex said quietly.

"Did she tell you about it?"

"Yeah, she told me about it."

"What did she say?"

"Been years, man. I don't remember."

"You've got to remember, Al. I've got to know."

"Let it alone, Carlyle. Just let it alone."

Alex had no expression on his face at all. Then he smiled slightly and threw his pack of cigarettes across the room. Evan caught it out of the air. He threw the lighter. Evan caught that; he lit a cigarette. Evan remembered the letters Elaine had written him from Detroit. They hadn't been love letters. They'd been chatty, full of ordinary details of her life—clothes, movies, and dates. He hadn't answered any of them. He ground the cigarette out under his heel.

"You ready now?" Alex said.

"Yeah," Evan said. "Let's get going."

Chapter Eight

The sky hurt. Above and behind the buildings of center Raysburg, evening was turning it gray, turning it to twilight. Up there in that sky, nighthawks calling out; they sounded just like rusty door-springs. Alex could see one of them up there, way up above the building, darting back and forth, catching bugs. High up in that sky riding on air currents coming up off the hot city streets. Maybe he could still see the sun from up there. Maybe he was just flying along in the gray-blue and catching bugs, yelling out because he liked it, making that funny noise like a door spring. Down here on the street, traffic was drifting on by, slow and crapped-out, end of a long, fucking boring day.

Elly gave him a free Dutch Masters cigar out of the case. The smoke of it smells like nights with Frank, loafing at the Cat's Eye, loafing at the P.A.C. Right now he can smell the cooking from inside the restaurant too. John's frying meat, crazy fucker. Alex looked back through the screen door, saw Elly walking across to him. Heard her coming first so he knew when to turn and look. Goddamn Elly Isaac, walking in her heels, looked just like a colt. She pushed through the door and out onto the sidewalk. Stood with him, back against the wall. The door spring. Nighthawk. "What's the matter, Al?" *Her eyes, black as coal. And her skin's white out here on the gray street.*

"Shit," he said. "Shit." And all of a sudden the streetlights popped on all at once. *Beautiful the way they done that, all at once.* He grinned at her. "Summer's over, huh?"

"Yeah, damned near." Her eyes.

"What the fuck you going to be doing, Elly?"

"I don't know. . . . Maybe go to New York. Saved all my tips for years, thinking I was going to New York. And now's the time to do it." She shrugged. White shoulders. "I'm scared of it, Al. I'm really scared of it."

"Yeah."

"Get up to New York, I'd just be another hick girl in the big city. I know all the stories."

"Don't know till you get there, do you?"

Cars drifted by on the street. Everything was slowed down. Easy and slow. Hot day, hot summer, and it was almost over. Maybe tonight was the night to do it. "What's the matter, Al?"

"Nothing. Just restless, that's all." *Because the sky hurt.* He jerked the screen door open, stuck his head in, and yelled back the length of the restaurant, "Hey, Carlyle!"

She looked at him quick. "What are you up to, Al?"

"Shit, Elly, don't know till you do it, do you?"

"Don't give me any of that bullshit, man," she said, laughing. "You know what you're going to do."

"Yeah."

Carlyle stepped through the screen door. Crazy Carlyle was wearing a yellow short-sleeved shirt with the sleeves rolled up a couple more turns. "What? What?" he says. *Always makes you feel good to see him, Carlyle. You can be feeling like shit, and you see him, and it makes you feel good, he's such a funny guy.*

"Let's take us a little walk, buddy."

"Walk? Where?"

"Oh, thought we might walk on down to the Cat's Eye, see if Frank's loafing in there."

"You watch yourself, Al," Elly said.

"Always watch myself. Right, Carlyle?"

Walking down through center Raysburg toward the river, know these fucking streets like the back of my hand. Know where the alleys go, know where all the cathouses are. Shit, walked back them alleys on a Saturday night, seen men lined up for blocks waiting to get in. They come from Columbus and Zanesville and Pittsburgh, they come from fucking everywhere just to get laid.

Gray-blue sky. It's in me, damn it, it's in my chest. Shit, it hurts. "Tonight?" Carlyle was saying, "Tonight? Is that what you're thinking about?" Alex didn't answer. "We've only got a week to go. You don't think we'll get arrested, do you?"

Oh, Carlyle, stay home if you want. I don't care. But just don't crap out on me, that's all. "Maybe," he said. *Walking down toward the river. Love to sit on the bank and watch the boats go by, love the way they swing their spotlights along the banks. Shit, case of cold beer and a couple cigars, sit on the bank over on the island under the bridge. Just me, nobody else, and maybe think things out. Going down to Morgantown? Live in a dorm? Shit! And only a week to go. But no, can't just sit and watch the river tonight. Hurts too much. Got to move, got to run.* "Jesus," Carlyle was saying, "that's all we'd need. Get arrested, right? A week before we were going to leave."

Felt like this the night he broke the record. It was all hurting in there, squeezed up tight so he couldn't breathe right. Same kind of sky, that blue-gray coming down, twilight. Same night-hawks up there over the stadium. He remembered the crunch of cinders under his spikes, jogging on the Canden track, warming up, Pilsudski jogging beside him. The sky's fading out, braking down for night. "How you going to run it, Warner?" Pilsudski says.

"Fast as I fucking can. Got no plans on it, Johnny. Just go out there and bury them bastards."

"Shit, Warner, this ain't just another high school meet. This is the goddamn *Invitational*. David Henderson from Canden's out for your ass. Nearly busted your record, you know. He did a four forty-four just a couple weeks ago. And there's Lyle Ledzinski from the Academy. This ain't been his year, but he's making a hell of a comeback. He's been under five lots of times. He could really surprise you, man."

Jump up and down, slap calves and thighs, tingle in all the muscles. Smells like wintergreen oil, pine trees. Track shoes, can't walk in them. All you can do is run in them. "Fuck, Johnny," he says, "goddamn Henderson . . . rich out-the-pike kid. He's going to think he's running with Roger Bannister when he sees me. Going to bury him. He's an even pacer, runs every lap the same, and I'm going to be long gone. . . . And Ledzinski, shit, let him take off and burn out that first fucking quarter. I need him to do that. And then I'm going to leave him."

"See, you *are* thinking about it," Pilsudski says with a grin.

"Just enough, man. But not too much."

Call for the mile run. He's tied in a knot. It fucking hurts: the sky, his chest. He's shaking, bouncing up and down. Official's handing out the pills, grab one, lane three. *Not bad. Where's Ledzinski? Lane five. Great. He'll sprint right out and cut in for the edge. Follow right behind him. He'll hear me right behind him, and he'll go, goddamn straight he will, always runs that first quarter like that's all the race there is.* Alex waves at Ledzinski. *Yeah, I need you, you fucking beautiful Polack.* Ledzinski smiles back, shyly, down his big nose. Skinny kid with acne all over his face; fast as a dash man, but he can't last.

Coach, old man Rurak: "You just hang on, Warner." Talking in his ear, almost whispering, "Don't go out too fast. Don't let Ledzinski scare you. You know how he runs the first quarter, and then he's got nothing left. Just stay in the middle. Right in the middle, you hear me?"

"Yeah."

"And make your break in the middle of the third lap, right? You hear me, Warner?"

"Yeah, I hear you, Mister Rurak."

He's shaking, shaking. Bouncing up and down. Can't wait much longer, *Christ, it's killing me. Fucking hell, fucking hell, fucking hell, goddamn all of them,* he's thinking: *They can all kiss my ass.* "Runners take your marks!"

Up to the line. Down in the cinders, hands right up to the line, fingers spread, knees on the cinders. "Get set!" Butt stuck up, tense, tense, tense.

Ledzinski breaks, false start. *Oh, I love you. You're going to be my rabbit today, man.* Ledzinski comes bouncing back, stringy muscles, jumping up and down, nervous as a cat. Try it again. "Runners take your marks ... Get set—"

Bang! The gun. Waiting's over. Ledzinski's fucking gone, sprinting like a hundred, cutting straight in for the edge, just what he's supposed to do. Alex is right behind him. Alex yells ahead to him in time to their feet: "Move it, move it, move it, move it!"

Rurak throws his hat flat down onto the ground, screams, "Slow down, Warner, you'll kill yourself!"

Ledzinski hears Alex behind him and he's moving it. *Goddamn, never felt the first quarter like this before.* Bent forward, elbows pumping, sprinter's kick. High knees, high knees. *Chop it on down, baby. Move, you beautiful Polack.* Ledzinski's knotty calves flashing away, his arms bunched up, working it hard as a fucking steam hammer. Alex stays right behind him, pushing him along. "Slow down, Warner!" Rurak's voice from the other side of the field sounds like a trumpet. Bent out sideways, floating the angle, scooting the curve back home. Coming into the end of the first lap right on Ledzinski's heels. "Sixty-seven!" Rurak yells out.

Shit, fastest first quarter I ever run. Shit, we're burning it. Shit, we're moving. "Too fast," Rurak yells. Pleading. "Save it, kid, save it." *What the fuck do you know, you old fart?*

Coming into the curve, kick right on by on Ledzinski's left shoulder. He sees me go by and drops back. Crazy fucker blows me a kiss as I go by. Shit, buddy, I love you . . . You knew what I wanted, didn't you? Alex is alone into the second lap. He glances back, just a quick shot to see, and fuck if they're not all twenty yards back. He's left the whole fucking pack. They're catching Ledzinski, and they're all way back, every fucking one of them. Alex is alone and pushing it out alone. The joy is more than he can bear. *Know what to do: Just run, that's all. Do you think you can run me? No one can touch me.*

Oh, God, it's beautiful, it's fucking beautiful. Breathing timed with his legs, skimming it along, moving it along, pushing it along, faster than he's ever done it before. *You're right on the edge, Warner,* he tells himself. *You've almost got it.* But what? *Jesus, just run it, that's all.* The joy is more than he can bear.

Push it, push it, push it, push it. Banging words to the footsteps. Floating light and easy, just on the edge. Coming by at the half, Rurak yells, "Two sixteen!" *Fucker's amazed. Don't know whether to shit or go blind. That time would win most of the half mile races in the fucking valley.* "Save something!" Rurak yells, begging him now.

Glance up at the sky. Gray-blue. It's quiet now. People in the bleachers all standing up. Nobody's yelling, nobody's saying a word. It's fucking quiet. *Beautiful. Look back again. Last time you let yourself look back. Shit, they're lost, all of them. Henderson's leading the pack, and no sign of Ledzinski, and they're all way back there. Damn near hundred yards back. Never seen them that far back before, never.* Alex is right at the edge. He's alone. He's into the third lap alone.

The pain comes down. No more joy, no more float, the pain comes down. And this would make or break him, the third lap. That dead third lap. That fucking terrible third lap. Never pain like this before. Mouth dry, sweat in the eyes. And fire in the chest, fire in the lungs, fire in the legs. Heart pounding. The pain is terrible. Can't stand this much pain. *Oh, Jesus, went out too fast and can't stand the pain! Ripped to shreds. Fucking dying in the pain. Oh, Warner, come on, coast it now, man, just coast it on through. Don't lose too much, just coast it on through. It's a good pace, just keep it.* But oh, God, the pain. *No one can touch me.*

"Three twenty-seven," from Rurak. "Just try to hold it, Warner. Just finish it, okay?" The third lap was the slowest lap, but the time's still fast. Incredibly fast. *Yeah, and now get it. Now's the time, baby, now or never.* But he can't do it. The pain is terrible. The pain is death. He can't do it. Hears a voice in his head say, "Slow down, kid. You're only human." *What? Like hell I am . . . Like hell I am! No one can touch me.* His lungs, burning. His legs, burning. Sprint, sprint, sprint, sprint. Never like this before. Never close to this. Burning lungs, burning air. Stadium burning. Sky burning. The whole fucking world's burning down. "You're only human." Trying to remember. Trying to remember for the last hundred yards. Screaming everywhere. People jumping up and down and screaming. Tape coming up. Burning through fire, burning through hellfire, burning it home. Cut the tape, still trying to remember.

The voices: "Warner, Warner!" He can't hold himself up. He's falling. Black spinning down like death. He's going down, fuck, right onto the cinders. But Pilsudski is there. Alex reaches out to him, falling. Pilsudski slides under his arm, catches him. Can't breathe, can't walk. But he breathes and walks. Stares up at the sky. Flashbulbs like lightning. He remembers: *Lark. The whore.* That's who said it: "Slow down, kid. You're only human." What a fucking stupid thing to think about the bad tail-end of a mile run. *No one can touch me.* Voices and voices: "Warner! Warner!" Roaring in his ears. Sky is pumping with his heart, beating back and forth, blue-gray. The joy is more than he can bear.

"Jesus, Warner!" Pilsudski's yelling in his ear. "You must have wanted to get that one over with."

He tries to laugh. He can't laugh. His lungs are burning. "I felt . . . strong."

"You broke the fucking record, man! Think you knocked four or five seconds off it."

"Warner! Warner!"

"Did I? . . . Shit." He hadn't once thought about the record. Flashbulbs. And silly old man Rurak: "Thought you'd moved out too soon, kid. Jesus, Al! Thought you'd blown it. But you knew what you was doing all right. Goddamn right. Yes sir, the best damned middle-distance runner the valley's produced in twenty-five years!"

Alex had barely heard him. He'd still been running.

They were walking through the crunchy gravel up to the screen door at the back of the Cat's Eye. ". . . get arrested, you know," Carlyle was saying, "just be our luck. Last fucking week, right? Just fuck everything up, right? Shit, maybe it's not the best thing to be . . ." He stopped and shrugged.

Dumb fuck's going to crap out on me, Alex thought. *Well shit, doesn't matter. Just so he does it before we get started and not in the middle.* He jerked the screen door open. Frank was at the table right inside drinking a quart of Bud. "Hey, Frank . . . come on out here a minute."

Almost dark now. Cooling down, end of August. Summer's almost over. "Hey, what the fuck you doing, Al?" Frank bending through the door, huge fucker.

Carlyle was still going on and on like a goddamned bug in his ear: "I don't know, Warner. If you're thinking about picking something off the street, well then that's kind of risky, you know what I mean? And shit, man, if we got ourselves arrested just before—"

"Hey, what the fuck you guys talking about?" Hospidarski said. "You talking about picking up pussy or something?"

Alex didn't answer him. The three of them stood silently in the parking lot. Alex turned to Carlyle: "All I want to know, man, is are you in or out?"

Carlyle stepped back a pace. He shook his head. "I'm out," he said.

"What the fuck you talking about, Al?" Frank said.

"Moving, Frank. I'm talking about moving."

They moved. In two stolen cars out the National Road.

Alex rammed the shift into second, felt like digging, grinding down like chopping in football, grinding away against a blocker, and he hauled the shift down into third and drove the accelerator down. The car fishtailed, then caught, grinding, driving. On the right the curve of the road streaked by, lights below streaked by, red, yellow, and green; he was right again, pushing hard.

Hospidarski on his tail in the left lane, slid and pulled through. In the rearview mirror Alex saw a flash of Polish grin. *Just try to catch me now, fuckoff*, he thought. A line of cars, stopped for a red light. Right fucking in front of them. Too close. Empty park lane to the right. Alex swung right, bounced against the curb, pulled to hold it straight, heard metal give, screaming, tearing. Glancing left, saw Hospidarski sail wide into the oncoming lane, sail wider yet, far left to avoid a tractor trailer: snapshot of the truck driver's fear. White face. Panic. And then he and Hospidarski were side by side again, the road open and clear in front of them. Behind, horns blew. *Christ, Frank*, Alex thought, *you're crazier than a fucking coot!*

Alex rolled down his window, yelled, "Where's that siren?" Hospidarski grinned. Alex couldn't tell whether he'd heard or not. But no siren yet, no sharp wail to add that edge to it like a knife in the guts. Another curve. The two cars banged together. Fuck! He held it straight, saw Hospidarski hold it straight. *Good boy.* They were both pushed to the floor. Curves ahead. *I'll get him on the curves*, Alex thought, *I'm better on the curves*. But things were already beginning to move too fast to plan. Alex couldn't think anymore, just had to let his hands do it for him, trust his hands and body to ride them through. Black, white, and red: just a smear behind a road sign. It had been a police car. *Here we go*, Alex thought. *Great. Wonderful.* He glanced at the speedometer. A hundred and twenty and still pushing.

The siren cut in behind them, frantic scream. *Come on, you motherfuckers, do you think you can run me?*

Rising high and easy over the crest of a hill, blue night sky streaming by overhead, Alex knew something. It was important. But he didn't have time to think about it, set it aside in himself to look at later. In the valley below the lights were lined out into whipping strips. Down the hill into Hallies Rise at a hundred and thirty. *Get her into the hills*, he thought, *and not a fucking cop in the state of West Virginia has the balls to stay with me. Get out in the hills, just bury them. I can run them mountain roads like nobody born. Keep her on the road when nobody else can. Can run her till she gives it up, run this fucking Chevy down to scrap. No one can touch me.* And they were through Hallies Rise in a flash, cop wailing away: siren! siren! and on into the country. Headed for Route 88, headed for the fucking hills.

Frank wants in. Nervous out there in that left lane. Don't blame him. Yeah, go ahead. Alex eases up, drops back to a hundred and ten, lets Frank goose that big Buick in ahead of him and burn it on down the road. *Guts in that fucking Buick, no lie. Bet he's got her wound out now, hundred and forty if he's doing anything. Didn't think them big cars could move like that. Shit, Detroit put something in there. But shit, hit 88, what's he going to do? Kill himself that's what, can't keep that big car on the road out there.* And checking his rearview, Alex saw the cop right on his fucking ass, running up his tailpipe. One driving. The other one's leaning out the window holding both hands on his fucking gun. *Oh, shit.*

Blam! Slug ripped up through the auto body, tearing metal.

*Fuck, not going to let me get to the fucking hills. Going to shoot
the fucking tires right out from under me. All right, you fuck
with me, and I'll fuck with you. Frank, you move your ass out.
You just move her straight for Little Washington and ditch her
first chance you get.* It was almost like Frank could hear him
talking. *Yeah, first chance, Frank, you ditch her. We're riding
the edge now, man.* Alex kicked the brakes hard.

Crash of metal as the police car rammed him. Kicked accelerator and dug out. *Yeah, you fuckers, how you like that one?
Blam!* Another slug, spraying glass. *Goddamn, going to shoot
me right through the fucking head?* Alex kicks the brakes again,
just a touch. Cop drops back, but Alex is already winding it out,
laughing. Back three car lengths now, but the fucker gets off
another shot: *Blam!* Wide, off into nowhere.

Little bridge just over the hill. *That's the ticket.* Alex stood
on the brakes, actually stood on them, his entire body clear of
the seat, his arms knotted behind white knuckles on the steering
wheel. Speedometer falling off fast, eighty, seventy, sixty. He's
sliding sideways, cop right on him. Bridge abutment coming up,
smack her out good, and the cop car right along with her. *Kill
you both, you fuckers, shooting at me like that!* He had to hold
it, had to hold it, goddamn it, until it hit. Hauled the wheel
around, just a little, not too much. Just keep her on the road.
Speedometer don't count now, sliding sideways. He jerked the
door handle with his left hand, gave the door a shove to flap in
the wind, grabbed the wheel again. Car sideways, just starting to
spin. Perfect. Easy on in. Fifty miles an hour probably, and he
felt like he had all the time in the world. Had to be just right or
that bridge abutment would catch him right in the teeth and
kill him dead as a post.

It's perfect where he wants it, left rear quarter panel. Explosion, glass metal, screaming tearing, impossible crash. He's
jumping out the open door. Lands, tumbling, fucking knees and
elbows in the dirt, slamming down the muddy bank and into the
creek. Feet under him in the water up to his knees, looks back.
Hospidarski's long gone, can hear that Buick winding out five

miles down the road. And the cops have creamed themselves right into the Chevy. Naturally. But they must have got her slowed down. They're not hurt. They're piling out. Oh, yeah, one is hurt. He's bleeding. Big gush of blood running down his face.

Alex took off at a run, digging hard, up the far side of the creek bank, sprinting, headed for the dark trees.

"Halt!"

Oh, come on, you assholes, do you think you can run me?

"Halt or I'll shoot!"

Yeah, do that, motherfucker.

Crack! Alex heard the bullet bite into wood on his left. Jesus, push, push, push! He drove himself hard through scrub and weeds, faking right and then left, left again, running a broken field for a touchdown.

Crack! Farther off this time. Way fucking off to the left. Dark up here. He's running out of light. *Keep on shooting, motherfucker, I'm in the trees. Crack!* Alex heard the bullet rip into the ground twenty feet below him. *Shit, he don't know where I am now. He's just shooting off his gun.* Alex allowed himself to look back again. Two cops, already far distant, were slogging through the creek. *You guys haven't got a prayer.* And Alex began to run.

He ran steadily up the hill, dodging in and out of the trees. He ran about two miles that way, making good time even though it was dark and uphill. He found a trail leading on up, and that made it easier. He kept on pushing back into the hills. He wasn't running away now, knew they'd already given up on him. He could hide out up in here a million years, and they knew that. And then, whenever he wanted, he could just walk down into Raysburg the back way, stroll into a bar, and sit down and have a drink. And Raysburg cops never liked to work too hard anyway.

He kept running it along because it felt so good. Not so fast that it hurt, just a nice easy, swinging pace. He wanted to run until he was high above the city. Finally he broke out of the trees and into a cleared area. He ran to the top of the hill and stopped to breathe. He looked back the way he had come and there, below him, very distant, were all the lights of Raysburg, tiny, like stars.

He felt great. He knew there was something he'd wanted to remember, but he couldn't find it. He stood breathing deeply and tried to remember. It had come to him like a punch just as he'd sailed up high and clear over the hill outside Hallies Rise with the siren loud behind him. That's when it had happened. But what the fuck was it? He didn't know.

It was something to do with running, he knew that much. But not running track. And not a fucking thing to do with cars either. Just something about running. But shit, what the hell was it then? Well, goddamn, anyhow you look at it, he'd had a hell of a good last run, a fucking fantastic last run. He felt great. But Jesus, if he could only remember! The night was warm and full of sound: bugs and crickets and frogs. Must be water around here somewhere. He looked up. The dark sky was alive with stars glittering, a million hard, silver points. For a moment he felt a huge motion underneath him, all around him. He didn't know what it was. "Aw, shit," he said out loud. He couldn't remember. The stars were like some bright dust out there, so fucking far away. He began to walk back down to the bars of Raysburg.